THE RAINBOW BRIDGE

Alyson Sheldrake is the author of the *Algarve Dream Series*, and the author/curator of the *Travel Stories Series* of anthologies. Her animal memoir, *Kat the Dog*, is a multi-award-winning bestseller about their rescued Spanish water dog. Alyson lives in the Algarve, Portugal.

"Alyson Sheldrake has woven her magic again! This book invites animal lovers to the place we hope exists: a gentle, timeless haven where cherished departed pets contentedly await their owners. **The Rainbow Bridge is a beautifully imagined journey that will stir the soul and heal grieving hearts everywhere.**"

— BETH HASLAM, AUTHOR OF THE FAT DOGS AND FRENCH ESTATES SERIES

"A contemporary heartwarming story of loss, but with a fantasy twist, and a hint of romance: **perfect for animal lovers and anyone who enjoys a well-written story.**"

— CHRIS MOORE, BETA READER

"**A heartwarming, emotional and beautiful story that really tugs at your heartstrings.** I don't *usually* like fantasy books. I don't read fantasy books. I read this and really loved it! A truly magical tale that will capture many readers' hearts."

— JULIE HAIGH, BETA READER

"A well-crafted portal fantasy with engaging characters and immersive settings that draw the reader to the heart of the tale. **The plot, though gripping and pacy, unfolds with compassion and tenderness befitting the theme of loss.** Those who have grieved for a cherished pet will recognise the hope that prevails amidst heartache, taking comfort in the message that the key to healing lies in the boundless capacity to love."

— LIZA GRANTHAM, AUTHOR OF THE MAD COW IN GALICIA MEMOIR SERIES

"If you're an animal lover, this book will enthral you. Alyson Sheldrake's wonderful, emotional story draws you into the Rainbow Bridge world of Archaven and its furry and human characters. **By the time you finish *The Rainbow Bridge*, you'll be wishing the story was true.** Recommended for all ages and for every pet owner."

— SIMON MICHAEL PRIOR, AUTHOR OF COZY MYSTERIES AND TRAVEL ADVENTURE MEMOIRS

THE RAINBOW BRIDGE

ALYSON SHELDRAKE

Copyright © 2025 Alyson Sheldrake

Cover designed by Miblart

Website: www.miblart.com

Formatted by Publish with Ant Press

Website: www.antpress.org

Published by Tadornini Publishing, 2025

Website: www.alysonsheldrake.com

First Edition

The Rainbow Bridge

ISBN (Paperback): 978-989-36398-0-1

ISBN (Hardback): 978-989-36398-1-8

The author asserts the moral right under the Copyright, Designs, and Patents Act 1988 to be identified as the author of this work.

All rights reserved.

No part of this publication may be reproduced, distributed, or transmitted in any form or by any electronic or mechanical means, including photocopying, recording, or other information storage and retrieval systems, without the prior written consent of the author, except for the use of brief quotations embodied in critical reviews and certain other non-commercial uses permitted by copyright law. For permission requests, contact the author, Alyson Sheldrake. Website: www.alysonsheldrake.com

This book is a work of creative fiction. Names, characters, places, and incidents are either the product of the author's imagination or used fictitiously. Any resemblance to actual persons, living or deceased, events, businesses, or locations is entirely coincidental.

NO AI TRAINING: Without in any way limiting the author's exclusive rights under copyright, any use of this publication to 'train' generative artificial intelligence (AI) technologies to generate text is expressly prohibited. This content is not licenced for use in training artificial intelligence models or tools and may not be copied, scraped, or processed by AI systems without the author's explicit permission. The author reserves all rights to licence uses of this work for generative AI training and development of machine learning language models.

The day my beloved Kat the Dog died was the worst day of my life. Writing this book helped me process the pain and begin to heal. May this story bring comfort and hope to anyone else who has experienced the devastating loss of a beloved pet.

Alyson Sheldrake
August 2025

CHAPTER ONE

That was such a strange dream. It almost felt real.

I stirred and pulled the duvet up closer around my neck. My hand brushed the pillow where Molly, my beloved golden retriever, would rest her head each night. I smiled as I recalled the cute snuffling noise she'd make as she chased imaginary rabbits, her paws scuffling and scrabbling in her sleep. Without her, the space beside me now seemed as wide as the ocean.

I never normally remembered my dreams, but this one was different. I could picture it all so clearly. A sloping field, long grass swaying in the soft breeze. In the distance a river, light sparkling across the surface of the water. A bird, high in the sky, swooping and swirling, dancing in the wind. Brilliant sunshine flickered through the leaves of a majestic magnolia tree. The heady scent of blossom; scattered blooms on the ground. And beneath the tree, lying down, her head resting on her paws, was Molly. My darling Molly.

She looked so peaceful there. As if she were waiting for someone. Waiting for me. I hesitated, not wanting to break the spell, but longing to run forward and hold her in my arms. She stirred, lifting her head, and her bright eyes, those gorgeous, melted milk chocolate brown eyes, focused on me.

"Not yet."

A tear rolled down my cheek, and I brushed it away, irritated that the dream had ended there and I'd woken up to reality. Molly had gone. I would never wake up and see her beautiful face again or take her on another walk. Never hold her, feel her gentle tongue licking my hand, or watch her play with her favourite old stuffed toy again.

It had been five weeks since Molly had died. Five long weeks since I'd kissed her one last time and cradled her in my arms as the vet gently let her go.

"Sweet dreams, darling. No more pain now. I will always love you."

I'd whispered those words to her as hot tears had streamed down my face and my heart had splintered into a million tiny shards of razor-sharp glass. The hushed whimper of that last goodbye had given way to an explosion of pain—a physical force that ripped through my chest, leaving me gasping for air in a dark and suffocating abyss of grief.

Not yet. I knew she'd spoken to me. *But what did she mean? Was she really there, under that tree, waiting for me?*

I'd read books about the so-called Rainbow Bridge. The place pets are supposed to go when they die. The place where they wait for us to join them. I didn't believe it, though. It sounded too good to be true. I glanced over at the decorative jar placed high on the shelf in my bedroom. *That's all that remains of my darling girl. Her ashes. How can she be sitting under a tree?*

I dragged myself out of bed. *This is hopeless. It was just a dream. Time to get on with my life.* I stared at my reflection in the mirror as I cleaned my teeth, my eyes all red and puffy. *But what if it's true?*

🐾 🐾 🐾 🐾 🐾

My studio was cold as I entered and turned on the lights. A series of acrylic paintings, wrapped and stacked against the wall, reminded me that today was the day they were being collected. The gallery, The Art Sanctuary, was a new venture in town. I'd visited them after their opening night and liked the owner straightaway. Mrs Thomas was an enigmatic and lively lady in her seventies, who wanted to know all about me and my work. I left the meeting promising her a dozen new paintings by the start of the summer and had set to work as soon as I arrived home.

It was the spur I'd needed to lift my spirits—a proper gallery representing me. I'd been selling my work through word of mouth and the occasional commission, but it wasn't easy. In a good month, I sold a couple of paintings and had some money left in the bank. Other months, it was beans on toast for tea. Several days in a row.

I checked the email on my phone. A driver would come to collect the twelve paintings at 10 am. I was to visit the gallery at 3 pm and check they'd hung everything correctly. A fizz of excitement sizzled up my arms at the prospect of seeing my work professionally displayed in a real gallery. My mum would have been so proud of me. She'd encouraged me from a young age, buying me proper paints and brushes, and hanging every single thing I painted onto the wall of our lounge.

We had a neighbour who was a professional artist, and I used to spend hours sitting in his studio beside him. The nutty aroma of linseed oil and the scrape of his palette knives were the backdrop to my own feeble attempts to fashion something pleasing to the eye. He taught me about the colour spectrum, how to hold and move my brush to create an atmosphere on the surface of the canvas, and when to leave things out rather than overdo a piece.

I smiled as I remembered those carefree days. Then enrolling at university alongside all the other students, innocent and excited. Everything seemed so easy then. There was no pressure. No bills to pay. Just lectures, assignments, and a social life full of bars, cheap beer, and late nights sat under the stars, laughing and talking. And Ben. My first love. Ben, with his long hair, straggly beard and shiny blue eyes. I'm sure Mum would have had something to say about him. But she never met him. Our love had exploded, then fizzled out long before the summer break arrived.

After Ben, no-one else quite matched up to the excitement I'd experienced with him. Sure, there had been others. Even one proposal. Which I politely, but firmly, turned down.

No good thinking about all that now. I shook myself and ran my hand along the side of my easel, the beechwood solid and reassuring beneath my fingers. The open frame taunted me. I hadn't painted a thing since Molly had died.

You need to get painting again. Be inspired.

I selected a new canvas and positioned it on the easel. Glancing at the bundle of finished paintings propped against the wall, I ran through each one in my mind. Scenes of the town, boats in the harbour, summer days at the beach. All depicted in my modern style, vibrant works with bold splashes of colour. All painted with love. And with Molly lying at my feet. But the floor beside my easel was bare now. A mournful reminder of her absence. I pictured her sweet face as she snuggled into her bed, eyes closing almost as soon as I started painting. She was so close to me that flecks of paint would sometimes land on her, and she would shake herself, curling around the soft fluffy cushion to find another comfortable spot before settling down again.

The studio was so empty without her. I wondered whether I should get another dog, but I couldn't imagine anyone else taking Molly's place. She had been my soulmate.

I'd found her through a local rescue centre and fell in love with her the minute I saw her. Metal kennels lined the walls, each housing a different dog longing to be adopted. Eager faces followed me as I edged past the cages, each inmate hoping I might be the special person who would take them home. Then I saw her—a small, scruffy bundle huddled in the corner of an enclosure, her eyes wide and scared, body hunched into a ball of matted fur.

I crouched down to her level and eased open the metal gate. She stepped out tentatively, her tail between her legs, but as soon as I whispered hello to her, she relaxed into my arms. I caressed her, feeling the softness and warmth of her body, and knew she was the one.

It was as if she'd known I was there to collect her, even though I'd only popped in to have a look that day. I'd already completed all the necessary paperwork and home check in advance with the charity. An hour later, we walked out of the building, her lead in my hand, the signed adoption papers in my bag. Her eager face, nose twitching as she sniffed the crisp morning air, made my heart soar. I had found her. My perfect companion. And from that very first day, we were inseparable.

Molly had no history or paperwork; the staff had found her tied to the gate of the shelter when they arrived for work one morning. They estimated her age to be about a year old, even though she was so underweight and unkempt, it was hard to be certain.

Thirteen years had passed by in a flash since the day I rescued her. *Or had she rescued me?* I'd had three relationships, all disasters, and Molly had survived them all. She'd given me a reason to get up each day and smile at the world.

I selected a pencil and closed my eyes, the warmth of the wood sinking into my fingers as my thoughts flickered and scuttled, unable to settle. I twirled the pencil around, chewing on the end as I tried to concentrate. An image of Molly, sat in her favourite spot by the river, flashed into my head. I knew I had to capture it quickly. It was how I started every new painting. I would envisage the finished piece in my mind, complete in all its glory before I'd even picked up a paintbrush. I made a quick sketch, the pencil sweeping over the surface of the canvas, leaving deft marks and scribbled notes. It was always like that —a few magical moments of pure clarity and sparkling energy before the hard work of painting began.

I stepped back and gasped, my breath catching in my throat. *There she is.* My beautiful girl, her head tilted to one side, one ear tipped upwards, her face quizzical. The river, glistening in the background. A winding path in the distance lined with trees, their branches bent forward as if to impart some secret wisdom to anyone who would take the time to stop and listen. The sun, low in the sky, casting shimmers of light across the water. And Molly, sniffing the air with delight. Probably smelling the rabbits and planning more mischief, knowing her.

I set the pencil down, content with my quick drawing, just as my phone rang.

"I'll be there in five minutes. Are the paintings ready?"

"Yes, all wrapped up. Great. I'll meet you outside."

I grabbed my keys and hurried through to the front door, opening it in time to greet a young man who was obviously in a hurry.

"It's through here. My studio's at the back of the shop."

In less than ten minutes, he'd loaded all my paintings into his van and driven off with a cheeky wave. The studio echoed with the sound of my footsteps; the noise reverberating off the empty walls.

I picked up a brush and started mixing my paints. The colours were like old friends as I squeezed the rich creamy pigments onto the palette and swirled my brush in a jar of clean water, mesmerised as always by the way the shades sparkled and came to life on the canvas.

The next thing I knew, it was almost 2.30 pm. *I've got to be at the gallery at three, and I haven't even had any lunch.* I looked down at my paint-splattered jeans. *Better get changed as well.* I hurried upstairs, flung on some clean clothes, grabbed a banana, filled up my water bottle, and raced out of the door.

CHAPTER TWO

"Well, what do you think, Laura? I hope you like it?"

Mrs Thomas had given me an entire wall of the main exhibition area, and my paintings looked fantastic. She had even selected one of my smaller pieces and placed it in the front window. I gasped as I saw the prices displayed. *Did she really believe I could sell them for that much?* Even with the gallery's 50% commission, it would still leave me with a healthy profit—if they sold, of course.

"It's amazing. I can't thank you enough."

"Don't thank me, girl. Your work is wonderful. Our customers are going to love them. You'll see." Mrs Thomas beamed at me. "And I've got a surprise for you. Look a little closer at that one over there." She pointed to one of my larger paintings.

"Is that... a red sticker? Already?"

"Yes. I sold it to a young gentleman and his wife. They came in at lunchtime, while we were still hanging them. Bought it straight away. He's coming back later to collect it. And they might be interested in another one as well." She patted my hand. "Congratulations. I told you folks would love your work. Now go paint me some more."

I said goodbye to her, my head spinning. *My first sale this month.* I walked past the local deli, then stopped and whirled around on my heels. *Time to celebrate.* I suddenly felt hungry as I stepped inside, smelling the freshly baked bread and looking at the cakes on display. I wedged myself into a corner table and picked up the menu. *Sourdough bread with avocado and smoked salmon. With a pot of green tea and then one of those slices of flapjack for afters. Why not?*

For the first time in ages, I felt good about myself as I tucked into the sandwich. The door opened, and a man popped his head around the doorframe.

"Is it okay to enter with my dog?"

The owner nodded. "Yes, of course. As long as they're well behaved. Come in."

He walked inside, and I froze as his companion trotted in beside him. The dog was the spitting image of Molly, even down to the same fluffy tail and soulful eyes. Identical colouring too.

My appetite deserted me, and I pushed the plate of food away. Snatching up my keys and bag, I made my way to the counter.

"I'm sorry, something's come up. I have to leave. Can I pay?"

"Yes, of course. Was everything alright with your meal?"

"Yes, yes, it was fine. Sorry, I just need to pay."

I stumbled out of the deli, my heart pounding as I gulped in gasps of air and forced myself to take some deep breaths. I almost bumped into a young woman and tumbled forward.

"Sorry," I muttered without looking up, my hands fluttering as I fumbled to replace my purse in my bag.

I walked home, hardly glancing at the shop windows or people as I passed them by, my heart aching with the unfamiliar void that Molly's absence had left behind. Walking anywhere used to be such a pleasure, with her padding along beside me. After Molly's passing, the world had slowed to a halt for me. Each day dragged by with the same monotonous routine, everything cloaked in shades of drab grey, like faded clothes that have seen better days.

I rounded the corner onto Queen Street, the familiar cobblestones uneven under my feet. The lights were still on in the Thread and Needle store; its windows glowing in the late afternoon sun. The little sewing and knitting shop was a welcome sight. Enid Pearce, the owner, had taken me under her wing after my mum had died, gently nurturing me, and making sure I looked after myself. She had become a second mother to me.

It had been fifteen years since the car accident that had changed my life in an instant. After her funeral, I discovered Mum had left me just enough money to buy the little flat above the shop. I barely survived each month on my meagre earnings as an artist, often struggling to make ends meet, but it was home, and I loved it.

The bell above the door tinkled as I walked in and waved hello to Enid, busy with a customer as usual. I wandered past the display area, inhaling the crisp scent of yarn, wool, and cotton, and wriggled past a bolt of vibrant patterned fabric balanced precariously on the counter. My hand trailed across the material, soft as a kitten's velvet fur. *Wonder what the customer is going to make with it? Curtains probably.*

The tension in my shoulders slipped away as I strolled over to the painted wooden door in the far corner of the shop floor. The memory of Enid leading me to this spot, her hands covering my face as she guided me forward, was unforgettable.

"There. That should solve your problem of where to work." She'd opened the door with a flourish, then stood aside, her eyes twinkling with excitement.

The doorway led to a large storage room Enid insisted she didn't need. The musty smell and piles of old boxes stacked in the corner confirmed Enid hadn't used the space for years, but the minute I stepped inside, I knew it had potential. As I swept away the dust on a shelf and opened the window to let in the sunshine, the room came alive. There was plenty of space to move around, and the north-facing window provided the perfect natural light for painting. I set up my easel and paints and realised I had found a special place. I'd finally realised my childhood dream. My own studio.

Fifteen years later, the easel's frame was a little worn and splattered with a kaleidoscope of paint colours, and I'd lost count of the number of paintings that had passed through my hands, each one a labour of love.

Heading back outside, I rifled through my bag for my keys, almost tripping over the post as I opened my front door. I picked up the ominous brown envelopes, stomped up the stairs, and dumped them on the small table in my hallway. *Another final demand, and my visa bill. Great.*

I dashed back down to my studio and slammed the door shut behind me in an attempt to banish all my financial problems. Flicking on the lights, I stood before my easel, studying the painting I'd started earlier. I picked up a fresh brush, mixing colours almost unconsciously, as I blocked in the background and bright blue sky. I lost all track of time as the images came to life beneath my brushes. It was midnight when I stopped, exhausted but satisfied with the new layers of paint picking out the sunlight glowing softly through the trees and glistening on the water. I washed up, leaving everything ready for the next morning, and went upstairs.

The following day, I was straight back into the studio after a hurried breakfast. Once a painting took hold of me, it was all I could focus on. It was an overwhelming compulsion; a passionate frenzy, forcing me to paint furiously until the work was complete. I marvelled at other artists I knew with their ability to juggle multiple paintings at different stages of completion, jumping between pieces as the mood inspired them. I could only ever have one canvas at a time on my easel. It was all-consuming to me. I could see the final piece in my mind, haunting and taunting me right through to the last brushstroke.

I was about to stop for lunch when Enid knocked softy on the door to my studio and asked me if I was okay.

"Yes, all fine, thanks. I'm working on a new piece. It's going well."

"That's good to hear, love. I've been worried about you. You're always so busy in here, and lately you've been so preoccupied. It's great to see you painting again."

She gently squeezed my shoulder and retreated as a customer came into the shop. *Enid's a good person. And she's right. I have been quiet* in here. But not anymore. I glanced back over at my easel. *Next step, painting Molly. But first, some food.*

I didn't need a reference photo of Molly. I knew every part of her—the gentle brown eyes, the tilt of her head, those velvet ears, and the curls that refused to behave themselves on the top of her head. Her beautiful, expressive face. I picked a soft brush and applied more layers of paint, only stopping once I'd captured her.

There you are. My darling girl. In our favourite spot beside the river.

I'd spent so many hours there, watching the water swirl and dance. Molly was content to snuffle and sniff her way along the path as I let the worries of the day float away on the breeze. It was my favourite place to go to escape the hustle and bustle of everyday life. The last time we'd been there, I'd almost fallen asleep, listening to the gentle lapping of the water as it ebbed and flowed its way down the river. I sat on the grass; the birds chirping and chattering in the trees above me, as a curious blackbird hopped around in the fallen leaves that cushioned the ground nearby. It was my secret place. Tucked away from the world.

There's something missing. There was a blank space waiting to be filled on the canvas. I checked the composition and realised I needed to be in the picture as well. *But I've never painted myself before?* In fact, I rarely painted human figures at all, preferring to capture nature, landscapes, even buildings and boats. But not humans. But the longer I stared at the painting, the stronger my belief grew. *I need to be there beside Molly.*

I sighed and picked up a brush. *Here goes.* It felt awkward depicting myself, and I spent several hours teasing the paint around the canvas until I was satisfied. I washed and dried off my brushes with a cloth before setting them down on the old wooden table beside my easel. I stroked the surface of the wood, the ridges and curves harsh beneath my hand. The table was like an old friend—paint-spattered, scratched, and marked with years of use.

I stepped back, pleased with my work. The painting almost glowed, the rich colours bouncing off each other, vying for attention. Molly settled at my feet, my arm draped around her, as we sat together with the river sparkling in the background. I tidied up my paints and took a last glance at the canvas before turning off the light and going back upstairs. Too tired to even prepare anything to eat, I curled up in bed and fell fast asleep.

CHAPTER THREE

I stared at Molly's portrait the next morning, brush in hand, as the memories came flooding back to me. The sterile smell of the vet clinic that filled my nostrils and made me retch as I took her in for a consultation, knowing something was terribly wrong. The coughing that had started when she rolled over onto her back had progressed to difficulty with her breathing, her breath coming in gasps and gulps. And yet, that very morning, she'd walked all the way around the river path. Our usual forty-minute walk had lasted well over an hour as she plodded along, determined to finish.

At the vet's, they'd run a series of tests, then said the words that had left me reeling. "We think she has something wrong with her lungs. There might be some fluid in there or an infection. We'd like to keep her in overnight to monitor her, then conduct a CAT scan in the morning."

I couldn't speak. The vet must have read my expression, as she tried to reassure me.

"We'll have to sedate her for the scan. But don't worry, we've checked everything, and she has a good strong heart. She'll be fine. But we need to see what's going on inside her."

I'd said goodbye to Molly, told her how much I loved her and tried not to notice her quizzical expression as I whispered, "I'll see you tomorrow, baby. Don't worry, it will all be okay." I knew I had to be strong for her as I held her close, but my head was reeling.

As they led her into the treatment area, I held it together until the last moment when she glanced back at me. Her brown eyes were full of questions. She didn't need to speak for me to know what she was asking. "Why am I staying here? Why can't I come home with you?"

I chewed the inside of my lip as she walked away, desperately wanting to grab hold of her lead and run back out to the car with her. *There's been a mistake. She's fine, really.* The frosted glass doors swooshed shut behind her, and I left the clinic in a daze.

I hardly slept that night, imagining her lying in a cage, lights and noise all around her. The bed felt so empty as I lay there, clutching her pillow to my chest, sobbing. *What if something happens to her? What if she never comes home again?* We'd never spent a night apart in thirteen years. It seemed so wrong to be lying there without her beside me.

At first light, I shot out of bed, then stood helplessly as I realised there would be no morning walk with Molly that day. The vet had told me to return at ten, and they would let me see Molly before they set up for the scan. I chewed on a piece of toast, the bread sticking in my throat as I tried to wash it down with a mug of tea. I couldn't taste a thing as I stared at the clock on the wall in the kitchen, willing it to move faster. Finally, it was time. I raced out to my car and drove to the vet. It was Sunday morning, and I breathed a sigh of relief—I could park right outside.

I entered the clinic; its white walls plastered in medical posters a stark reminder of why I was there. The receptionist nodded at me and made a phone call. The doors to the treatment room opened, and there she was. My darling Molly, racing towards me, tail wagging. She crashed into my waiting arms as I buried my head in her fur.

"Oh, I've missed you so much. Are you okay? Did you miss me?"

She whirled around; her face breaking into a grin as she woofed at me. She looked fine, her breathing normal. *Perhaps I've been too hasty. Maybe there's nothing wrong after all. We'll just do this scan and then go home again. Everything's going to be alright.*

"Why don't you take her out for a quick walk while we get things ready here?" The vet handed me her lead. "She's a wonderful girl. She's been no trouble at all."

I took my time outside, ambling beside Molly as she stopped to sniff her way along the road. My feet dragged as I retraced our steps, hesitating at the entrance to the clinic. My stomach churning, I walked inside, crouching down to give Molly one last hug and kiss before the vet led her away.

"We'll take good care of her, don't worry. There are a few forms we need you to complete and sign now, ready for the procedure. And we'll call you as soon as we're done. Go have some lunch. There's a nice café down the road. She'll be fine."

Lunch? How can she possibly think I could eat anything? And yet, I had time to kill and nothing to do. The thought of staying in the waiting room didn't appeal to me, which is why I found myself sitting at a formica table staring at a menu. The words all blurred together on the page as I wiped away the tears brimming in my eyes.

After a lacklustre lunch, I trudged through the park, my heart sinking as I kept checking my phone. *Nothing. No calls. How long does it take to do a scan?*

🐾 🐾 🐾 🐾 🐾

Suddenly my phone sprang into life, the ringtone jolting me. My fingers were shaking as I swiped across the screen.

"Yes, hello, is everything okay?"

"Hello Miss Adams. Yes, it's Doctor Wilson here. I'm calling you from the surgery room. We've found the problem. I'm sorry, but I was right. Molly's lungs are full of liquid. I need your permission to drain them. It's not part of the procedure you signed for, so I need you to confirm it's in order for us to go ahead."

Lungs. Liquid. Drain them. The words shot through my head like flashes of lightning scorching a blackened sky.

"Sorry, I'm just trying to process this. Can I ask, is it dangerous? How long will it take?"

In truth, I didn't know what to say. All I could focus on was that, at that very moment, my baby girl was lying on an operating table.

The vet reassured me they were doing everything they could for Molly, and she was being monitored carefully.

"Yes, of course, if that's what you need to do." My voice caught in my throat. "Go ahead."

"Thank you. I'll get straight onto it. Don't worry."

Don't worry? It was all I could do to stop myself from collapsing as I rushed over to a nearby bench. My chest heaved as I gasped for breath, my heart pounding a frantic rhythm against my ribs. I sat hunched on the bench, willing her to survive the operation. *She's fourteen. How long has she been in there? How long can she stay under an anaesthetic? What if...?*

Suddenly, a white butterfly flew right up to me and perched on the arm of the seat beside me. Its wings shimmered in the afternoon sunlight as it sat there, a tiny ballerina quivering in the gentle breeze. It was so close to me I could almost touch it. I sat motionless, not wanting to scare it away. The creature spun around, as if it were trying to hold my attention. Trying to tell me something.

I shook my head. *Now you're being stupid. As if a butterfly could talk.* And yet, the longer it remained there, the more convinced I became it was a sign. I felt the tension lift from my shoulders and the throbbing pain in my head dissolve as the butterfly floated up into the air, circled around me, and gently fluttered away.

My phone rang, and I rushed to answer it.

"Molly's alright. The surgery went well, but the vet would like to talk to you."

I ran back to the clinic, then took a deep breath before I pushed open the glass door and stepped inside.

I knew the minute I saw the vet's face. It was serious.

"Is she okay?"

"Yes, Molly's fine. She's in our recovery room, coming round slowly."

"Can I see her?"

"Not right now, I'm sorry." The vet took my hand, her eyes soft and full of sympathy. "It was worse than we thought, I'm afraid. We removed almost two litres of fluid from her lungs."

What? That's impossible. How can her lungs even hold that much liquid?

The vet continued. "We've left the drains in on either side of her body, so we can monitor things. She's going to be groggy for a while, and she's had quite a day. The operation lasted almost three hours. Go home, come back tomorrow morning, and you can see her then. I'm sorry it's not better news, but we'll know more tomorrow when we have the results of the CAT scan."

I drove home, almost crashing into the kerb as I parked outside my flat, and walked upstairs, not even bothering to turn on the lights as I collapsed onto my bed and sobbed.

Sadly, the results the next day confirmed the vet's worst fears: Molly had a severe infection and more fluid already gathering in her lungs. As they brought her out to me, with drains attached to her sides and bandages enveloping her body, the room grew silent. She still seemed groggy as she padded over to me and licked my hand, then slumped down beside me. I dropped to the floor and held her in my arms, kissing her nose and stroking her gently. *I can't break down here. Not in front of everyone. Molly needs me to be strong.*

I glanced up at the vet and saw the concern etched across her face, her eyes shining with tears.

"We'll do everything we can for her. Let's take things one day at a time. We can start a course of antibiotics today, and you can take her home tomorrow. For now, she needs to rest and recover from the surgery."

I gathered Molly into my arms, kissed her one last time, then staggered out of the vet's, my heart breaking as I stumbled down the street.

CHAPTER FOUR

The final few weeks after I brought Molly home were dreadful: the drains protruding from each side of her body, the daily trips to the vet to have more liquid removed, the awful antibiotic injections she endured. Sometimes, as I sat in the waiting room, I even heard her yelp of pain from the treatment room as the needle went in. And every day she stoically trotted into the vet's beside me, knowing what lay ahead. Each morning, she still strolled along the river path with me, sniffing and snuffling, taking everything in. Despite her ragged gasps and laboured breathing, she was determined to walk everywhere as normal. Some days, the medication appeared to be working. The fluid levels dropped, and her breathing was easier. And then the latest test results would come back. The purple graphs on the paper showing the infection was still there. It was a cloying poison searing through her veins; a hidden enemy that haunted us and refused to go away.

Seven long weeks of treatment followed, and Molly battled on. But the fluid stubbornly refused to disappear, and each day she grew weaker.

The vet was kind but firm. "It's her lungs. I'm sorry. There's nothing more we can do for her. We've tried everything, but we can't clear the infection. She's fourteen; she's had a good life. It's time to let her go."

That day would haunt me forever.

I shook my head. The pain was unbearable; the memories slicing through me like a jagged knife tearing through stale bread. I turned around to face the canvas balanced on my easel, willing myself to recall what I'd been thinking about before those dark, haunting visions had once again burrowed their way into my mind.

A butterfly. That's what's missing from the painting. A white butterfly. I smiled. How many times had a white butterfly appeared while Molly was ill? It had to be more than a coincidence. One afternoon, a butterfly had even followed us as we strolled up the hill beside the river. It was skittering and flittering over Molly's head like a bejewelled dancer as the sun caught its wings and set it on fire.

"After I'm gone, every time you see a white butterfly, think of me."

Those words had leapt into my mind as I watched Molly sniff the air, the butterfly almost landing on her nose. At the time, I had dismissed the thought. *How could Molly be telling me that?* And yet, it really felt as if Molly *was* talking to me, planting that idea in my mind, trying to reassure me. But back then, I had not wanted to even acknowledge the notion that one day she would no longer be beside me.

I wonder if the concept of a white butterfly is significant? I grabbed my phone and started searching for butterfly symbolism online.

> Folklore and legend are full of white butterflies. Some people say they represent prosperity or good fortune. Others say their presence is a sign of an angel watching over you. Sometimes they signify healing on a physical or spiritual level.

Yeah, well, that sure didn't work, did it? Molly didn't heal, did she?

As I read on, the surrounding air grew noticeably colder, and goose bumps gathered on my arms.

A white butterfly is a message from heaven. Someone you had a close relationship with is visiting you through this beautiful creature. After someone passes and you see a white butterfly, it is proof your loved one is safe and has eternal peace.

I picked up my paintbrush, knowing what I needed to do. A few deft strokes of paint and it was complete. A white butterfly, dancing elegantly on the breeze, finished the portrait. Molly, her face turned towards me, sat at my feet, the sunlight glowing over the field and a river glistening in the distance.

As I stared at the painting, the butterfly seemed to lift its wings and float above the canvas. *Now I'm imagining things. Good grief, I need to get a grip.* I tried to walk away, but something drew me back to the painting. *That butterfly is shining. That's ridiculous. It must be a trick of the light.*

The paint felt warm as my hand caressed Molly's head, then skimmed over the butterfly. *My sweet girl. How I miss you.*

A rush of heat flooded through my fingers and raced up my arm. My heart pounded as the room spun, then everything went dark as I tumbled through the air. After a few seconds of frenzied whirling, I landed on something cushioned. I stretched out my hand, touched soft grass and opened my eyes.

Bright sunlight made me squint as I took in my surroundings. I was in a meadow full of wildflowers, their stems lifting and swaying as a gentle breeze ruffled their tips. The sun was high in the clear blue sky, casting a golden glow. A swallow, wings tipped with black, swooped in front of me, flying inches above the ground. White daisies nestled in the grass, creating a subtle carpet of colour. I straightened up, patting my arms and legs in disbelief.

I'm still alive. I'm still breathing, and my body feels the same. A gentle gust of wind swept across my cheeks as the warm sun caressed my face. I glanced down at my hands, noticing the flecks of acrylic paint on my fingers. *White paint. From the butterfly. What on earth is going on? Where am I? I must be dreaming.*

It didn't seem like a dream. It felt very real. More real than anything I'd ever experienced before. I took a tentative step forward, the grass soft and springy underfoot. I rubbed my eyes. The sun's heat on my arms and the silky breeze on my face sent a shiver down my spine. And then I saw her. Sat beneath a giant blossom tree in the middle of the field. My Molly. My darling girl. Watching me.

I raced over to her, crying out as I reached her and wrapped my arms around her as she licked my face and yipped with joy. She spun round; her face sparkling, eyes shining as she pranced in front of me.

"My baby. My precious baby girl." I buried my head in her fur, feeling her body quivering, her tail wagging furiously. "I've missed you so much."

Hot tears rolled down my cheeks as I looked at her. Gone were the drains, the bandages, the tired expression. She was young once more, full of life, her curly coat soft as velvet, her eyes that beautiful, melted milk chocolate colour I knew so well.

"How can this be happening? If it's a dream, I never want to wake up again."

"It's not a dream. It's real. I've been sitting here waiting for you. I knew you'd come." Molly licked my hand, her tongue soft as it caressed me.

I sensed, rather than heard, her. It was as if we didn't need actual words.

"You can talk?" It was more of a statement than a question.

"Of course I can. I've always talked to you. You just haven't always been able to hear me."

I thought back to the times when I'd sensed what Molly was thinking. *Had I been able to 'hear' her all along? What had I been missing? And why can I understand her now?*

"It's easier here. This is a special place." Molly read my thoughts.

"Have I died? Is that it?"

"No. You're still alive. But I don't understand how you managed to find me here like this. I don't think we're supposed to meet yet." She lay down, curling herself around my legs. "I was just advised to wait here for you."

"Who told you that? Where are we? Is this heaven?"

"The Keeper. He met me here and explained you would join me one day. And then we'd be together again. But this doesn't feel right. I've watched other pets when their owners arrive. They look different. You still seem human. Older. Not ready."

"Ready for what?" My head was spinning. I touched Molly's face; her fur was silky and soft beneath my fingers.

"All I know is what happens when the other animals reunite with their owners. They bound up to them and then they walk off together."

"But where do they go?"

Molly turned her head. "There's a bridge over there that crosses the river. I'll show you."

She stretched and padded off towards the river. I jumped up and followed her, noticing how easily and gracefully she walked, her tail raised in the air as she placed each paw on the ground.

"You're not in pain anymore?" I rested my hand on her side.

"No, watch me. I'm like a young pup again."

She raced ahead, bounding across the meadow, then turned back and woofed at me. I caught up with her, then gasped as we reached the river. It was beautiful, a cascading torrent of fresh, pale green water flecked with flashes of white, tumbling and dancing. It almost sounded like it was singing to us.

Molly spun around in a wide circle as if she were looking for something, her nose twitching.

"That's strange. There's no bridge here. Every time I've seen an animal and its owner reach this point; a bridge has appeared above the water. It shimmers, a stunning display of rainbow colours glowing as they walk across. But it's not here today. I guess it's not our time yet." She sighed and lay down, resting her head on her paws.

"So, what do we do next? I don't know why I'm here, but it's so wonderful to be with you again. Do I stay here now?" I couldn't see anything but fields and the river stretching far into the distance, as we wandered slowly back towards the magnolia blossom tree.

"There's no food here. Or other people. I was simply told to wait for you. It's alright though. Time doesn't seem the same here. It's as if

I've only just arrived." Molly settled down under the tree as I paced back and forth, my hands trembling.

"You mentioned The Keeper. Who is that? Where is he?" My chest tightened, and I took a deep, slow breath. As marvellous as it was to see Molly, I suddenly realised I had no way of knowing how to get home again. Or even if I could return home.

"The Keeper only spoke to me once, when I arrived here. He's tiny, not like a human at all, with the face and tail of a lion. He scared me at first, so I tried to hide. But he reassured me, settled me down and explained about the bridge and that I should wait for you to collect me. He said this place is called Archaven. The land of the Rainbow Bridge. That's all I know."

I could hear my heart pounding in my ears, and that was making it hard for me to focus on anything. My mouth filled with a horrible metallic taste as I tried to make sense of it all. *A Keeper that looks like a lion. A bridge that's a rainbow. Archaven. What is this place?*

My body trembled as a wave of dizziness washed over me. The world tilted as tiredness engulfed me, and I struggled to keep my eyes open. *What's happening to me?* The ground appeared to surge upwards as my legs gave way beneath me and I stumbled, losing my footing.

I curled up beside Molly, her presence comforting me as she rested her head on my lap, my hand caressing her side. A dark shadow crept across the grass towards us. Overwhelmed by weariness, I closed my eyes and slumped forward into a deep sleep.

CHAPTER FIVE

I woke with a start, expecting it all to have been a dream. I looked down and saw Molly still curled up asleep beside me. She stirred, yawned, and stretched out her soft paws. She licked my hand as I stroked her fur, feeling the familiar tangles between my fingers.

The sun was low in the sky, casting long shadows across the meadow. A strong breeze rippled along my arm, making me shiver.

"How can this be happening to me? All I did was touch my painting, and now I find myself here, beside you."

Molly looked up at me. "A painting? I used to love watching you paint. Maybe that's the key to this."

"It was a portrait of you and me. Down by the river, in your favourite spot. The place you loved to explore. And then I added a white butterfly."

The memories hurtled back into my mind, raw and painful. The walks we took together at the end, Molly panting, moving slowly, refusing to give in to the infection that inflamed her lungs. Nights filled with restless sleep, listening to her ragged breathing, wishing and praying she would get better.

Seeing her now as a young pup was incredible. The beautiful girl I loved from the first day I rescued her. She radiated life, her eyes sparkling, coat shining. Healthy.

"You're okay here? You're happy, safe?"

"Yes, it's lovely here. Peaceful. There are lots of us here, fields full of other animals, dogs, cats, horses. All kinds of creatures. All waiting. But I like it here on my own. If I want company, I can hunt out friends to play with. I'm fine here, just waiting for you."

"And then what?"

"I'm not sure. All I know is what I've seen. When the owners arrive, they meet up with their pets and cross the bridge together. I never see them again."

My head was spinning. "And you don't think I should be here yet?"

"No, it doesn't feel right. You don't seem ready. You still look human. Normal. Not like the others."

What did the 'others' look like? Who were they, and how did they get here? Is this the fabled Rainbow Bridge? Does it really exist then? It was all too overwhelming for me to process. My mind was a whirl as I looked around, seeing the leaves on the blossom tree above us twirling in the breeze. A few petals floated to the ground, one of them landing on Molly's back. I swept it away, tenderly stroking her body and feeling the fizz of her long tail as it brushed the grass. It all felt so real.

"That painting must have transported you here somehow." Molly cocked her head to one side, her ear flopping. That special pose always made me smile.

"I don't know. As I stood in front of that canvas in my studio, I experienced such an overwhelming love for you. I wanted to be with you so desperately. Maybe that's why I'm here? Maybe our love for each other was so strong it brought us back together. Losing you was the worst day of my life. I've cried so much."

Molly shifted closer to me, resting her head on my thigh as I sat on the grass, picking at the daisy plants at my feet.

"I know. I've sensed your pain. Your tears. I tried to comfort you, reassure you, but I couldn't reach you."

The tears flowed as I whispered to her, burying my face in her fur.

"I told you I would love you forever. I never thought I would see you again, though. Or that forever is an actual place. That one day we would never be apart again. All those stories of a Rainbow Bridge. I thought they were just fantasy."

My breath came in ragged gasps as I struggled to remain calm. I could feel my eyes closing, my limbs heavy as I slumped onto the grass.

Molly nudged me, her nose pressing against my leg. "Please don't fall asleep. You must stay awake. Alert."

"I don't know what to do now. I want to stay here with you, but you told me there's no food here. Or other people. And this place makes me feel so tired. But how do I get home? And even if I manage to find a way home, how can I possibly leave you behind?"

Molly stretched out her long body, front legs extended in a yoga pose. "You came from the far side of the meadow. Shall we go back and see if we can find something there that might help us?"

I walked beside her, ruffling the fur behind her ears as we reached the place I'd first landed.

"Over there. What's that?" Molly raced over and stood sniffing the ground, her tail wagging.

It was my canvas, lying face down on the grass. I picked it up and propped it against a rock, as a chill wind whipped around me. The colours of the painting seemed brighter here, the butterfly glowing, almost luminescent.

I shivered, instinctively knowing what I had to do.

With a trembling hand, I reached down to caress Molly, memorising every tiny detail of her gentle expression, desperate to hold on to and preserve each precious moment in my mind.

The breeze picked up speed, sending leaves scurrying across the grass. The branches of the trees by the river creaked as they shifted and bent under the weight of the wind. Clouds scurried across the sky, cancelling out the sunshine as I wrapped my arms around my body. A strange and unsettling feeling washed over me, a sense of foreboding that only intensified as the wind whipped around me.

"I don't want to leave you. But I know I can't stay here. It just doesn't feel right."

The sun burst forth from behind a cloud, casting a radiant golden spotlight on my darling girl.

"I understand. But now you know I'm alright. I'm safe here. This place is so beautiful and peaceful. I guess this just isn't your time yet. Remember that I'll always be here, waiting for you."

"Perhaps I can come back and visit you one more time?" I couldn't bear the thought of saying goodbye to Molly. Of leaving her. Again. "That day at the vet's. Your last day. It almost killed me. Taking you there. Knowing what would happen. You trusted me right to the end."

The pain surged in my heart as I remembered each dreadful minute as if it were only yesterday.

"You stood there at the door that morning, waiting to leave home for the last time with me. You realised what was happening, didn't you? The way you looked at me as I picked up your lead. It was as if I knew what you were saying."

Molly leant closer to me. "I tried so hard to reassure you. To let you know it was time. That I had to go. And that I loved you. Would always love you."

"We had such fun together, didn't we? From the very first day I took you home, I knew you were special. I loved you the minute I saw you sitting there in that rescue centre. Your eyes were so sad, yet hopeful, too. You rescued me, too. You do know that, don't you? My life was such a mess before. You changed me. Made me a better person. You gave me a reason to get up every morning. I loved our walks, watching you frolic in the sunshine, sniffing your way along the river path. Digging holes in the sand at the beach. Getting food stuck in your whiskers in your excitement at eating breakfast each day. That little yip of joy when we played catch. Curling up beside you on the sofa, your legs twitching in your sleep as you dreamt about chasing rabbits. I loved every single day with you, my sweet girl."

I bent down to hug her, her soft fur tickling my face as she gently licked away the tears that were spilling down my cheeks.

"I'm not sure I can do this. How can I say goodbye and leave you here?" I wiped my eyes, my heart pounding in my chest like an instrumental drum solo, loud and fast.

Molly stared at me; her eyes glowing brightly. "I know. I don't want you to go either. But you must. You can't stay here. You still have a life to live. And I'll be here. Waiting for you. You know where I am. And that I'm safe. It's going to be alright."

I stepped forward and touched the painting, my tears making it almost impossible to see the images on the canvas. The butterfly sprung to life beneath my hand as I reached out one last time to embrace Molly. I closed my eyes and whispered, "I love you," as the world turned upside down in a dizzying surge of colour and noise.

CHAPTER SIX

Crawling out of a deep sleep, my head swimming as I rubbed my eyes, I glanced at the clock on the wall. I blinked, shook myself, and looked again. *Twenty past eleven. How can that be?* I remembered hearing the church clock strike eleven when I reached forward to touch the butterfly on the painting in my studio. That moment before everything changed. *Was that really only twenty minutes ago?*

I must have been dreaming. But it felt so real. I stretched, kneading the stiff tension in my neck with my fingers as I tried to make sense of what had just happened. I could picture Molly so clearly—the field, her gentle face, the river. My heart thumped as I dropped my hands to my side, grasping the edge of the blanket on the sofa beneath me. I brushed my fingers through the tasselled edges, remembering all the times I had gently placed the same soft blanket over Molly as she lay sleeping beside me.

I tried to process everything logically. It seemed as if I'd been there with her for ages. Hours. And yet, only twenty minutes had passed on the clock. *It must have all just been a dream.*

I looked at my paint-spattered and tatty clothes and frowned. *What's that near my ankle?* I reached down, carefully lifting a single daisy flower balancing on a thin strip of grass from the hem of my jeans.

I twirled the delicate white and yellow flower around my fingers. *Where's this from? It wasn't there when I got dressed this morning. I'm sure I would have noticed it.* I pictured the field again; the sun pouring across the grass; the daisies spread before me like a patchwork blanket.

This can't be happening to me. I need to get out of here for a while. Go for a walk. Anything but this.

I laid the flower on my desk, grabbed my coat, purse, and keys and shot out of the studio, almost crashing into Enid in my haste to escape.

"Are you alright, dear?" She held out her hand, her face etched with concern.

I must have looked a sight. My heart was thumping as I gasped a hurried reply.

"Yes, sorry, all fine. Just need to go for a walk. I'll be back soon."

Stumbling through the shop door, I took a deep breath as I lifted my head up to the sky and rubbed my hands together briskly. I tried to avoid the stream of shoppers as I headed down the main street, not even thinking about where I was going.

A dream. It had to be a dream. It couldn't possibly be anything else.

The sound of a dog barking brought me back to earth. Ahead of me was a man struggling to catch up with a large Alsatian hurtling along the pavement towards me. The dog halted in front of me, and I reached out instinctively and grabbed his collar. Large brown eyes stared up at me as the dog wagged his tail, almost knocking me over as he leant into my side, his tongue lolling as he grinned up at me.

The man raced up to us, his face flushed as he clipped the lead dangling in his hand to the dog's collar.

"Sorry about that. He doesn't normally act like that when he sees someone. I don't know what got into him. I thought I'd attached the lead when I jumped out of the car, but he wriggled away so quickly."

"Oh, that's okay. No harm done. He must have known I love dogs."

I looked at the man again, thinking that his face looked familiar, but I couldn't remember where I'd seen him before.

I stroked the dog's head, smiling as he shuffled his bum on the ground to get closer to me.

"What's his name?"

"Buster. And he's going to have to learn some manners, daft boy running off like that." The man smiled as he held out his hand to me. "And I'm Tom."

"I'm Laura." I shook his hand, feeling the warmth in his fingers, then pulled away sharply. "So, it was nice meeting you and Buster. Take care and watch out for that lead."

"I will. And thanks again for catching him for me."

He sauntered away with Buster, lead firmly wrapped around his hand, then turned and crossed the road. *Tall, dark wavy hair, a bit longer than it should be. But friendly eyes. I definitely know you from somewhere.*

The deli sign was glowing orange, reminding me it was lunchtime, and I was hungry. *That's who he reminds me of. The man the other day in the deli. With a dog that looked exactly like Molly. But it can't be him. Different dog.*

It was busy inside, and I had to wriggle past several tables full of people before I found a free seat in the corner. I sank down in a chair, slipped off my coat, and picked up the menu.

"Sorry, we're short-staffed today. Might be some time before we can cook food for you." The young girl stood in front of me, notepad at the ready.

"That's okay. A coffee and a doughnut will be fine."

I closed my eyes for a second, then opened them again as someone bumped into my table.

"I'm sorry. Is anyone sitting here? It's bursting at the seams in here; this is literally the only seat left."

A woman was standing beside my table, hugging a carrier bag to her chest.

"Oh, my! Don't I know you?" she added.

Just what I need right now. Not.

"Yes, we went to school together. I'm Sadie. Remember me?"

The woman kept talking as she pulled back the chair opposite me.

"May I?" she said, already sliding onto the chair and settling down with a smile on her face.

"Ah, that's better. Thanks ever so much. I've never seen it so full in here before. Now, where's that waitress I saw a minute ago?"

I hadn't said a word to her. It didn't seem to matter as she busied herself getting settled and ordered a large latte and a cake from the poor hassled server, who rolled her eyes at me as she took the order.

"Where were we? Oh yes. School. I remember you. You were always the quiet one, sitting at the back, drawing all over your notepads. You still do that?"

"Yes, actually I do. I'm an artist now." I stifled the urge to scoff my doughnut and run. *Maybe I'll chat with her for a while. It's not as if I'm in a hurry or have anywhere else to go today. Or anyone else to talk to.*

"Gosh, that's exciting. Good for you. I'm in banking. Very boring. But it pays well. So, what are you doing here today? Do you live near here? And sorry, I can't remember your name."

"Yes, I'm literally around the corner. Got a little studio behind the sewing shop. I've been here ever since I graduated. And it's Laura. Laura Adams."

I took a bite of my doughnut, revelling in the sugary hit as the creamy centre exploded in my mouth. I wiped my lips with a napkin and took a long sip of coffee before looking up at my unintended company.

"So, what sort of things do you paint?"

"Um, well, all sorts really. Landscapes, still life. And I've recently added pet portraits to my repertoire."

Sadie was staring at me and leant forward, resting her chin on her fingers. I looked away, embarrassed at being watched so closely.

"Mmm. Something tells me you're not very happy, though. Your eyes. They're so sad."

I felt a jolt inside. *Is it that obvious? Can everyone see my pain?*

"Well, I... I've had a tough time of it lately." My body shuddered as I gulped down the hot coffee. *I'll finish this and then leave.*

"I'm sorry. Forgive me. I didn't mean to pry. It's just that..." Sadie's voice trailed off as a different server approached and placed a latte and a chocolate brownie on the table. Sadie waited until he'd gone, then reached out and patted my hand gently.

Her touch was the trigger as I blurted out everything about Molly's illness and her passing.

"I'm so sorry. You must miss her so much."

"I do, but then today..." I hesitated. *I can't tell her about that. She'll think I'm nuts. Well, there was this painting. And a butterfly. And the next thing I knew, I was in a field and Molly was there. Madness.*

"What happened today?" Sadie pushed her empty plate to one side of the table.

"You'll think I'm crazy if I tell you."

"Go on. Try me. I'm all ears."

I told her about my morning, watching as her expression went from amazement to disbelief.

"So, what do you make of that, then?" I wrapped my arms around my body and jutted my chin out. "Mad, huh?"

"I don't know. You certainly seem convinced it happened. But the mind can play strange tricks, that's for sure. Especially when we're upset. I bet you fell asleep and you miss your dog so much that you dreamt about her. Dreams can feel awfully real, you know."

Sadie slurped the last of her drink and glanced at her watch.

"Is that the time? Gosh, I must dash. Need to get home. Well, it was lovely talking to you today, um... sorry, I've forgotten your name again?"

"Laura. It's Laura."

Sadie left in the same flurry of activity that marked her arrival. I folded my paper napkin into a tiny square, cursing myself for being so stupid as to share everything with her. *And she definitely didn't believe me. She probably thinks I'm a nutter. She couldn't wait to leave either. It doesn't matter; I doubt I'll ever see her again.*

I paid up and trudged home. *Am I going mad? Was it all just an illusion? But the daisy flower. That was real. And I've not been anywhere lately with daisy plants. So how did that get there?*

I was glad I hadn't told Sadie that part. That would definitely have made me sound crazy. I slowed down as I reached the Thread and Needle store, now all in darkness. Enid must have gone home for the day. It was Wednesday. Half-day closing.

There's only one way to find out whether it was real or not. Can I go back there again? I turned the key in the door and headed for my studio, switched on the overhead light, and walked towards my painting of Molly.

CHAPTER SEVEN

The butterfly was glowing on the canvas in front of me. *This is unbelievable. Crazy. It can't be real.* Sitting cross-legged in my favourite ancient armchair in the corner of my studio, I noticed something sticking out from underneath the cushion. I pulled out Molly's favourite toy. An old, battered little teddy bear with one ear chewed, eyes missing. I had called it Toffee one day for a joke, and the name had stuck. One of my most treasured photos showed Molly snuggled up fast asleep in bed, one front paw wrapped around Toffee, her face a picture of contentment.

I stuffed the bear into my pocket and reached out to the painting, my fingertips tingling as I gently touched the butterfly. I closed my eyes as the room whirled and spun like a washing machine. A rush of colours, vivid and swirling, filled my senses as I stretched out my arms, almost toppling over as my feet landed on soft ground. A wisp of wind danced across my face as I opened my eyes, blinking in the bright sunlight.

I was in the same sun-drenched field, backed by tall willowy trees, the dense carpet of daisy-strewn grass beneath my feet. The sky seemed to stretch on forever, a vivid blue expanse dotted with fluffy white clouds, while a small group of birds sang out a cheerful chorus in the distance. Behind me, the trees swayed and rustled, their leaves spiralling and twirling in the gentle breeze.

I tiptoed forward, my feet sinking into the soft grass with each step. It was like walking on a quilted bedspread. I breathed in the sweet air, soaking in the beauty and peace around me. The sun's rays warmed my face, and the birds sang a joyous song, uninhibited and carefree.

My initial delight was short-lived as a thread of panic spiralled inside me. *I need to find the painting. Put it somewhere safe, where I can find it again. I bet it's over in the wooded area.* I hunted through the scattered leaves and plants, twisting and weaving my way through the undergrowth. The ground abruptly sloped downhill, and my foot slipped forward. I snagged my hand on a jagged branch and squealed as a sharp spike skewered my index finger.

A trickle of blood seeped through the tattered piece of skin. I sucked my finger, drawing the salty liquid into my mouth. *Trust me to cut myself. Interesting, though, that I bleed here. I'm still human. Mortal.* Another set of thoughts rushed into my head, making me catch my breath. *What if I were seriously hurt here? Who'd help me? How would I get back?* The reality of my situation hit home as I wiped my hand on my jeans. *I need to be more careful.*

I picked my way through the trees, suddenly more cautious than before. A pile of leaves, freshly heaped up, caught my attention, and underneath them was my painting. I dusted off the leaves and propped the canvas against a large boulder, satisfied I could easily locate it again.

Molly's tree. I set off, wading through the longer grass, eager to see her once more. I wriggled my fingers into the pocket of my jacket, feeling soft fur nestled inside. *Her teddy. That's brilliant. It looks like I can bring things over here with me.* I stored that thought away as I picked up speed, my heart thumping as I reached the magnolia tree.

Where is she?

A sudden movement on the far side of the field stopped me in my tracks. I panicked, then relaxed as I saw Molly, ears flapping, racing towards me.

She bounded up to me and fell into my arms, licking my face and yipping with joy. "I thought it was you. I was just over there chatting with some other dogs."

She whirled around, tail wagging, then sat down, panting gently. I wrapped my arms around her, nuzzling into her neck, feeling the warm, fluffy fur tickling my face.

"I have a surprise for you."

As I handed her the teddy, her eyes lit up at the sight of her old friend.

"Toffee. My favourite toy. I've missed him. Thank you so much."

I curled up on the grass beside her, twirling my fingers in her coat, kissing her face over and over.

"And you made it back here! I wasn't sure whether you could visit me again. It's so lovely to see you." She rolled onto her back, legs dangling in the air.

"I can't believe it. I still think this is all a dream. But when I'm here with you, it seems so real. You feel real." I stroked her tummy, the steady beat of her heart thrumming beneath her golden coat. "It's like we've never been apart. And I can talk to you. Understand you."

I kissed her nose, revelling in the love pouring from her eyes, as a white butterfly flittered across the grass in front of us.

"The moment I saw you in that shelter, I knew you were special. And that we were meant to be together." My mind drifted back to that day. "How did you end up there? I always wondered about your story. You were such a beautiful girl, even then, sat forlornly in that kennel."

Molly curled up closer to me, resting a paw gently on my arm.

"It's not something I like to remember. I was with a family before you. They had me from a young puppy. I hated being taken away from my mother. She felt so warm and safe. But a man arrived and picked me from the litter and drove me back to his house. A woman was there, and they made a real fuss of me at first. Took me everywhere with them. Fed me well. Played with me. But then one day she arrived home with a baby. And everything changed."

Molly sighed and stared across the field, her tail quivering.

"The baby cried all the time. It was a boy, and he never seemed to sleep. They were so busy with him; they hardly noticed me anymore. And when they did, they shouted at me. I was always in the way. The baby grew and started to crawl. Then, before I knew it, he was walking. He would chase me, pull my tail, hit me on the head with his toys. I tried not to mind, but one day he threw a metal toy car at me, and I reacted. It hurt so much, I snarled and snapped at him. The man grabbed me by the collar, shouting, 'That's it. I've had enough. She can live outside.' He dragged me out into the garden and tied my collar to a hook on the wall with a length of rope. He returned later that day and placed a small plastic kennel on the ground beside me. It was barely big enough for me to curl up inside. He left my water bowl outside the kennel and went back into the house, slamming the door shut behind him. And that became my life, sitting there tied to the wall. They would walk me sometimes around the block, but most of the time they just left me there alone."

My eyes filled with tears as I pictured her life. "That's no way to treat you."

"I was so sad. I didn't mean to snap at the boy, and I would never have actually hurt him. But I couldn't tell them that."

"So what happened? How did you escape?"

"Winter came, and I kept hoping they would let me inside the house. I could see them from where I was sitting. If they left the curtains open at night and the lights on, I could watch them for hours. I sat huddled in the damp kennel, shivering and longing to be back in the warmth of the house beside the fire. One night it was so cold my teeth were chattering, and I couldn't get warm. I know I was supposed to be loyal to them. They were my family. But I'd had enough. I gnawed through the rope that tied me to the wall. The cold weather had made it brittle, and I soon broke free. I jumped over the wall and set off down the street. It was dark, and I didn't know where I was going, but I just kept running. I was free at last."

I held her closer, feeling her body tremble as she told her story, her eyes a dull, flat brown, all the sparkle gone from her face.

"After what seemed like hours, I saw the faint twinkle of lights in the distance. I ran faster and faster until I reached a small town. The chill of the frosty night air seeped into me as I padded onto the main street. I looked around in wonder, taking in the unfamiliar sights, sounds, and smells. I spent a few days hiding in the park and kept to the edge of town, eating rubbish from the bins. Part of me wanted my family to find me, to miss me. I thought maybe they would treat me better if they realised I'd escaped because I was sad. But they never found me. I doubt they even looked for me. After a few weeks, a man in a uniform called to me, and I was so hungry I let him lift me up and put me in the back of his van. The next thing I knew, I was in a concrete kennel, surrounded by other dogs all caged up. And then you found me. That was the best day of my life."

Tears spilled down my face as I smiled at her. "That was the best day of my life, too."

I sat quietly, stroking her side as Molly drifted asleep, Toffee tucked between her paws. Memories of our time together cascaded through my mind, tumbling over each other like children scrambling to the gate at the end of the school day. All the special times we'd spent together, our daily walks, the holidays, curling up on the sofa side by side, Molly scoffing biscuits and treats from my pockets, nestling together each night in bed, listening to her gentle breathing as she slept.

Molly stirred and gazed up at me. The look in her eyes was one of total love and adoration, and a surge of intense emotions rushed through my body. I bent down and kissed her head, my heart filled with gratitude and pure, unconditional love. We stayed like that for a while, wrapped in a blanket of blissful peace and unity, until finally I stood up to stretch my legs, a wide yawn escaping my body.

A flash of gold between the trees caught my eye, and I jumped backwards, startled.

"Did you see that? Something is down there, moving between the trees."

"No, I didn't see anything." Molly seemed unconcerned as she licked her paws.

"There it is again. There's definitely something—or someone—over there."

The long grass parted, and I sensed someone staring at me, even from that distance. A strange sensation, like a strand of silk swirling around my neck and the soft brush of a fingertip on my ear, sent a chill slithering down my spine. As the mysterious figure stepped out of the shadows, I backed away, my heart beating wildly in my chest.

The figure strode forward with a confidence that was almost tangible. My breath caught in my throat, and I couldn't speak. When he was about six feet away from me, the man stopped, stomped his foot on the ground, and glared up at me. There was something unsettling, piercing about his eyes. Steadfast. Ruthless. His demeanour made me even more nervous as I glanced around, realising there was nowhere I could go to escape him.

He was like nothing I'd ever seen before. He had the stocky body of a man, with the head and tail of a lion. Work boots and khaki trousers splattered with mud, a shirt, sleeves rolled up, revealed tanned and muscular arms. He could have been mistaken for a park ranger, were it not for the golden tresses flaring out like a fan around his face, a mesmerising beard of fire. A lion's mane in all its glory. His amber eyes were glowing, as if they could see deep inside me. My hands trembled as I tried, and failed, to hold his gaze.

His locks shimmered as he turned his head slowly to one side, then the other, his nose twitching. The wind carried the intoxicating scent of cinnamon and honey, with a hint of cedar, across to me, as I took a deep breath and checked that Molly was still beside me.

"This is The Keeper I told you about." Molly seemed unperturbed by the creature's appearance.

I could almost taste his disapproval as the man continued to stare at me. His tail swished from side to side, his muscles tense as if ready to pounce. He curled his top lip back, revealing a set of sharp teeth, pointed fangs poised, as his nose wrinkled upwards. A quiet, yet penetrating snarl escaped his mouth as he took a single step forward.

Is this it? Is he going to attack me? Am I to die today? He's obviously not happy I'm here. But what can he do to me? I couldn't think straight, couldn't move. His fierce glare held me captive, my legs pinned to the spot.

His golden-yellow fur sparkled as he shook his head, gave a roar that vibrated the very earth beneath my feet, then spun around and departed as silently and stealthily as he had arrived. My knees buckled as the shockwaves passed, and I crashed to the ground.

CHAPTER EIGHT

My heart was pounding as I rested my hand on Molly's head, soaking up the reassuring steadiness of her presence alongside me.

"So, that was The Keeper." I took a deep breath. "He really frightened me. Will he be back? What should I do now?"

"I don't know. He's never been like that with me. He always leaves me alone."

"What do you know about him?" I shivered as I pictured his face again.

"Not much. One of the other dogs told me that The Keeper sometimes mentions that he's been here 'since the war'. But no-one knows which war he means. Apparently, Archaven is divided into areas, and a designated keeper or guardian oversees each section. I don't know what the other keepers look like; I've only ever seen ours."

Molly glanced around as I leant back against the tree trunk and clutched at the grass beneath my hand. My fingers curled through the soft tendrils, then dug into the soil underneath. It was warm to the touch, comforting and calming me as I attempted to process everything that was happening.

"It's as if I've stepped into a childhood storybook. A man who looks like a lion and a butterfly on a painting that can transport me to another world. A world where you are waiting for me. And a rainbow for a bridge. It's madness."

I caressed Molly's head, stroking the soft tender spot behind her ears. Her favourite thing in the world. The meadow hummed with life. A bumblebee darted between the flowers, and a bird soared high above us in the ultramarine blue sky. Molly had fallen asleep, her head in my lap, ears twitching as her breath slowed to a peaceful rhythm. I felt myself joining her as my eyes closed, then I sat up with a sudden jolt.

"My painting!" I realised the menacing lion figure had first appeared exactly where I'd left my canvas.

"What if The Keeper has taken it? How will I get home?"

Molly raced over to the line of trees with me as I stumbled into the undergrowth, hunting for my canvas, my hands scrabbling through the leaves in desperation.

"It's not here. I left it propped up against that rock." I sank to the ground, reaching my arms out to Molly as she padded over to me. My hands shook as I stroked her, trying to breathe and think calmly.

"I didn't see him carry anything away. It must be here somewhere." Molly looked around, her nose twitching.

"What if he's still here? Will he attack me?"

Molly's face had its usual relaxed, soft expression. "No, I don't think he'd hurt you. He's The Keeper. He's always been very gentle with me."

"But you're supposed to be here. I'm not. I still don't really understand how this can be happening. But I need to find that painting. I know I can't stay here forever with you. It's just not right. And without my painting, I'm trapped."

A glint of sunlight lit up a patch of grass beneath the trees. I set off towards it, not knowing what else to do. As I followed the glittering trail of light, I glanced down at Molly, relieved to see her walking calmly beside me, her paws padding gracefully. I reached down and placed my hand on her head, the tension slowly soaking away from my body.

She gambolled ahead, turning to woof at me as her tail lifted and shimmied in the air. Suddenly she shot forward, head down, tail wagging ferociously as she pawed the earth beneath her.

"Here it is."

I ran over and fell to my knees in front of my painting. I swept away the leaves that surrounded it and held up the canvas. It was still intact. *This was definitely not the place where I'd left it.* Maybe The Keeper was sending me a warning. A shiver snaked its way across my back and swirled around my neck, making me shudder.

"It's time for you to say goodbye again, isn't it?" Molly looked up at me, the question in her eyes leaving me racked with guilt.

"Yes, I think so. I hate to leave you. But now I know I can return. You've no idea how wonderful that feels, knowing that you're here and I'm able to visit you. I just need to protect this painting when I'm here. I'll keep it with me next time."

Molly circled around me, her tail swishing, eyes shining. "I'll wait for you. That's all I have to do. Time means nothing to me here. And there are so many other animals around. I won't be lonely."

"I hate saying goodbye to you, though. Leaving you here. And going back into the world without you. You know I miss you every day, don't you?"

Her eyes softened as I caressed her. "I know. I can feel your pain, and I count every one of your tears. But you can see I'm alright. You can't stay here. I know that now. But one day we'll be together again in an unbreakable bond. Forever. But I guess your time to be here hasn't arrived yet. Don't worry. I'll be here, waiting for you."

I gripped the painting, squeezing my eyes shut as hot tears spilled down my face. The sun disappeared behind a cloud, and the sky took on an ominous hint of grey, almost as if it knew how I was feeling.

"I'll come back soon. I promise."

The image of the lion man, his mane bristling as he roared, sprang to mind. I shuddered. "Nothing can stop me from seeing you again. Not even The Keeper."

I touched the painted butterfly, and kissed Molly on the tip of her nose, as the earth spun beneath my feet. I caressed her fur one last time, then everything went dark. Opening my eyes slowly, my throat constricted as I found myself back in my studio. The clock on the wall was ticking, with the afternoon sunlight streaming through the window. I was home again. Without her.

I opened the back door and listened to the birds twittering and chattering in the trees. Everything was exactly as I'd left it. I rubbed my hands up and down my arms. *Home. What does that even mean?*

A picture of my mum, arms folded over her pinafore, hands covered in flour, leapt into my mind. She loved baking. Every Saturday she would pull out her old cake tins and bakeware mixing bowl, dust down the worktop with a sprinkling of flour, and roll out an enticing gooey dough mixture. I closed my eyes, remembering the heady aroma of the cakes as they bubbled, their edges turning golden brown in the oven. Then the wonderful moment when she pulled on her oven gloves, opened the hot oven door and eased out the trays. I always made sure I was hovering around the kitchen door, ready to inhale the comforting sweet smell and snaffle a still-warm cake from the cooling rack as she swatted me away with her tea towel. *Home. That's what it should feel like. Not this empty existence.*

Molly's last words haunted me. *Live your life. Adopt another dog.* I couldn't imagine doing that yet. My heart and life were so full of her memories. Her presence was still hovering in the room, even now. Her toys remained scattered around the flat, her favourite blanket crumpled on the sofa.

My phone ringing jarred me back to the present as I looked at the caller ID. Anna White. My best friend since university. I swiped to answer the call and smiled as her voice crashed through the speaker, warm and bubbly as ever.

"Hello! It's me! I've missed you."

"How was Spain? Too hot, I bet." I settled down into my armchair, arranged the cushion behind my head, and curled my feet up underneath me. Anna's calls were never short affairs.

"Ooh, it was lovely. Lots of long days spent lazing by the pool, then wandering into the village to eat in the evenings. Geoff had to come back early, some emergency or other at the hospital. So, I had the last ten days all to myself. I missed Bayley, though. The dog sitter said he was fine, but he sulked the whole day yesterday. I think he's punishing me for leaving him."

I could picture Bayley, their beloved, slightly overweight and spoilt cocker spaniel, doing exactly that. "How old is he now? He's probably just set in his ways."

Anna chuckled. "Who, Bayley? Or Geoff?"

"Ha ha, both."

I tried to imagine Geoff sulking and failed. A cardiologist at the local hospital, he was a well-respected, if somewhat stuffy man, who always wore a smart suit and tie even on his days off. But he had a ready smile and adored Anna. Childhood sweethearts, married at twenty-two when Anna completed her university degree, they had everything they wanted in life. Or so it seemed. I pulled myself back into the conversation, as I realised Anna had continued chatting away to me.

"So, how are you? Are you feeling any better about dear Molly yet?"

"Well, not really. Some days are easier than others. But I'm getting there slowly."

I decided not to say anything about what had happened since Molly had passed away.

"What you need is a night out. Take your mind off things. And luckily for you, I know just the person to take you out."

"But you're over two hours away. You can't drop everything and come down here. And it's almost seven already." I pictured her sitting in the lounge of her house, with designer furniture and paintings all around her. Being married to a top doctor had its advantages.

"Ah well, that's where you're wrong, you see. Geoff's home with Bayley, but I'm down here, staying at a hotel in Honiton. In fact, I'm less than ten minutes' walk away from you. And I've got lots of news to share with you. So grab your coat and meet me at the pub. The Dirty Duck, you know the one."

The phone clicked, and Anna was gone.

Just what I don't need tonight. All I wanted to do was relive every minute of my time with Molly, and a shiver ran down my spine as I thought about The Keeper. *I hope she's okay over there. He'd better look after her.* The streetlight flickered on outside, and I forced myself up out of my comfortable armchair. *I wish I could pop back and give her one more kiss goodnight. Maybe later.*

Better get ready and go to the pub. I smiled, remembering the nickname we had given it all those years ago as students. The White Swan. But it had always been The Dirty Duck to us. I rushed up to my flat, pulled a brush through my hair and smeared on a layer of lip gloss, then grabbed my coat from the back of the door. *That'll have to do. I wonder what news Anna has in store for me?*

CHAPTER NINE

A rush of warm air hit me as I pushed open the pub door and stepped inside. Already busy for a Wednesday evening, I wriggled my way to the bar and ordered a small beer, certain that Anna would want to share a bottle of wine with our meals once she arrived. The door crashing open again a few minutes later signalled her arrival as she waved and bounded up to me, enveloping me in a hug.

"You look good. Your hair's getting really long now. It suits you. Boy, it's packed in here tonight. Quick, let's grab a table over there." She led the way, and I followed, happy to sink into a chair and check out the menu written on the chalkboard behind us.

"They've got their special pot roast on tonight."

"Two of those then, please." Anna caught the eye of the server as he walked past us, notepad in hand. "And a bottle of house red?" She glanced at me as I nodded, the server departing with our order complete.

"Tell me all about Spain then."

Anna unwound the scarf wrapped around her neck and dropped it onto the seat beside her. My thoughts wandered as she chattered away, telling me all about her holiday. *Molly, I miss you so much. I wonder what you're doing right now?*

The sharp sound of Anna clapping her hands together hurled me back into the room. "But that's not why I'm here tonight. Just to talk about Spain. I've got big news." She grabbed a handful of nuts from the bowl the server had dumped on the table and grinned at me.

I forced myself to appear interested as she continued. "I've got a new job. A promotion. Starting in September. And you're going to be seeing much more of me now, as we're moving back down here to Devon. You're looking at the new deputy headteacher of The Park Primary School. It's a Church of England school, and I can't believe they gave me the job!"

"Oh, that's fantastic! Well done."

Anna was beaming at me, excitement etched across her face, and I felt a tinge of envy ripple inside me. *That could have been me if I'd kept up with my training. Too late now, though.*

"But a church school. Are you sure about that? And what will Geoff do?"

"He's moving down here. They advertised for a senior cardiologist at Exeter, and he's been biding his time, waiting to see if I could get a job down here too. So, I'm busy house-hunting. Which is where you come in. I need a second opinion. Can you take some time off and look at properties with me? Geoff can't get away, so it's just me down here for a few days."

"Well, yes, of course. That's such great news. You're really coming back home? Fab."

Anna reached into her bag and pulled out a sheaf of papers, full of properties for sale. I gasped as I saw the price range. Cardiologists certainly earned a lot of money.

The evening sped by as we reviewed all the listings, discarding most of them and shortlisting a handful Anna was interested in viewing. It was going to be a busy few days. She set the papers aside as the server brought over our desserts. Apple pie and ice cream. The combination of warm buttery pastry, tangy fruit with a hint of cinnamon and sweet vanilla ice cream, was always a winner for me. I finished and put my spoon down, wiping my mouth with a paper napkin, and sighed. Life with Anna was never boring, as she signalled for two large brandies to be delivered to our table.

"But enough about me." Anna reached over and held my hand. "Now, how are you really?"

"I'm okay. Surviving, you know."

"You don't fool me, kiddo. We've been friends for far too long. You miss Molly, don't you?"

Tears sprang up behind my eyes, and I fought to keep them from spilling over.

"Yes. Every day. But…"

Do I tell her or not? She might think I'm crazy. Best not to say anything.

"But what? Come on, there's something you're not telling me, isn't there?"

"Promise you won't think I'm mad?"

"Well, everyone already knows you're bonkers." She chuckled as I raised my eyebrows and tutted.

"Gee, thanks."

"No, seriously, what's up?"

I wrapped my hands around the brandy glass, swirling the amber liquid, and took a large gulp, spluttering as its warmth trickled down my throat. *Okay, here goes.*

I told her everything that had happened with Molly and how I'd visited her in a magical land called Archaven, then sank back in my chair, waiting for her response. She stared at me, her eyes sharp darts, and in that moment, I knew I'd made a grave mistake opening up to her.

"You're joking, right? You actually think you've seen her in some Rainbow Bridge land? Just by touching your painting? Do you know how ridiculous that sounds—even after a bottle of wine and a double brandy?"

"Yes, I know. I thought I was dreaming at first. But it feels so real when I'm there. Molly is fit and well again, and I get to hold her and be with her."

"And the lion thing? You do know that's not possible, don't you?

It's straight out of a Tolkien novel. Are you sure you're getting enough sleep? You're not hallucinating? Or taking something?" She glared at me as I sank down in my chair.

"What—like pills or drugs? Surely you know me better than that?" I curled my hands up into tight fists, feeling my fingernails bite into my palms. "Forget I told you. It's not important."

"Of course it's important to you. I can see that. But honestly, the whole thing sounds a bit far-fetched, doesn't it?" She tossed her napkin onto her plate. "You know what the church would say about something like that, don't you?"

"Oh, right, so you're going all religious on me now, are you? Just because of your new job? That's great." I stood up, knocking my chair over in my haste to escape.

"Hey, stop. Sit down, silly. Don't spoil a lovely evening." Anna pleaded with me as I puffed out a deep breath, then perched on the edge of my seat.

"Anyway, you can't fall out with me. I need you to house-hunt with me tomorrow. Let's get the bill and call it a night, shall we?"

I shrugged my arms into my coat as Anna insisted on paying for our meals, then walked out of the pub behind her. I felt like a naughty schoolgirl caught cheating on a test as I slumped along beside her.

She pulled me into a hug and kissed my cheek. "Take care of yourself. Get some rest, and we'll meet up at the deli for breakfast tomorrow. Nine thirty alright for you?"

The next morning, I rose early, determined to show Anna I was fine. I took my time getting dressed, putting on a new top, and the matching scarf I knew made my eyes sparkle. I brushed my hair until it shone and tied it into a ponytail, then grabbed my bag and rushed out of the door, only just making it to the deli in time. Anna was already sitting at a table, and she stood up as I walked in, her eyes wary as she glanced over at me. I hesitated for a second, then put on my brightest voice as I sat down and cheerily wished her a good morning.

"We're okay then? Still friends?" Her hand hovered over mine.

"Yes, of course, we're fine. Let's forget last night ever happened. Put it down to the wine talking. Now, come on, which house is up first today?" I grabbed the menu off the table and signalled to the server to take our breakfast order. "A fresh croissant with ham and cheese for me, and a large cappuccino. I'm going to need plenty of sustenance today."

The day passed in a blur of houses and estate agents, as Anna marched round each property, making notes and asking questions. I trailed behind her, trying to keep up, and pretended to be interested, amused by the look of terror on the face of most of the agents as they saw her striding towards them, paperwork in hand.

When we'd exhausted all the options on her list and then grabbed a quick bite to eat at the local Chinese restaurant, Anna dropped me off outside my flat.

"Same time again tomorrow? There's one here on my list I'm really excited about, but the agent couldn't meet us today."

"Um, yes, that's okay. But I need to be back here in the afternoon. I must get some work done."

Anna waved as she raced off, her flashy sports car soon a haze of red at the end of the road. The sky was a riot of twinkling stars, a dazzling display of nature's artistry, as my thoughts turned once again to Molly. *I wonder if she can see the same stars tonight in Archaven? Maybe I can sneak over there to see her tomorrow. Just for a few minutes.*

The sight of my studio in darkness as I walked through the sewing shop made me sigh. I jumped as Enid appeared from the kitchen, clutching a mug of tea in her hand.

"Looks like you could do with a cuppa, love. Has Anna been driving you mad again?"

"What are you still doing here so late? And how did you know?" I smiled as I took the warm mug from her and cradled it in my hands.

"Well, I saw her drop you off. I was busy sorting through my inventory. Figured you could do with some company. You looked so sad. What's she been up to this time?"

I sipped my tea as Enid bustled around, tidying up and setting things ready for the following morning. As I told her Anna's news, she frowned, her eyes questioning me.

"And that's it? There's nothing else bothering you? Surely Anna's return is a good thing? But you don't seem thrilled?"

"No, I'm fine. Just tired. You know what Anna's like. She's always full-on with everything. I lost count of how many properties we checked out today. And there was something wrong with all of them. Hopefully, she'll like one of the houses we look at tomorrow."

"Well, as long as that's all it is. Don't forget I'm always here for you. If you ever want to talk." Enid smiled as I gave her a hug.

"Thank you. You're wonderful. I don't know what I'd do without you. It's been a long day. But I'm okay, really."

Best not tell her about Molly, in case she thinks I'm crazy, too.

I washed up my mug and said goodnight to Enid. As I trudged up to my flat, I vowed not to talk to anyone else about Archaven. It would be my secret. It was better that way.

CHAPTER TEN

The cottage was perfect. I knew it would be the instant Anna parked up, and we saw the enchanting wisteria plant enveloping the archway leading up the drive. Anna clapped her hands together and beamed as she grabbed the details and squeezed my hand.

"Let's hope it's as nice inside as it looks." She hooked her arm through mine as she glanced at her phone. "The agent should be here any minute."

As we stood there, a car pulled up outside, and a man got out and waved over at us. I gasped. *It's him. The man with the dogs.* He gathered up a folder from the passenger seat and strode over.

"You must be Anna. I'm Tom Bryant. We spoke on the phone. And hello again. It's Laura, isn't it? Fancy seeing you here!"

Anna stared at me. "You two know each other?"

"Um, no, not really. We met the other day. Bit of a problem with an escaped Alsatian dog. That was you, wasn't it?"

"Yes, that was me. Chasing after Buster. I'm not sure who needs more training—him or me." Tom brushed the hair away from his eyes and looked sheepish as he glanced at me.

"So, you're an estate agent? And a dog trainer? How does that work, then?" I tried to feign a lack of interest, but he intrigued me.

"Oh, I'm not a dog trainer. Far from it. I just help out at the local rescue centre. Walk the dogs. Clean up. That sort of thing. Anyway, let's get started. Wilson's Cottage. Lovely place. Three bedrooms. Deceptively spacious. Big garden. Shall we?"

Tom gestured for us to go ahead of him up the path as he reached into his pocket and jangled a set of keys.

Half an hour later, it was obvious Anna was itching to make an offer on the cottage. The current owners had modernised it nicely, retaining original features like the old fireplace and chimney breast in the spacious lounge. But it was the kitchen Anna kept returning to, with its stainless-steel appliances, sleek worktops and fabulous big picture window overlooking the garden. A children's plastic slide and a wooden sandpit sat in the centre of the lawn. As Anna stared out of the window, a wistful smile dancing on her lips, I realised with a jolt she was thinking about starting a family. She didn't need to say anything; it was there, written all over her face.

Anna promised to contact Tom later that afternoon with her offer. As he walked away to his car, he glanced back, smiled and waved.

Anna nudged me. "He fancies you."

"Don't be silly. He's just being polite."

"Yeah right. All estate agents wave and smile like that, don't they?"

"You haven't changed a bit, have you? Forever matchmaking for me. I'm fine as I am, thank you."

Anna giggled as she waggled her car keys at me. I slid into the passenger seat of her flashy Audi sports car, marvelling at how polished and tidy it was inside. A stark contrast to the state of my old, battered little Nissan Micra. Anna drove around the village, smiling broadly as she checked out the local amenities.

"I think this is going to be perfect. It's less than half an hour to Exeter, but it's so peaceful. I hope Geoff approves. I've sent him all the details, and I'm just waiting to hear from him."

"He trusts you. I'm sure he'll love it."

The drive through the open countryside back to my flat gave me time to think about Tom, as Anna sang along to the music now blaring out from her car stereo. *Fancies me indeed. Chance would be a fine thing.* Although I had to admit to myself, he was a nice man. And he volunteered at the rescue centre. So, he liked animals. That was always a bonus point in my book.

Anna dropped me off, and I gave her a gentle pat on the arm and asked her to call me that evening with an update on the house offer.

I pushed open the door to Enid's shop and jumped backwards as she scurried towards me, waving her hand in the direction of my studio. "You've got a visitor. She's been waiting ages for you. I told her I didn't know how long you'd be, but she insisted on staying. She's in the kitchen with a cup of tea."

"Who is it?"

"I've no idea. Never seen her before. She said her name was Sadie, and you'd know who she was."

I shrugged off my coat. *That's all I need. I was hoping to grab a bite to eat and then sneak off to spend some time with Molly again.*

"Thanks Enid. I'll see what she wants."

Enid gave me a friendly shove. "Try to smile! You never know, she might want to commission you."

I trudged through the shop, then forced myself to look interested as I opened the kitchen door.

"Laura. There you are! How are you?"

"Hello Sadie. Sorry you had to wait. I was out and forgot to tell Enid how long I would be. Normally, she knows where I am."

"That's okay. She's been looking after me. I really needed to see you." She set her mug down on the worktop counter. "I remembered you saying you did pet portraits, and my gran has recently lost her beloved miniature poodle. I was hoping you could do a painting for me. A memory piece."

I led her through to my studio and offered her a seat, but she wandered round looking at my paints and brushes, then stopped in front of my easel, where I'd propped up my painting of Molly.

"Is that your girl? The one who died? She's beautiful."

"Yes, that's my Molly." I felt my heart leap as I thought of her, sitting on the grass, waiting for me.

I grabbed a pad and a pen. "Tell me more about your gran and her dog. And what sort of thing did you have in mind for her?"

"It's probably best if you come round and meet her with me. Iris, my gran, is a wonderful lady, eighty-three years old and bright as a button. She lives near here, in a flat on Rumbold Street. It's a lovely spot, easy to get into town, bus stop right outside. She's had Poppy since she was a pup—fifteen years. A gorgeous girl. Gran's devastated now that she's gone."

I tried to concentrate as Sadie rattled off her gran's life story, noticing the way she twisted her long hair around her fingers.

"So, what do you think? Would that be alright?"

What did she just say?

"Um, yes, sorry, that'll be fine."

"Okay, great, we can walk there now if you like. She'll be delighted to meet you, and she's got loads of photos of Poppy." Sadie picked up her handbag and headed for the door, and I realised she expected me to follow her. I stuffed my notebook, pen, and camera into a rucksack and raced after her. *That'll teach me not to pay attention. I guess we're off to meet her gran now. What did she say her name was again?*

Sadie chatted non-stop as we walked down the road, and within minutes had stopped in front of a block of flats. "Here we are. Gran is going to be so pleased to see us."

Sadie rang the doorbell with a flourish and grinned at me. "She loves surprises!"

The door to the flats buzzed open, and we went inside, Sadie bounding over to a ground-floor apartment door that was already opening. A perfectly coiffed grey-haired lady was smiling at us, her arms open wide as she greeted Sadie.

"Darling, what a marvellous surprise! Do come in. I've just baked some shortbread; you must have known! And who's this with you?"

"Gran, this is Laura, my artist friend. Laura, meet my gran, Iris."

Iris held out her hand. "Nice to meet you, dear. Come in, come in, don't stand out there."

I quickly found myself sitting on a sofa, mug of tea in hand, plate of shortbread on the table in front of me. Her flat wasn't quite what I expected, with its clean lines, no mess, and modern Ikea furniture. Lots of plants. And Gran, Iris, wearing wide-legged trousers, an embroidered hippy-style top and a smart pair of soft pink moccasins.

Sadie held her gran's hand. "Laura's going to paint a portrait of Poppy for you. I want you to have something special to remember her with."

Iris's eyes filled with tears as she pulled a handkerchief from her pocket. "That's so nice of you, dear. I've got a favourite photograph of us here. Would that be useful to you?" She handed me a framed photo of her with Poppy sitting on her lap, staring up at her. The look of love and adoration between them was clear. It was a special moment captured on camera, and I knew it would make a wonderful painting.

"That's perfect. May I borrow this? I promise I'll take good care of it."

"Yes, of course. She was such a special girl. Loved to sit on my lap every afternoon and have a little snooze. I miss her so much. She was such a beauty. Sadie said I should get another dog, but I could never replace my Poppy. And anyway, I'm getting too old for that now. I'll just treasure the memories of my precious girl."

Iris dabbed her eyes with her handkerchief. "I'm sorry, dear. Silly old me. Take no notice; I'll be alright in a minute."

"Laura lost her own dog recently, Gran. I'm sure she understands. We all know how much you loved Poppy."

"Do you have any idea where you might like to hang the painting?" I changed the subject, not trusting myself to talk about Molly.

"She'll have pride of place in here, right above my television, I think. That way I'll see her when I sit in my favourite chair." Iris pointed to the wall in question, and I made a note of the rough size of the space.

"I can paint a custom-sized canvas for you. I'm not busy this week, so I'll make a start on it straight away."

"We can talk pricing via email." Sadie winked at me. "Don't want Gran here to know about that!"

I gathered up my things, placing the framed photo carefully into my rucksack.

"It was lovely to meet you. And I'm sorry about Poppy. I'll do my very best to honour her for you."

Iris stood up and patted my arm. "I'm sure you will, my dear. And thank you."

We left, and Sadie reached over and hugged me as we walked out of the building. "Thank you, thank you. I know she's going to love it. Here's my card; just drop me an email when it's ready. Whatever it costs, no problem."

She waved as she raced away, and I turned and walked slowly home.

CHAPTER ELEVEN

The next morning, I skipped down to my studio, my heart feeling lighter than it had done in a long while. *I'm going to do the best I can with this painting, as it means so much to Iris. I know how hard it is to lose a precious soulmate.*

I propped a new canvas, freshly primed and ready for action, on my easel. As soon as Iris showed me the framed photograph of Poppy and her, I knew this was going to be a special tribute. The deep-rooted love that flourished between them as Poppy nestled into her owner's arms was priceless. I hoped I could do it justice.

The outlines took longer to pencil in than I expected, and I picked up my phone to take a screenshot of the photograph. I zoomed in, studying the pattern on Iris' scarf, knotted loosely around her neck, and made a few notes on a pad of paper; reminders of things to feature and remember about her outfit and Poppy's decorative collar.

Suddenly, I froze, staring at my screen. *Surely, that's not... it can't be?* I magnified a section of the image. *There. No way! It is.* Pinned to her jumper was a butterfly brooch, sparkling with tiny diamonds on each wing. I squinted and looked at it again, just to be certain. *Yes, it's definitely a butterfly.*

My heart fluttered with anticipation as I stood up and added a quick pencil outline of the brooch to the canvas. *Well, this should be interesting. What if?... No, don't be silly. It's not going to happen again. Or could it?*

My phone ringing startled me, and I grabbed it to see who was calling. *Anna. Of course, it would be. Perfect timing.*

"Hello, I'm glad I caught you. How are you? I've got some exciting news."

I sat down. "Hi, I'm fine, thanks. I've started a painting for a new client today."

"Ooh, that's great. I can't wait to see it. And guess what? I put in an offer on the property yesterday, and the agent called me back this morning. The owners have accepted. It's all agreed. Full steam ahead. It's perfect for us. The minute I saw the cottage, I knew it was going to be our new home."

"That's fantastic. Well done, you…"

"And that's not all." Anna interrupted me, her voice loaded with excitement. "Guess who asked after you? Only our young, handsome estate agent."

"Yeah, well, I'm sure he was only being polite."

"No, he was very specific. 'How's my favourite artist?' That's what he said."

I heard the teasing tone in her voice as she tried to cajole me into responding, but I refused to take the bait.

"Great news about the cottage."

"Yes, Geoff is really pleased, too. It's amazing that he trusts me, as he's only seen the details I emailed him. I'm off back home today, and we're hoping to come down the weekend after next to view the place together. It's going to be fabulous, being so close to you again, too. I've got a million things to do before I leave, so I don't think I'll be able to see you today, but we'll all go out to dinner when we're next down here. Must dash. Love you. Bye."

The 'call ended' message flashed up on my screen. I tutted at the whirlwind that was always Anna in her ultra-busy mode, then returned to my canvas with a smile. *Better get painting.*

Hours later, I stepped back, pleased with my day's work. The portrait was coming along nicely, and as I washed out my brushes, my thoughts turned once again to Molly. I glanced at my watch. *I wonder if I have time to pop over there, just for a few minutes?* The thought of being able to hold her, even briefly, and see the sparkle in her eyes, was too tempting to ignore. *I won't stay long.*

I rested her painting on the table in front of me, and the canvas pulled me in, as if it had a force of its own that I was powerless to resist. The butterfly shimmered, dancing in the evening light, as I hovered my fingers above it and closed my eyes.

Molly. My darling girl. Mummy's coming.

Darkness surrounded me as I plummeted forward. My breath caught in my throat as a tornado of noise cascaded around me. Thunder roared as a burst of lightning spiralled, sending me spinning. *It's never been like this before.* A strong wind lifted me up into the air, twisting me round and round. Panic filled my veins as the painting started to slide through my fingers. I snatched at the canvas, gripping it tightly.

Then, instantly, it was daylight. Everything was calm and silent, the flower-strewn field beneath me. Archaven. Exactly as I had left it. I pitched over onto my side, gasping for air, and held the painting across my chest. I lay motionless, trying to steady my breathing, my head still reeling.

Suddenly, Molly was there beside me, licking my arm as I leant forward to greet her.

"What happened? You look scared." Molly sat down, nudging me with her nose.

"It was nothing. I lost my footing. Just being clumsy as usual. I'm fine." I didn't want to worry her or tell her what had really happened. All I wanted to do was be with her.

She rolled over onto her back, grinning at me as I gently stroked her tummy. *That smile. I've missed it so much.*

"You always loved your tummy rubs."

Molly groaned and wriggled her body closer to me, resting her head on my arm.

"I missed you. I can't stay long, but I couldn't resist coming over to see you."

I brushed my hand along her back, feeling her steady breathing as she settled down in my arms, and all the tension in my body disappeared. *If only I could stay here with you.* And yet, I knew it wasn't possible. A few stolen moments with her were all I could hope for.

A rustling in the trees startled me. *I must have dozed off. I don't even remember falling asleep.* Molly stirred beside me and stretched her front legs out, yawning loudly. There, standing in the shadow of the trees, was The Keeper. His fur blazed as he moved forward, his steps measured, unwavering. Molly tensed as she stood up, her tail erect, her forehead wrinkled as we watched him approach us.

Everything seems different today. I don't like this at all. I leapt to my feet, determined not to show The Keeper I was afraid, but a bead of sweat trickled down my neck.

"You again." His voice reverberated around the field as a flock of birds shot up from the grass and swooped away, cackling and cawing as they left. The air above me seemed to grow thick and dark, like treacle dripping from a spoon. *Don't panic. Molly's here. It's going to be alright.* I tucked my fingers into the curls of fur around her neck, the warmth of her body bolstering my courage as I faced The Keeper.

"It's not right. You shouldn't be here." He flicked his tail from side to side, his golden eyes glaring at me. As he stretched out his arms, he threw his head back and emitted a deep, menacing growl. The sound was like a train approaching, a low rumble that gathered speed and volume until it slammed into me. He spun around and marched back into the line of trees, disappearing from view.

Molly looked up at me and shook her head, her ears flapping, then yawned again. "Well, it looks like he's not going to do anything about it, though." Molly seemed unconcerned as she lay down and closed her eyes.

The word 'yet' almost escaped my mouth as I fought to regain my composure. *He's not going to do anything about it—yet.* I forced myself to stay quiet, not wanting to worry Molly.

All too soon it grew dark, and it was time to say goodbye. "I'll be back again before you know it, my darling. Don't worry. The Keeper doesn't frighten me."

I patted her head, bent down to kiss her on the nose, and then held the painting aloft. The butterfly glowed as I reached out, took a deep breath, and felt the ground beneath me disappear.

The return journey was instant, and I collapsed down onto my chair in the studio, the painting clutched in my hands. *Oh, Molly, what am I going to do?* I thought back to the sensations I'd experienced travelling there, but already the memory of how scared I had been was fading. *It'll all be okay next time. Next time? Of course there will be a next time.* I was already looking forward to seeing Molly again. *Nothing will stop me from visiting her. Not even The Keeper.*

The unfinished painting of Iris and Poppy perched on my easel brought me back down to earth with a jolt. The pencil sketch of the butterfly brooch taunted me as I stared at the canvas. *I wonder if there's any way that Iris might visit Poppy?* I couldn't even begin to imagine how that might happen. But then I had never expected to see Molly again. I glanced at the portrait one last time as I switched off the studio lights, my head buzzing with ideas.

CHAPTER TWELVE

I hesitated at the door, the canvas, covered in bubble wrap, clutched in my hands. Beside me, Sadie hopped from foot to foot.

"Gran is going to be so thrilled. Hurry, let's go inside and surprise her."

The painting had taken me over a week to complete. I worked long into the evening almost every day, and when I finally laid down my brushes, I knew it was the best work I'd ever done. I had captured the love between Iris and her cherished dog on canvas. Poppy sat on her lap looking up at her with pure adoration, Iris with her head to one side, her face soft and full of affection as she held her girl in her arms.

Sadie had come round to the studio almost as soon as I'd called her and gasped in delight when she saw the finished painting.

"It's perfect. Thank you. You've done an amazing job. Little Poppy looks so precious sitting there."

She had paid immediately using my portable card machine and even added a generous tip. And then, of course, she wanted us to take the painting straight round to her gran's.

She rang the bell and skipped inside the apartment. I held back, letting Sadie hug her gran, as she waved towards me with a flourish.

"'Ta-da, look what I've got for you!" Sadie pointed to the package and stepped aside as I walked forward to greet Iris.

"Come in; don't stand there outside. I'll put the kettle on."

I sat down on the sofa, the painting resting beside me, and listened to Sadie chatting with her gran in the kitchen. Soon they reappeared with a tray laden with cups of tea and a plate of digestive biscuits. The malty taste reminded me of my childhood. My mum always had a tin full of those biscuits on the dining table. They were her comfort food, often sharing them with our family's pet Labrador. *Happy times.* I dragged my mind back to the present.

"So, here it is, Gran. Your painting. It's all finished, and I know you're going to love it." Sadie handed her the package and winked at me.

Iris unwrapped it carefully, folding the bubble wrap neatly, then tears filled her eyes as she looked down at the painting.

"Oh, Laura, it's perfect. My darling Poppy. And you've caught her face so beautifully. Thank you so much."

Sadie glanced at her watch, then leapt to her feet.

"Is that the time? I've got to go, sorry, Gran."

I started to get up, but Sadie stopped me.

"No, stay. Finish your tea and chat to Gran for me. No need for you to rush off."

Sadie kissed Iris on the cheek, then left, crashing the front door shut behind her.

Iris placed the canvas on her lap. "Let me have a closer look at this wonderful painting. You're so clever. I wish I could paint like this. I miss my little Poppy so much. She really was my world. The flat seems so empty without her."

I sank back further onto the sofa, wrapping my arms around myself. *Now, do I tell her about the butterfly effect or not? What if it worked and she could actually see Poppy again? For one last time? If that were me, I'd want to go. Of course. But what if she has an awful time getting there—like I did last week? And don't forget The Keeper? She's in her eighties, for goodness' sake. The shock might be too much for her.*

My mind spun, thoughts swirling and wheeling round so fast I gasped aloud.

"Are you okay, dear? I'm sorry, I do talk a lot, don't I? I'm just so delighted with the painting. It will have pride of place in here, where I can enjoy it every day."

"No, I'm fine. Sorry. I'm so pleased you love it."

"You've even captured my butterfly brooch, too. That one means so much to me. My late husband, Arthur, gave it to me when we were courting. It was his mother's. He couldn't afford an engagement ring, but he gave me that brooch instead. Promised me as soon as he'd saved up enough money to buy me a ring, he would ask me to marry him. That all seems so long ago now. But I've always loved that brooch."

She sighed as she ran her hand over the painting.

"That's strange." Iris stared at the portrait and twisted it so the canvas caught the light from the window. "I could have sworn that butterfly moved. Must be my eyesight playing tricks on me."

This is it. Now or never.

"Funny you should say that. I have a painting at home of my dog, Molly. She was my soulmate. I lost her a few weeks ago, and it almost broke my heart. I painted her sitting beside me and added a butterfly to that picture too."

Iris leant forward, her brow furrowed. "There's more to it than that, isn't there? There's something you're not telling me. About the butterfly. What is it?"

I took a deep breath and then told her everything. The glowing butterfly, Molly and the field. Archaven and The Keeper, how I thought the painting might transport Iris there, and how to find her way back home.

"But that's wonderful! You mean I can actually visit this place? And see my girl again?"

"Yes, well, maybe. I'm not sure. I've never done this with anyone else before. You're not scared then? And you don't think this is all a bit weird or ridiculous?"

"My dear, I'm eighty-three years old. Nothing surprises me

anymore. What have I got to lose by trying?" Iris patted my arm. "Let's do this!"

"Okay. But you need to be careful. I don't know if this will work, but if you decide to do it, you must keep a tight hold of the painting. Don't let it out of your sight, not even for a moment. And you can't stay there too long. Don't fall asleep. And watch out for The Keeper. He's pretty scary, but he's never hurt me."

I looked over at Iris, unsure of what her reaction would be, but instead of the shocked expression I expected, she was glowing. A huge smile lit up her face as she clapped her hands together.

"I knew it. I knew there was something special about you the instant I met you. Let's do it. I so want to see my Poppy again. Just once. So I know she's safe and happy."

"Are you absolutely sure?"

"Yes, yes, of course I am. Never been more sure of anything in my life before. It'll be fine. Now, what do I need to do again?"

She held the painting on her lap and whispered the words I'd said to her, my reminders to be careful, not to fall asleep. Not to stay too long. I held my breath as she caressed the butterfly brooch in the painting. Time seemed to freeze; our silence filling the space with expectation. The steady tick-tock of the clock in the room got louder and louder as we sat there in anticipation. *Maybe nothing is going to happen.*

Suddenly, a flicker of light leapt from the painting, and she was gone. And yet, the ghostly outline of the painting remained, perched on the chair where Iris had been sitting. I shot out of my seat and marched around the room, a sudden panic setting in like a car crashing in front of me, my heartbeat thrumming in my ears. *What if something happens to her? What would I tell Sadie? Oh heck. What if Sadie comes back now and asks where her gran is? I didn't think this through. We shouldn't have done this. Telling Iris was a mistake. What am I going to do now?*

I stopped beside Iris' chair. The outline of my painting fizzled and then disappeared. In its place, a window appeared, and a field beyond it came into focus. A field full of daffodils, the flowers fluttering and dipping in the breeze, and at the centre was Iris, her arms outstretched, sunlight streaming across her face. She was radiant; her face beaming as a small white poodle raced up to her and jumped into her arms. *Poppy. She made it then. And there's the painting beside her on the ground. Phew.*

I scanned every inch of the scene before me, but everything seemed serene and calm. *It's a different field from Molly's. But it looks so peaceful, and Iris is glowing with love and happiness.* I couldn't hear what Iris was saying, but it was obvious she was telling Poppy how much she loved and missed her. *Maybe it will all be okay.*

I sat down, feeling awkward as I watched them interact. It was such a private moment, but I justified it to myself by remembering I wanted to make sure Iris was safe. Poppy romped around her owner's feet, gambolling through the flowers and rolling around in the grass, tail wagging, tongue lolling, relaxed and carefree. It didn't seem long before Iris was wrapping Poppy in her arms and kissing her over and over—I presumed, saying goodbye. Iris picked up the painting, tears streaming down her face, as Poppy scampered off across the field.

Iris' return to the room was as sudden as her departure, as she plopped down in the same chair, still clutching the painting. Her tears continued to fall as she uttered one gut-wrenching, heaving sob, then looked up at me, the corners of her mouth twitching upwards, her head nodding.

"Well, that was something else. I can't believe I've seen my Poppy again. She looks so well, too. Full of life. And she could talk to me. Imagine that! I'm not sure I'll ever be able to thank you enough." Iris grabbed my hand and squeezed it gently. "I think this should be our little secret, though, don't you? I doubt my Sadie would believe me, anyway." She nudged the plate of biscuits towards me. "Another cup of tea?"

I couldn't string a sentence together. My mind was reeling from what had transpired, in stark contrast to Iris's calm and almost nonchalant demeanour, which only heightened my shock.

"You're alright then? I mean, with all of this? Going over there? Seeing Poppy? You don't even look that surprised."

I thought back to how I'd felt the first time I'd visited Molly, the total confusion that filled my brain afterwards. I'd struggled to comprehend or believe what had happened, as if my view of the world had somehow been irrevocably and permanently altered. And yet Iris appeared unscathed by it all, except for her obvious distress at having to say goodbye to Poppy at the end.

"Yes, dear, I'm fine. That was such an unexpected and lovely thing to happen. I'm content now, knowing she's alright. I've always thought there had to be something more after we die. You called it the Rainbow Bridge, is that right? I've heard that name before. The special place we go to be reunited with our beloved pets again. I never thought about what happened before we joined them to cross the bridge together, though. That beautiful meadow with all those flowers. Daffodils have always been my favourites. Archaven. I like that name. It reminds me of archangels and heaven. Now I'm reassured, knowing Poppy will be there waiting for me. You don't know how much comfort that gives me. You're a very special young lady."

I stared at her in amazement. *I wish I could be so calm and collected. This changes everything. I need to think through the implications of all this. I mean, what if more people could visit their pets too? What have I started here?*

As I gathered up my things and handed back the framed photograph I'd borrowed, Iris stood up and gave me a hug. "Thank you again, my dear. I'll never forget this."

I walked home in a daze, struggling to make sense of everything that had taken place. And then I remembered the conversation I'd had with Sadie that day in the café. *Blast. I've already told her about my trip over to see Molly. Now what do I do?* I was glad Iris had decided not to tell Sadie about her journey. *If we add that to the mix, it might completely freak her out. Probably best to keep quiet. I dread to think what Sadie would say if she knew I'd encouraged her gran into such a reckless act.*

CHAPTER THIRTEEN

I desperately needed to see Molly again. Just to reassure myself she was okay and check I could still travel there at will. But I had so many things to consider before that. Seeing the window image appear in place of Iris' painting had scared me. Did that happen every time I visited Molly? The painting was with me when I travelled. It was always there on the 'other side' with me. It was my only way back home. But what if the echo of my visit was also being broadcast in my studio—or wherever I set off from? *I need to be more careful. Make sure there's no way anyone could stumble upon that window in my absence.*

And the timings too—they were confusing me. Each time I had crossed over, it had seemed like I'd spent hours there with Molly. And yet, the clock in my studio hardly moved. Time was obviously a different concept over there. *I must ask Iris how long she thought she'd been with Poppy. And how it felt. Was she afraid? She certainly didn't appear scared. She was positively glowing when she returned. What does this all mean for me? And how will The Keeper react to this?* Something told me he wouldn't be too pleased. *Well, there's only one way to find out.*

I quickened my step and rushed home, grabbing my painting of Molly from the studio, and scampered upstairs to my flat. I shut and locked the door, breathing a sigh of relief. *Time to see my girl again.*

The journey over was quick and painless as I set the painting down on the grass and waited for Molly to race over to me. She was circling around the bottom of the field, but this time she moved at a snail's pace, her tail hovering above her body. She seemed different, almost reticent, as she approached me, and I held back, unsure of what was happening.

"We need to talk." She settled down at my feet, licked my hand, then stared up at me. "The Keeper. He came to see me. He wants an explanation. Who was the lady you sent over? Her dog has been going wild since that visit, racing round telling everyone about how wonderful it was to be with her owner again."

"Oh no. I never thought about the consequences of what might happen over here. She's called Iris. And she just wanted to see her little Poppy again. She was missing her—the same way I've missed you."

I explained about the butterfly brooch and the painting as I sat stroking Molly. "I wasn't sure if it would work, if she could travel here the way I can."

"Well, obviously she did. And now The Keeper is on the warpath. I've never seen him angry before. But he was storming around here, bursts of fire escaping from his mouth as he roared. He sees himself as the king of the pride, I guess. His job is to protect us and this place. And he's not happy. He said he wants to talk to you."

"Where is he anyway? I can't see him anywhere." I shuddered at the thought of his menacing figure.

"I don't know. I've not seen him today. Let's go for a walk, and we can worry about him later." Molly stood up and shook herself. "There's something I want to check out."

I picked up her painting, tucking it under my arm, and followed her as she trotted down to the river and then turned right, walking away through the line of trees. Soon we were in a different field. The grass was longer, and the entire area looked derelict and abandoned. Molly circled around, her nose twitching, ears flat against her head. Suddenly she leapt over to a pile of rocks and growled. I'd never seen her like that before, as she scrabbled at the ground with her paws. Frantic. Unsettled.

I walked up to her, and then I heard it. The faintest of sounds. A groan. Followed by a shuffling noise. The pile of rocks bordered the edge of a disused well, overgrown with weeds and rubble. As I peered down, a sudden movement made me jump back. There was someone or something trapped in the well.

"Help me. Is someone there?"

It was The Keeper. His golden mane was matted, clothes covered in dust. But it was definitely him.

"I'm stuck down here. Help me. Please."

My mind raced. "Okay, hang on. Let me think about what we can do."

Molly circled around the well, her head swishing from side to side, as I racked my brains for a solution.

"I'll need a rope. I'm sure Enid has one in her garden shed."

"There's a donkey in the field nearby. I've heard him braying." Molly looked at me. "What if I ask him to help? If The Keeper ties one end of the rope around his body, the donkey could pull him free."

"Great idea." I'd no idea how we were going to heave The Keeper up out of the well, and that seemed like the perfect solution. "I'll need to go back and get the rope. Meet you back here in about ten minutes?"

I cupped my hands round my mouth and shouted down to The Keeper. I explained our plan and told him to hang tight. He nodded and sat down.

I shot back home, racing to the garden behind my studio. Enid had a thriving vegetable plot there, centred around a large cherry blossom tree, but it was the shed I needed. Coiled in the corner, under a pile of wooden fruit boxes, was an old but thick rope. I secured it around my waist and hurried back over to Archaven, landing just as Molly returned with a sturdy and composed donkey trailing behind her.

"This is Charlie. He used to pull a plough when he lived on a farm, so I'm sure he'll manage to lift The Keeper out of the well."

I tied one end of the rope around the donkey and then dropped the rest down the well. It wasn't perfect, but I had to hope our plan would work. The Keeper signalled he was ready, and Charlie slowly walked away, pulling the rope taught behind him. Soon the head of The Keeper emerged, and I leant forward, tucking my hands under his armpits and helped to lift him clear of the well. I untied Charlie, thanked him, and watched as he trotted away.

"You're alright?" The Keeper seemed unharmed, but I wanted to make sure.

"Yes. No broken bones. Thank you." He shook himself, dusting off his clothes, and stared down at the well. "I heard a noise. I thought it was an animal in distress. And then, as I leant over to check, the wall crumbled. I lost my balance and ended up falling headfirst into the well. The ladder inside had disintegrated, and I was stuck."

He shuffled his feet, his expression guarded. "You saved me today. Thank you. I don't know what I'd have done if you hadn't found me. But I think you have some explaining to do. Why are you here again?"

I bowed my head and took a deep breath. *Don't be afraid of him. Whatever he is, or whoever he is, he's in charge here. And I must respond. I need to protect Molly, and not annoy him. Otherwise, he might not let me come back again. And he owes me one now. I rescued him. Saved him. That must mean something.*

"I'm only here to visit Molly. I mean you no harm. Honestly. I've no idea how or why this is happening. It's a complete shock to me that I can be here. I didn't ask for this. But I love this girl so much. I thought my heart would break when she died. And now I have the chance to be with her again. Please understand, I don't want to cause any trouble for you or anyone else." My voice caught in my throat as I willed myself not to choke or cry. Even after everything that had just happened, The Keeper was still an imposing figure.

He took a step forward, and the earth trembled beneath us. Molly spun around and sat at my feet. I placed my hand on her head, her warmth and calmness giving me strength as I stood there, facing the impressive lion-man figure.

"And the other lady? How did she get here? You know I cannot let that happen again, don't you?" He stood before me, arms folded, eyes glaring, as his dusty mane shimmered in the early evening light. Even the trees behind us seemed in awe of him, unmoving in the breeze that swirled around us, the birds all silent. Watching.

"I'm sorry. I didn't think it through. The lady missed her poodle so much. The connection between them was incredibly strong, and she was distraught without her little dog beside her. I didn't know whether she could even travel here. It was just an experiment. I'll make sure she doesn't return."

"See that you do."

"And what about Molly and me?"

"You're not disturbing anyone else, but no-one has ever passed through time and space in this way before. It is a complete mystery to me. But today, you did a brave thing. You could have walked away and left me there, trapped in the well. So I owe you something in return." He stroked his beard, deep in thought. "You may visit Molly. For now. But this cannot last forever. And you cannot keep sending others over here. If you're quiet and don't cause any trouble, you may return. But I will be watching you carefully. If any problems arise, then your visits to Archaven will have to stop. Do I make myself clear?"

"Yes. I understand. Thank you."

He swished his tail and strode away, leaving me breathless and dismissed.

"I think I ought to go now, Molly. This has been one strange day. Will you be alright?" I looked down into her gorgeous eyes and couldn't hold back the tears. "I'm not sure it ever gets any easier, saying goodbye to you."

Molly nuzzled into me. "I'll be fine. You know where I am, and it would appear you're free to come and go as you please. For the moment, anyway. Let's just make the most of this time and enjoy being together again. I'll always be here, waiting for you. Only a wish and a step away."

I grasped the painting and touched the shining white butterfly, feeling it quiver beneath my fingertips.

"I'll be back soon. Take care. I love you, my darling."

🐾 🐾 🐾 🐾 🐾

The next morning I headed over to Iris' flat, hoping to catch her at home. I was in luck as she answered the doorbell straight away.

"Come in, Laura. How lovely to see you again! Shall I put the kettle on?"

"No, thank you, Iris. I can't stay. I just wanted to talk to you about yesterday."

"My dear, I hope you haven't been worrying about that. It was a lovely experience, one I'll treasure forever. I have to pinch myself to believe it happened. But then I remember the look of pure joy and excitement on Poppy's face when she saw me, and I know it was real. What I wouldn't give to do it all again, though. Could I go back—just one more time? Please?"

I touched her arm. "That's why I'm here. It's, well, it's complicated. Remember, I warned you to watch out for The Keeper—the lion figure?"

Iris interrupted me. "Oh him. I shouldn't worry about him. I doubt he's bothered at all."

"That's just it. He's not happy. I went over there after I left here yesterday and met with him. He's the guardian of Archaven. And he warned me you can't go back there again. He's allowing me to visit Molly at the moment. But not anyone else."

Iris' top lip quivered as she grabbed a hankie and blotted her eyes. "I so wanted to see her again. To hold her in my arms and kiss her darling face." Iris looked up at my painting on the wall. "Just once more?"

"I can't risk it. The Keeper was adamant that you can't return. I'm sorry."

"That's alright, dear. I quite understand, and I wouldn't want to get you in any trouble. I know Poppy is safe there, waiting for me to join her. That will have to be enough for me."

"Thank you. I'm still finding my way with all of this, to be honest. It was such a shock the first time I found myself over there. I thought I was dreaming. Hallucinating. Lack of sleep, I told myself. But then, well, as you know, it was really happening. The whole Rainbow Bridge story come to life. In my hands. Simply by adding a butterfly to a painting. If I told people, they'd think I was crazy. I'm so glad I have someone to share it with now."

"Let's have that cup of tea, shall we? And then we can talk some more." Iris busied herself in the kitchen as I sat looking out of her window onto the street below. I didn't hear her come back into the lounge and jumped as she set a tray down on the coffee table, crockery clattering as it skidded across the tiled surface.

"Can I ask you something?" I sipped my tea, shaking my head at the plate of biscuits on offer. "What was it like over there for you?"

"Oh, it was wonderful. It felt like the most alive I have ever been. All my senses were on fire. When you get to my age, everything starts to fall apart. My eyesight and hearing aren't what they used to be. And my bones ache, you know? But over there, I was alert. Animated. Pain free. I guess that's how Poppy felt too. She had such bad arthritis before she died. But she was bouncing and running around like a little puppy again."

"And how much time did you think had passed while you were over there?"

"Not that long, really. I think I could have stayed longer. But your stories of the lion character made me nervous. I just wanted to hold Poppy in my arms. Check she was okay. After that, I was happy to return home. But then last night, I couldn't stop thinking about her. Wishing I could be back with her again."

I told her about the window and watched as her expression darkened.

"I think you need to tread carefully, Laura. If the wrong people find out about this…" Her voice trailed away as she gazed at me. "Well, who knows what could happen? Promise me you'll take care of yourself, please?"

"Of course I will." I tried to reassure her, but alarm bells were ringing in my head. *She's right. I must be more careful.*

I gathered up my coat and bag and headed for the door. "Don't worry about me. I'll be alright."

CHAPTER FOURTEEN

After that, I tried to carry on with my life. Mrs Thomas at the art gallery informed me they'd sold two more paintings, and I promised her I would get straight to work and create some new pieces. But every time I picked up a paintbrush, I just stared blankly at the canvas, thinking about Molly.

I went out to dinner with Anna and her husband Geoff as planned and tried to look interested as they told me all about their plans for the new cottage. Anna would leave her current post at the end of term, and they were hoping to exchange contracts before that date. My mind wandered away to Molly, wondering what she was doing.

"That gives me the whole of the summer holidays to get the new place up to scratch. Isn't that great? Laura… you are listening to me, aren't you?"

"Oh yes, of course. The whole summer. Lots of plans. It's very exciting."

"Naturally, I'll be looking for new artwork for the walls of the cottage. Do you know any decent artists around these parts?"

That comment made me smile. "Well, I know of one. She's rather busy, though. But I'm sure she can fit you in."

"Great. I've got loads of ideas to run past you. I'll pop into the studio next time we're down, and we can start plotting."

They left in a rush of kisses and hugs, with Anna promising to call me to meet up again. I wandered home, my head far away in a land of daisy-filled fields and Molly.

Something drew me back to Molly the next morning. I promised myself I wouldn't stay long, but it was almost as if I could hear her calling me. After what happened with Iris, I kept the painting of Molly in my flat, just to be on the safe side. And in case there was a window when I departed, and anyone saw me while I was over there. I couldn't risk that.

I laid a finger on the butterfly, feeling the room sway as I spun around. A whoosh of cold air enveloped me as I landed, and I dusted myself down and strode over towards Molly's tree.

"Oh good, you're here." Molly licked my arm, her touch tender and full of love.

"I just had a feeling you wanted to see me today."

"Let's go for a walk, shall we? Like we always used to." Molly got up and shook herself, her tail whipping around, ears quivering, as she faced the river. "This way. I want to show you something."

I ambled along, Molly prancing ahead of me, her eyes full of mischief. The heady scent of the flowers scattered in the grass reminded me of long, hot summer days as a child, playing in the fields near my house. My mother watching as I carefully created daisy chains to drape around her neck. I bent forward to trail my hand through the tall stems, their caress like a soft skein of velvet yarn brushing my fingertips. A swallow in flight danced around us, whirling and tipping its wings as it darted across the grass.

As we reached the edge of the field, I could hear the ripple of waves tumbling down the river.

"The tide's racing along today. Is it always like this?"

Molly pranced around, carefree and unperturbed by the torrent ahead of us. "Sometimes. I think it depends on the weather. Or The Keeper. One of the other animals told me he controls the flow of the water."

The river stretched for miles in either direction. There seemed to be no way across, no bridges or breaks in the swell, and it was impossible to see what was on the other side. The water was endless. All-consuming. And foreboding, too.

Suddenly, in the distance, a spark of colour rose above the tide. A flash of rainbow hues that hovered and glistened in the air. I couldn't take my eyes off the spectacle as I gasped and pointed at the sparkling lights. I was desperate to find out what was happening, but it was too far away.

"What's that? Molly, can you see it?"

Molly wrinkled her nose.

"Oh, that's the Rainbow Bridge. It hasn't fully formed yet, but someone will walk over there with their pet. Or pets. I've watched people meet up with several of their beloved animals in the past. Dogs. Cats. I even saw a donkey once. They cross the rainbow structure together like I told you."

"But where do they go? What's on the other side?"

"I've no idea. But it's always so peaceful and calm. Nothing to be afraid of. I'm sure of that."

A scrabbling sound behind us made me jump as a small cairn terrier approached us. Molly trotted over to say hello to him as they tentatively sniffed noses. Content with the greeting, Molly came back to me as the little dog sat down on the grass facing the river. He peered around as if he were looking for someone.

"Let's sit over there, out of the way." Molly nudged my leg. "That's Monty. He's waiting for his owner."

Molly sped over to a grassy mound nearby, and I hurried over to join her. As soon as I sat down, the air changed above us, and the sky seemed to glow. I could hear the river roaring in the distance, and the earth vibrated as a vivid tide of colour appeared, hovering at the water's edge. An exquisite rainbow stretched across the river. Each blazing colour was in perfect balance, dazzling and glittering in the sky.

Monty barked once as an old man came hiking across the field. He had a walking stick, which he threw into the air as soon as he saw the grey terrier racing towards him. The man lifted him up into his arms, shouting with joy and then spun him around, the little dog yipping with excitement.

I found myself utterly mesmerised as they made their way over to the riverbank. The closer they got to the bridge, the more youthful the man became, until he transformed before my eyes into a fit and healthy young man. It was incredible.

How can this be happening? It's a miracle. Nothing short of a miracle.

The man and dog were oblivious to anything or anyone else around them as they moved as one towards the bridge. Time seemed to stop as the man bent down to pat Monty's head. Then he strode forward beside his dog, stepping vigorously onto the rainbow. The arch held firm as they walked resolutely side by side, each step taking them further away from us over the river.

I strained my eyes to follow their path, but the light was so bright it was almost impossible to see them. Soon they were completely out of sight, and the rainbow faded away.

I jumped up and raced over to the riverbank. "But where are they? Where have they gone?"

A booming voice startled me, and I jolted forward, struggling to stay on my feet.

"They have gone to a better place. One day, you may join them. Perhaps."

I swivelled round to face The Keeper, who was standing beside Molly, a clipboard and pen in his hands. He stroked his mane and pointed at the river.

"There are things here you know nothing about. Things beyond your comprehension. It's best you don't ask so many questions."

I lowered my gaze.

"I have work to do. See that you don't stay here too long today. And speak of this to no-one." The Keeper swept around and was gone in a blast of golden light.

Molly crept over to me and lay down. "He's right. One day that will be us crossing the bridge together. And we'll discover what's on the other side. But I know you're not ready for that yet. It's not your time. You still have things to do in your life first. I'm content to wait for you, however long that takes. Time is irrelevant here, as I told you before. I'll be safe here, just waiting for you."

I nestled my face into her body, breathing in her unique scent. A heady mixture of sunshine mixed with a cocktail of fruit and freshly mown grass assaulted my senses as I buried my head further into her side, trying to absorb the very fragrance of her. I wished it were possible to capture her sweet smell in a glass jar; something I could take back with me to open at leisure each time I missed her. I settled for picking up strands of her fur that had fallen onto my jeans, determined to keep them hidden in my purse.

"I'm not sure I can go on like you said. Without you by my side. Life just isn't the same now you're gone."

A part of me almost wished I could simply grab hold of Molly and run across the Rainbow Bridge with her the next time it appeared, but I knew deep down that wasn't a possibility.

Molly nuzzled in closer to me, softly licking my face as I stroked her muzzle and tickled her ears.

"You must go on. Be brave. Visit me when you can, for as long as you can. But you must keep living. For me. And for yourself. You've been given a rare gift. The knowledge that I'm here waiting for you, and that there's so much more for us to experience together in the future. But for now, go back, live well. Please adopt another dog. Fall in love. Live your life. I will always be here."

I dissolved into tears as I cradled her face, my hands shaking as I stared into her eyes. Darkness was falling, the stars tiny pinpricks of light in the distance as I held her one last time.

"I promise I will. For you, my darling girl. And I'll return soon. I love you so much."

CHAPTER FIFTEEN

A text message pinged on my phone as I stared at the blank canvas on my easel.

> Can I pick you up tomorrow morning? I'm off to see the cottage again. Need your help!

Anna. Well, why not? I'm not exactly busy here. Maybe it will inspire me.

> Of course. See you then.

I headed off to the local supermarket to stock up. My cupboards and fridge were empty, and I knew it was time I pulled myself together. I grabbed a box of Cherry Bakewells as I pushed my trolley around the store. The little cakes with the fondant icing and a cherry on top were Enid's favourites. *I must catch up with her. It's been ages since we had a proper chat.*

The Thread and Needle store was quiet as I slogged up to my flat, lugging three heavy shopping bags. I put all the fridge and frozen goods away, then raced back downstairs to make some tea. Five minutes later, balancing two mugs of tea and a plate of cakes on a tray, I crept into the shop, hoping to surprise her.

Enid smiled. "I heard you put the kettle on. Ooh, and Cherry Bakewells too. How lovely." She patted the stool beside her. "Come and sit here and tell me what you've been up to. It's been a quiet morning. Hopefully, we won't have any customers disturbing us for a while. I know you're up to something; I can just tell." She took a bite of cake, dusting stray crumbs off her lap.

"No, nothing special. Anna's picking me up tomorrow to view her cottage again. She's had her offer accepted, and they're moving in at the end of term. I'm hoping she wants to commission some paintings, although I'll only charge her mate's rates. And the gallery wants some more paintings too, so that should keep me busy."

"I'm sensing there's a 'but' in there somewhere."

Enid knows me far too well.

"I've enjoyed painting animals and pets lately. I'd love to do more of those. Capturing the personality of the dog—or cat—with my brushes. It's a real challenge. I like that. But the gallery won't want those. They're hoping for more of my landscapes."

"I saw the one you did of Molly. It was beautiful. I'm guessing it has pride of place in your flat now?"

"Yes. And I painted a miniature poodle last week. The owner loved it." *Don't tell her about the brooch. Or Iris and her visit to Archaven. Enid will think I'm barmy.*

"Well, why don't you get some posters printed advertising your work? I'll put one up in the window here, and I'm sure Mrs Thomas at the gallery would have some. See if you can drum up some new business?"

"What a great idea! I'll get straight onto it today. Thank you. You're always such a wholehearted supporter of my work."

Enid patted my hand. "It's my pleasure, dear." The little bell above the door jingled as a customer walked into the shop. "Must get back to work, then."

"Yes, me too." I washed up the empty mugs and plates and went into my studio, closing the door behind me. *Time to make some posters. Pet Portraits. Why not? But no more butterflies.*

Bright and early the next morning, Anna rang my doorbell. She swept up the stairs into my flat, unravelling the patterned silk scarf wrapped around her neck, and plopped herself onto my sofa with a loud, "Oof."

"Any chance of a coffee before we have to leave?" She glanced at her watch, a delicate gold number that probably cost a small fortune. "I think we've got time before we meet Tom."

"Tom? Who's Tom?"

"Oh, Laura, pay attention! Tom Bryant—the estate agent. You know, the one that fancies you. He's meeting us at the cottage with the keys, silly."

"He does not fancy me. For goodness' sake, Anna, pack it in. I'm not looking for anyone. I'm happy as I am."

"Rubbish. You're as lonely as can be. Anyone can see that. He'd be good for you. Nice looking. Steady income. And he likes animals. In fact, come to think of it, he's perfect for you."

Here we go again. Anna playing matchmaker for me. I don't need a man, thank you very much. Just Molly. I'm only lonely because Molly isn't here with me.

"Coffee. Here you are." I placed the mug on the coffee table. "I'm ignoring the rest of what you said."

"Oh well. Fair enough. But I'm not giving up."

I'm sure you won't.

I kept myself busy tidying up the lounge until Anna rose to her feet.

"Time to go. You ready?"

"Yep. Let's do it."

We arrived at the property early, and Anna snapped some shots of the front garden with her phone. She was buzzing with ideas for plants and paint colours for the outside walls.

A car pulled up, and Tom jumped out, grabbing his phone and briefcase. "Gosh, sorry, I'm not late, am I?"

"No, we were early. Thank you so much for coming today. It's so good of you to open up for us. You are wonderful. I just wanted to have another look around and take some measurements, ready for the big day. The current owners don't mind?"

Anna had turned on the charm, and I tried to cover up the smile that hovered on my lips.

"Nope, they're fine with it. They live up in Yorkshire. This was just their holiday home. I've got about an hour before my next appointment." He glanced at his watch. "I've some work to do, so I'll sit out here in the garden if that's okay with you. I'll trust you not to steal anything."

Just their holiday home. Blimey. Some people have too much money!

"Ooh, you are funny! As if I would steal anything." Anna patted Tom's arm and, I'm certain, engulfed him in a wave of her expensive perfume as she kissed him on the cheek. Pulling out a notebook, pen, and tape measure from her designer handbag, she grabbed me by the arm and pulled me into the cottage. "Come on, Laura, let's get started."

Tom's shoulders were shaking as he chuckled and gave me a knowing nod of the head. "I'll be in the garden if you need me."

An hour later, my head was spinning. Anna had covered every inch of the property with her trusty tape measure, scribbling down copious notes and muttering frequently to herself. "We'll need a plumber. That downstairs bathroom just won't do. And someone to check the boiler and those radiators. They look ancient. And that sofa will have to go. I wonder if they're planning to leave any furniture, though? The dining table is nice."

I lost all interest and wandered around, nosing at the pictures on the wall of a bright, jolly family. I counted three dogs and five grandchildren. They looked happy, full of life, content. *Lucky people.*

"Right, so, Laura. You've got all that? Four paintings, one for each bedroom and the fourth for the dining room?"

"Um, yes. Remind me again… sorry… themes? Colours? Anything in particular?" Anna's voice dragged me back to the present as she rattled off her plans to me.

"I'll send you everything in an email. Sizes, colours, ideas. Can you have them all ready before the summer holidays?"

I counted out the weeks in my head. Six weeks. Four paintings. I gulped. "I'll do my best. Okay, are you all finished? Can we leave now?"

We walked out to the garden and caught Tom lying back in his chair sunbathing, his eyes half closed.

"Wakey, wakey!" Anna's lack of subtlety was legendary. I smirked as Tom shot up out of his seat, patting his pockets and searching for his mobile phone.

"There you are. All done? Great. My eleven o'clock has just cancelled, so I'm free for another hour. Got time for a coffee? There's a fab teashop in the village. They do the best cream cakes this side of Exeter."

Before I could speak, Anna leapt in. "Oh, that sounds so nice. But I'm afraid I've got to dash off. I have another meeting. But I'm sure Laura would love to join you. Actually, could you give her a lift back home afterwards as well? That would save me such a detour." Anna winked at me, and I could have cheerfully throttled her.

"That's no problem at all. It will be my pleasure." Tom walked over to his car as I wheeled round, ready to say something rude to Anna.

"Now's your chance to get to know him better. You can thank me later." She grabbed her bag as I dramatically drew my finger across my throat at her.

Anna wiggled her fingers at me in response and hopped into her car. "Bye. Have fun!"

I climbed into the worn leather passenger seat of Tom's car, muttering expletives in my head.

"She's quite a force of nature, your friend, isn't she?" Tom drove through the village, coming to a stop outside a pretty little old-fashioned tearoom a few minutes later.

"Well, that's one way to describe her." I clicked my tongue, then smiled as Tom grinned at me.

The interior of the tearoom was barely larger than the front room of a house and boasted a beautiful vintage décor of patterned wallpaper and a wood-beamed ceiling. It was like stepping back fifty years in time, with small round tables covered with damask tablecloths. A display in the far corner was full of homemade cakes and pastries, and the entire room smelled of freshly baked scones and bread.

We settled down at a table, and the server, dressed in a pretty white pinafore, came to take our order. She suggested we tried the lavender Earl Grey tea with a slice of Victoria sponge cake, and we both agreed.

The tea and cake were sublime, and I devoured every crumb whilst chatting to Tom like an old friend.

"I feel like I've known you for ages. We have so much in common. The same childhood, similar schools, and university. So, how did you end up as an estate agent?"

Tom filled me in on his career to date, and I was happy to let him talk.

"So, it's just a job for now, really. I don't want to be doing it forever, but it pays well and I enjoy meeting people."

"What would you do if you could do anything, then?" I had to admit I was warming to him. He seemed a good person. Humble. Hard working.

"Honestly?" He blinked and glanced up at the ceiling. "I'd love to work with animals. Run my own rescue centre one day. I always wanted to be a vet, but I didn't have the science qualifications I needed to study veterinary medicine. So, I did a degree in geography instead. But ever since I was a child, I've always loved animals. Especially dogs. We had a dog at home when I was growing up. He was my best friend; we went everywhere together. His name was Max. No idea what breed he was. My dad called him our 'Heinz 57 mutt'. There might have been some lurcher in there somewhere. He had dark grey wiry fur with the cutest white muzzle and beard. Piercing light blue eyes. I was heartbroken when he died. If I'm honest, I still miss him today. I bet you think that's daft, right?"

"No, not at all. I completely understand."

Tom nodded. "That's why I help out at the local rescue centre. Second Chance. Don't laugh, but every time I'm there I check all the cages hoping to find another Max waiting for me. Crazy I know. But he was so special. You should come over one day and see what we do there. It's a remarkable place."

That's where I found Molly.

"I, well, I think it would be too painful for me to go there. I'm sorry."

After that statement, I had no choice but to open up. I blurted out the entire story of losing Molly and how painful that had been. Tom sat quietly and let me talk, only reaching over to touch my hand as I finished speaking.

"I'm so sorry. You must be devastated. I know only too well how that feels. I bet you wish you could see her and hold her just one more time. That's how I feel about Max. Even after all these years."

Careful. Don't say anything. Don't spoil this moment. If you tell him about Archaven, he'll think you're crazy.

"Yes, it's hard. Gosh, look at the time. I've sat here chatting to you for far too long. You must have work to do, and so have I."

"You're right, but it's been very nice talking to you today. Let's do this again sometime."

Tom insisted on paying, as I gathered up my things and walked with him to his car. He drove me back into town, pulling up outside the Thread and Needle shop.

"How did you know where I live? Oh, hang on, let me guess. Anna, right?"

Tom laughed. "Yes, she's a regular matchmaker, isn't she? I, for one, am glad, though. I feel as if I've made a new friend today. Thank you. And you know where I am if you change your mind about volunteering at the rescue centre."

Well, that's not likely to happen. But maybe I could track down Max. Wouldn't that be something?

CHAPTER SIXTEEN

The canvas was taunting me, its mottled white surface completely blank. I threw down my pencil. *I don't know what to paint.*

Maybe a brief foray over to see Molly might stimulate me. Give me some fresh ideas. Inspiration. Just a quick visit.

I dashed upstairs, grabbed her painting, and within seconds, I was there. *Archaven. Every time I'm here, the grass is lush and fresh, and the sky is an impossible shade of blue. It's so perfect. And there she is. My girl. How lucky am I?*

She trotted up to me, her tail whisking itself into a frenzy as I hugged her.

"I'm so glad you're here. I've got someone I want you to meet."

That surprised me. Molly was usually on her own, seeming to prefer her own company, even though she'd told me there were lots of other animals around. She nodded as a dog plodded towards us.

"This is Jack. He's got quite a story to tell, and I'm hoping you can help him." Molly's soft eyes were full of compassion and love, and I hugged her again.

"Of course, if I can."

Jack advanced slowly, his head darting from side to side as he sidled up to us. A collie dog, crossed with who knows what, peered up at me. He had the most amazing eyes. One brown, the other a brilliant shiny blue. He scuffed his front paws on the ground and then huddled down; his head slumped on the grass.

I sat down a little way away, facing side on to him, and settled my hands in my lap, hoping not to scare him.

After a few seconds, Molly nudged Jack's paw with her nose. "Go on, lad. Tell her your story. I promise you're safe here, and no-one is going to hurt you. Or judge you."

"I've always been a street dog. It's all I've ever known since I was a young pup." He glanced over at me. "Dirty pavements, hidden corners, prowling around, trying to stay out of trouble. Rummaging through bins for the next meal, hunting for fresh water. Shivering through the cold winters and hiding from the summer heatwaves."

I nodded. "I try to stop and feed a stray dog if I see one. I've always imagined it would be tough surviving on the streets. Not easy to stay safe. Or find enough food to eat." As I listened to Jack, I sensed there wasn't a happy ending to his tale.

"I was good at scrounging food, but there's a real skill to being able to read a situation quickly. Sometimes the people who seem the nicest are the ones who tempt you towards them, fingers outstretched, holding an enticing morsel of chicken or fish. But then, when you get closer, they lash out and kick you. Usually it's easier to wait until darkness and scrabble around the bins and back alleyways, hunting for something to eat. But I was used to it. Like I said, it was all I ever knew."

Jack stared out over the distant fields. "It was so rare that anyone cared about me or even looked interested in me. Sometimes, a café owner would come out at the end of the day and throw me some scraps, or someone would whistle to me. But I was always wary. I'd been hit and kicked too many times. Had stones thrown at me. Even had a drunk person vomit over me once. And then, one day, everything changed. I walked past a girl sitting on the pavement, huddled into her coat, hat cast on the floor in front of her. Homeless, like me. She seemed so sad. I crept up to her. Slowly. Just in case. But she smiled when she saw me and stretched out her arm towards me. I sensed straight away she was alright. That she wouldn't hurt me."

Molly nuzzled closer to him. I think she could sense his distress as he continued talking.

"The girl gently reached out to me. 'You okay, boy?' she said, stroking my fur. 'You look as lost as me. We make a fine pair, don't we?' She dipped into her rucksack and drew out a sandwich, unwrapping it and sharing it with me. Cheese and ham. I can still taste it now. It was wonderful. From that moment, we were inseparable. We went everywhere together. I curled up at night with her in a makeshift shelter under the old railway bridge. She kept me warm, fed me and showed me love. For the first time in my life, I felt I belonged somewhere. That I meant something to someone."

"What happened then?" I hesitated, not wanting to push him.

"It was my fault." Jack seemed to shrink further into himself. "I'd trotted off to the park, as I often did during the day, leaving my friend sat in her usual empty shop doorway. But the police must have moved her on, or something, because when I returned, she'd gone. I tried to pick up her trail, scenting around to work out which direction she'd walked, but I panicked. It was so busy on the high street, with people marching past me, traffic roaring. I spun round, barking, trying to find her, and then I thought I saw her. On the other side of the road. I raced across, but there was a car. It was silent. It seemed to glide along the road. No engine noise. I didn't see it. Too late. There was an enormous bang. I rolled and rolled on the ground. The pain was intense. I knew it was bad. The last thing I remember was my girl running over to me as I lay there. I couldn't move. As I felt myself slipping away, darkness descending all around me, I heard her crying and saying, 'It's all my fault. I should have stayed. Waited for you to come back. I made a mistake. I'm so sorry.' And then I woke up here. In this place. With no way to let her know she wasn't to blame. And every day, I live with the guilt. It's like a physical pain eating me up inside."

"Can you tell me anything more about her—your girl? What does she look like? What's her name? Where were you sleeping rough? Do you remember the name of the place? Anything that can help me find her for you?"

"Why? What can you do to help? It's too late for me now. I know that." Jack dropped his head, not even making eye contact with me.

"What has Molly told you so far? About the fact that I can come here to visit her, even though I'm still alive?"

"Nothing much. Just that you might help me. But I don't see how."

"What if I could find your girl for you? Tell her you're okay? That you don't blame her. That it really wasn't her fault. It was just an accident. A rotten, painful accident."

"But how would she believe you—even if you could find her?" Jack shook his head, his ears flopping as he stood up and stretched. "It's not like she knows you or anything."

"Why don't you leave that up to me, eh? Let me try to help. Now, tell me everything you remember about her."

Jack described the girl's clothes and her old army green rucksack, and the path under the bridge where they slept each night. "She has long dark hair. It's always tied up on top of her head. And I know we were in Exeter. She told me once she was a student at the university there. But she got caught up with a bad crowd. Drugs, I think. She lost her place, and the landlady of her digs threw her out. She said she was too embarrassed to go home and tell her folks what had happened. So that's how she ended up on the streets. I never knew her name. She called me Jack. Or sometimes Jackaroo. 'Cos she said when I stood up on two legs and hopped around, I looked like a kangaroo. I didn't know what that meant, but it always made her laugh, which was good enough for me."

"And the empty shop? Can you recall what it was near? Or the name of anything that might help me?" I thought it was a really long shot, but as I glanced over at Molly and saw the trust in her eyes, I knew I had to try. *At least she's in Exeter. I know that city well.*

"I don't know any more than that. I'm sorry."

Jack stood up, and I had a sudden idea. "Let me take a couple of photos of you. They might come in useful if I find your girl."

I pulled my phone out of my pocket and took a few shots. "You too, Molly. I'll snap some of you as well."

"Thank you for listening to me today." Jack's tail was curled under his body as he circled around us. "I'm not sure you'll find my friend, but if you do, tell her I love her. And that it was never her fault."

Jack departed, his figure shrinking into the distance, head down, as he disappeared across the field. The rich scent of the flowers woven in the grass filled my senses as I trailed my fingers through their stems and did my best to remember everything he'd told me.

Molly burrowed in beside me, and I rested my hand on her back. "It's such a coincidence, isn't it? That Jack was in Exeter. So close to us. Thank goodness they weren't in a city or town at the other end of the country."

"Actually, I've met several pets over here recently, and they all lived around the same area in Devon." Molly paused, her eyes squinting. "It's as if this place has replicated our previous lives. In fact, you remember Mrs Williams, who used to live in the bungalow down the street from us? I saw her cat here last week. Toby."

"You mean, Toby, the ginger tabby cat that you always used to chase?"

Molly had the decency to look a little abashed as she wagged her tail and grinned at me. "Yes, that's the one."

"I didn't know he'd passed away. Mrs Williams must be so upset. She loved that cat. At least Toby's life was a long and happy one, and his owner spoilt him rotten. Poor Jack. He didn't have much of a life, and then he finally met someone who loved him, and he lost it all. It doesn't seem fair, does it? He looks so sad. My heart aches for him. I hope I can trace this girl for him."

Molly nuzzled me gently. "I knew you'd understand and want to help him. Do you really think you can find her and talk to her?"

I leant back against the trunk of the blossom tree as the birds raced across the sky above us. "I honestly don't know. Even if I find her, I'll have to tread carefully. I can hardly go up to a complete stranger and say, 'Hey, you're not going to believe this, but I've seen your dead dog, Jack. He's in a rainbow land waiting for you, and he wants to tell you he's okay. And that what happened wasn't your fault.' Yeah, I really think that would go down well. I need to think this through. But first, I have to locate a homeless girl. In a big city. With not a lot of information to go on. Not even her name. It's not going to be easy."

"I have faith in you. You can do it." Molly settled down, resting her head on her paws, and closed her eyes.

"I guess that's my cue to get going, then. Take care, my darling. I'll be back again soon. I love you."

The minute I landed in my flat, I grabbed my phone and scrolled through my photo album. All the shots I'd taken were blank. There was just a plain black screen.

I wandered into the kitchen and stared out of the window. *What have I got myself into?*

CHAPTER SEVENTEEN

Well, there's no time like the present. Might as well get out there and look for this girl. I promised Molly and Jack—so I have to try.

I decided not to tell anyone what I was doing. I could just imagine what Anna would say if I told her. And if I said anything to Enid, I knew she would only worry. "So, I'm off out looking for a homeless girl. Might be on drugs. Sleeps rough under the railway bridge in Exeter. Don't worry about me; I'll be fine." *Yeah, best not to mention it.*

I had a vague plan for what I'd do if I found the girl. I figured I couldn't just march up to her and tell her about Jack. So, I was going to use my art as an excuse. I'd ask if I could do a painting of her and say it was for a project. See if I could get to know her first. Scope her out. It wasn't perfect, but it was the best idea I could come up with.

It took me two weeks to find her. Two weeks when I juggled working in my studio on the paintings for Anna each morning and then driving over to Exeter in the afternoon. Parking up, walking around, asking people. Hoping to bump into her. And then, early one evening, there she was in front of me on the street. A bedraggled girl, clutching an old dirty sleeping bag under her arm, a green rucksack on her back. Exactly as Jack described. She trudged down the unmade path that led to the railway line, climbing over piles of rubble and rubbish. I followed her cautiously, checking to see if anyone else was nearby. The stink of rotting fish and stale urine made me grimace as I stumbled forward, stubbing my toe on a rock.

The girl spun round, her head jerking back as she gripped the sleeping bag closer to her body.

"What do you want?"

I held up my hand. "It's okay. I don't mean you any harm."

"Who are you? Get away from me!"

She stood looking ready to bolt at any second, her eyes darting around.

I'm not sure my art idea is going to work. She seems far more scared than I imagined. Now what am I going to do?

My mind raced as I took a step forward. "I won't hurt you. Look, I've got some food in my bag if you're hungry? I just want to talk to you."

"You're not from the welfare or anything then?"

"No, I promise. Just someone who wants to help you if I can. I'm an artist, doing a project. That's all."

She kicked a stone and smirked at me. "So, you want to draw me, is that it? Got a thing for homeless kids, have you?"

"Only one. But if I told you the real reason, I doubt you'd believe me."

"Try me. I ain't in a hurry. As you can see, I've got nowhere else to go. Just here, sleeping in this dump of a place."

It's no good. I'll have to tell her. This isn't going to work any other way.

"How about I buy you a coffee and we can talk?"

She hefted the rucksack further up onto her shoulders and pushed past me. "Alright, I won't say no to a coffee. And a sandwich, if you're offering. But that's all. And only because I haven't eaten anything today."

I followed her, picking my way slowly back up the path. I had to rush to catch up with her as she marched down the street, stopping at a little café that was still open.

"They know me in here. They don't mind if I come in with my bag and stuff. The owner's a nice guy. He stays open late and often gives us homeless folks free food. They do a good cheese toastie here." She eyed me up as I sat down opposite her and called the server over.

"Whatever she wants, and a latte for me, please."

She stared at me. I felt as if I was being thoroughly checked out and squirmed in my seat as she set down her mug of tea and snorted with laughter, wiping her nose on her sleeve.

"I'm guessing you don't know many homeless folks, do you? You're not from a charity, that's for sure. You're not official enough. And you don't look the church type, either. So, who are you and what do you want from me?"

"I'm Laura. And I am an artist. That much is true." I handed her a business card from my purse. "If that helps."

"Pleased to meet you, Laura Adams." She spun the card down onto the table. "I'm Scarlett."

Her face softened a little as the server brought over the food. She grabbed the toastie with both hands and sunk her teeth in, groaning quietly. "Man, that tastes good."

I dived straight in. There didn't seem to be any other way to turn the conversation around.

"I have a bit of a strange story. I confess I've been looking for you. To tell you something important. About your dog."

She interrupted me, snatching her hand away from the tabletop where it had been resting. "I don't have a dog."

"I know. But you did, didn't you? Jack. He was a beautiful dog. A collie."

"So what? You must have seen me around with him." She paused. "But how did you know his name?"

I leant forward. "Because I've met him. Recently. Since the accident."

"Yeah, right? Now I know you're insane. He's dead, okay? It was all my fault. I killed him. So why don't you leave me alone?" Scarlett scraped back her chair and shot up, fists clenched.

"He loved you, you know. Worshipped you. You were the first person to show him any affection. He loved it when you called him 'your Jackaroo'. It made him feel so special."

She sank back down onto her chair and whispered, "Who told you that name?"

"He did. When I saw him. Look, this is going to take some time. Why don't I order us another drink, and I can try to explain?"

It was dark outside by the time I'd told her everything. She sat frowning at me, shredding a paper napkin into tiny pieces. But she didn't leave. And when I'd finished, she looked dazed.

"You know that sounds bonkers, don't you? You're not on drugs, are you? I've met people like you before, out on the street. They're loopy, mad as a box of frogs."

"I know. I have a hard time believing it myself. But I promise you, it's true. I really went over there and met Jack. And he wanted to tell you it wasn't your fault. The accident. That you mustn't feel guilty. That he loves you, and he's waiting for you."

Scarlett had tears in her eyes as she scrubbed her hand over her face. "You actually met him?" She paused. "Could I go over there? See him myself? Like you did?"

"I'm not sure. But it's possible." I thought back to Iris and the joy on her face when she returned from visiting her Poppy. "Maybe. But it's not without its risks. There's a dangerous side to it all."

"Hey, it's not like I don't know about danger. I live on the street, for goodness' sake."

"Okay, fair enough. I'll need to do a portrait of you and Jack. And there's a butterfly to be added in there too. I'll explain it all later. Can we meet up tomorrow afternoon? So I can take some photos of you and make a few quick sketches. It's too late to do it now. Where will you be tomorrow?"

"I'll meet you by the railway bridge, if that's alright with you? It was the one place I always felt safe, with Jack tucked beside me at night. He would alert me to anything. Protected me. If you're going to do a painting of us, I'd like it to be there."

I paid the bill and left her chatting with the owner. "Three o'clock tomorrow. See you then."

I drove home, mulling over everything that had happened. *I wonder if she'll actually be there tomorrow? Or will she think I'm completely nuts and not show up?*

The next afternoon, I arrived early, convinced that Scarlett wouldn't appear. I was on the brink of leaving as she came striding along the pavement towards me.

"You're here. I really thought it was all a joke. That you were just winding me up." She dumped her rucksack on the ground and looked me up and down, her eyes narrowing.

"No, it's all true. I'm here, and I've got my gear with me. I need to do a few quick sketches to take back to my studio. Then I can get started on your painting. And then you can see Jack."

"Okay. I still think you're barmy. But let's do this." She ran ahead, jumping down into the depths of the underbridge. "Where do you want me to stand or sit?"

"Why don't you show me how you used to settle down with Jack? I can work on something from that."

I took a few photos and made some notes and pencil drawings in my sketchbook.

"Right, I think I've got everything I need. But how will I reach you again? We'll need to meet up once the painting is ready. And are you sure you're going to be alright here?" I offered to help her find somewhere to stay, but she was adamant she didn't want any support.

And somehow I need to get a better image of Jack to paint, too. That means another trip to Archaven. I hope I can find him again. Wait until I tell him I've found Scarlett.

"I'll be here every evening. I'm not going anywhere. You're really going to do this for me? I can't believe I might see my Jackaroo again." Scarlett hugged her knees tight to her chest as I waved her goodbye and promised to be in touch.

CHAPTER EIGHTEEN

I couldn't wait to tell Jack the good news. *I hope he's there when I arrive. He's going to be so pleased.* I checked to make sure I had securely zipped my sketchbook and pen inside my pocket before placing Molly's painting on the chair in front of me.

The journey felt familiar, almost second nature, as my fingers brushed the butterfly's wings, and the air below me soared and unfurled with a soft whoosh. I landed gently, marvelling at the verdant landscape that now was like a second home to me. The golden sun warmed my face as I stood, arms outstretched, enjoying the peace and serene beauty of the view.

Molly bounded up to me, and I noted with relief that Jack was trailing along behind her. He sped up when he saw me, and they both circled around the blossom tree, tails wagging, sending stray petals sailing into the air.

"I found her, Jack. I found her for you. And I told her everything you asked me to."

He looked up at me with wonder in his eyes. "No way? You actually found her? That's amazing. I can't believe it."

"I know. She's called Scarlett, by the way. And she really misses you."

"She's alright? She's safe, not in any trouble?"

"Yes, she seems okay. Still sleeping in the same place each night. I had a hard time convincing her of all of this to start with." I waved my hand around and laughed. "Well, I mean, it's not every day you meet someone who tells you they've just talked to your dog. Not after they've died, anyway."

Molly sat down beside me, leaning her weight against my leg. I curled my fingers through the soft fur behind her ears, relishing the warmth of her body nestled against mine.

"That's not all my news though, Jack. Scarlett wants to come here. To see you one more time."

"What, like how you visit Molly? Is that even possible?" Jack's ears perked up as he cocked his head to one side.

"I've arranged it once before. A lady called Iris travelled over here to see her dog, a poodle called Poppy."

"So that really happened?" Jack looked down at the ground, his face changing in an instant. "We all thought she was mad and making it all up. But then I met you and Molly." He looked sheepish as he admitted he had teased Poppy until she eventually ran away. "No-one has seen her for days. Now I feel guilty. I promise I'll try to find her."

"You should. She's a sweet little dog, and her owner adored her."

I pulled out my sketchbook. "The thing is, for this to work, I have to give Scarlett a painting. Of you and her together. I tried to take some photos of you the last time I was here, but they didn't come out at all. My phone obviously doesn't work here. So, I need to resort to some old-fashioned methods. Sketching you, making some notes, enough for me to paint from. Are you okay with hanging around for a while?"

Jack settled down beside Molly, and I sat peacefully, roughing out some outlines. I was so engrossed in my sketches I didn't notice The Keeper had crept up behind me. I flinched as a blast of hot air shot across my back and then screamed. The Keeper was leaning right over my shoulder, the hairs in his mane tickling my neck.

"Nice work. But why are you drawing this dog here?" His question seemed innocuous, but I shuddered inside.

What do I say?

Instinctively, I knew I couldn't lie to him. His eyes penetrated mine, two piercing globes of gold, laser sharp and unwavering. It was as if he could actually read my mind.

Before I could answer, he briefly nodded his head. It was subtle, but I saw it. The faintest hint of danger in his movement. He was calmness personified. Ice cool. Composed.

"You're going to send another one over here, aren't you? Why are you doing this?"

"Because I want to help, I guess. Give some comfort and support to a grieving owner. I never asked for this to happen. But somehow, I've been given this gift. The ability to visit my darling Molly. And I want to share it if I can. I don't mean you any harm. And I don't want to put Molly, or anyone else, in any danger."

I waited for his reply. My hands trembled, though I fought to keep them still, as my heart pounded.

With a loud huff, The Keeper shook his head, his mane gleaming in the sun, and stormed away.

"I think it's time I left." My voice was a mere whisper as I gathered up my things, hugged Molly and patted Jack on the head, before picking up my precious painting of Molly. My hands were still shaking as I touched the butterfly, closing my eyes until the floor of my flat was solid beneath my feet. Somehow, The Keeper's complete silence and lack of response had unnerved me more than if he had replied.

🐾 🐾 🐾 🐾 🐾

That afternoon, I went downstairs to say hello to Enid. As I entered the shop, I could hear her talking to someone who was obviously distraught. I turned back, intending to leave it until later, but Enid heard me and called me over.

"Laura, do you remember Mrs Williams? She used to live down the road. Dorothy, this is Laura. My artist friend and neighbour."

Mrs Williams. Why is that name familiar? Of course, Molly mentioned her. She lost her cat. Toby.

"Hello Mrs Williams. I'm so sorry to hear about your cat. Toby, wasn't it?"

"Yes, that's right. But how did you know? I haven't been able to talk to anyone about it since it happened. Enid is the first person I've told. I was so upset I couldn't bear to leave the house."

Enid scowled at me, and I squirmed under her gaze.

"Well, I…" My voice tailed off. *I need to think of an answer, and quick.*

"I overheard you talking just now."

"Oh, well, that makes sense, I suppose." Mrs Williams dabbed her eyes with a tissue. "He was such a lovely boy. I'm lost without him. I wish I could believe we get to see our loved ones again one day. Across some Rainbow Bridge. But that's all nonsense."

Enid gave me one of her 'I'll talk to you later' glares as I made my apologies and left in a hurry.

Whoops! I almost got caught out there. And I'm sure Enid knows something is up.

I knew I wouldn't get away with it. I was busy in my studio when I heard a quiet 'tap tap' on the door before it opened. Enid stood in the doorway, her arms folded.

"Got five minutes for a cuppa? I think we need to have a little chat, don't you?"

I laid down my pencil and followed her into the kitchen.

"I don't know what you mean," I blustered, playing for time.

"Oh, I think you do, young lady. You don't fool me, my dear. I know you're up to something." She carried two mugs of tea back into my studio and set them down on the table. "So, come on, spill the beans."

"I'm not sure where to begin, to be honest. Or if you'd believe me if I told you."

"You can start at the beginning. The shop's shut. Take your time." Enid settled herself down on the sofa and stared at me. I took a deep breath and confessed everything that had been happening, starting with my painting of Molly and the butterfly effect.

Enid's face grew more incredulous as I unravelled my story, but she didn't say a word until I'd finished talking. The studio was silent. A sudden chill in the air made me pull the arms down on my jumper as I felt the weight of Enid's unwavering gaze upon me.

"Well, say something. Please. Don't just sit there."

"You're right. That's one heck of a tale. If I didn't know you better, I'd think you were mad. But I do know you. Probably too well. And I can't imagine you'd make this up. But are you sure? You can visit Molly? In some special rainbow place? What did you call it? Archaven?"

Enid shook her head. I could tell she was having a hard time believing my story. And I couldn't blame her. Every time I talked about it to someone, it sounded preposterous. Even to me. And I'd been there. Several times.

"Hang on a minute. I've had an idea." I motioned to Enid, then raced up to my flat, and returned with Molly's painting under my arm.

"Here you go. I'll prove it to you. I'll go over there and see Molly for a few minutes. Once I disappear, a window will emerge in place of the painting, and you can watch me."

Enid's eyes widened as she leant forward. "Really? You'll visit this other land, and I can see it happen? From here? You're going to disappear right in front of me?"

"Yes, don't worry. You can just sit there and observe everything. You'll get to see Molly again as well. How amazing is that?"

Enid held her hands up to her face. "Oh my! Well, okay, if you think you can do this." She hesitated. "Give her a big kiss on the nose from me then."

I knew Enid was still doubtful as I gripped the canvas and took a deep breath. I touched the butterfly and glanced over at Enid as the room tipped on its side, and I rocketed through the air, landing on the soft green grass of Archaven.

Molly bounded up to me, tail wagging as she woofed with pleasure.

"You're back again so soon. I wasn't expecting to see you again today."

"I know. I can't stay long. But I needed to show Enid this is really happening. She didn't believe me when I told her about us. About all of this. She's back in my studio right now watching us through the window that appears each time I'm over here. It was the easiest way to prove it to her. I still can't believe it myself some days. That you're here. And I can be with you."

I ruffled her fur. "I don't want to push things, though. The Keeper made it clear he doesn't want lots of people finding their way over here. I'm already committed to helping Jack find Scarlett. So, I need to be careful. I'd better go back now and see Enid. She sent you her love. And I love you too, my darling girl."

I hugged her goodbye and then held her painting aloft. The late afternoon sun warmed the canvas as I tapped the butterfly and then landed back in my studio in a rush of air.

Enid's expression was priceless. It took her several minutes to compose herself as she stared at me.

"That was incredible. I've never seen anything quite like it. Dear Molly. And you were talking to her, weren't you? She looked so young. Full of mischief. Just how I remember her. Goodness me."

"I know." I grinned at Enid as I laid down the painting. "It's mad, isn't it? So, do you believe me now?"

"Yes, of course I do. After that performance, I'm convinced you're telling the truth. But I guess my burning question is, is it safe?"

I had omitted to mention The Keeper earlier, not wanting to scare Enid.

"Oh, yes. Perfectly safe." I flapped my hand at her. "And I've even sent another person over there to visit her pet dog, too. Remember the girl who was waiting for me in my studio that afternoon? It was her gran she wanted a painting for. I added a butterfly to that one as well, and that all went fine, too."

Do I tell her about Scarlett? Maybe I'll leave that for another day. Too much, perhaps, in one go.

"As long as you know it's safe. That's quite some gift you have, being able to visit Molly. I miss her. She used to love sneaking into the shop when you weren't looking and scoffing a biscuit or two. Such a dear girl. Well, I guess I'd better get on." Enid swept her hands down her thighs and groaned as she stood up. "Oh, my old aching bones. I've got a few things to tidy in the shop before I finish for the day."

She touched my arm as she walked past me. "Look after yourself, won't you? You mean so much to me."

"I will. And please don't tell anyone else. The last thing I need is for people to hear about this and start contacting me. I'm still trying to get my head round it all and figure out what to do."

After she'd gone, I picked up my sketchpad. *That went okay. I think she believes me now. Although there are some days I struggle to believe it all myself.*

I flipped through my sketches of Jack and Scarlett, wondering how I could interpret them in the best light. It wasn't exactly an inspiring location, the old railway line with its dark underbelly. *How about if I add some images of Exeter in the background? The cathedral perhaps, and part of the River Exe along the quay?*

Energised by my ideas, I set to work and soon had the design sketched out, ready to add paint the next morning. Satisfied, I tidied up the studio, switched off the lights, and headed upstairs for some supper.

CHAPTER NINETEEN

Scarlett and Jack turned out to be one tough painting. I kept scrubbing out and reworking sections until I achieved the desired finish. In my head, I knew how I wanted it to be, but it proved to be more difficult than I imagined. Eventually, satisfied with my work, I laid down my brush and cleaned off my palette.

There's something missing. What am I not seeing? Then, suddenly, I realised what I'd forgotten. *Of course. The butterfly. I need to add a butterfly.* I thought back to the bejewelled butterfly brooch I'd added to Iris' painting. It seemed that it didn't matter if it was a white butterfly after all. Any butterfly design would work. *Now, what type would suit Scarlett?*

A quick Google search and I had my answer. The Scarlet Peacock. A stunning, vivid red creature with distinctive black and white markings and a brown centre. *Perfect.*

I carefully added it to the background, hovering near Jack's head. I checked his colouring against my notes one last time, content that I'd captured his gentle expression and his distinguishing trait—one blue and one brown eye. He was a very handsome boy.

I thought about how to deliver the finished painting. It wouldn't be any use to Scarlett turning up with a mounted canvas painting that she couldn't easily carry with her, so I painstakingly unpicked all the metal clips that held the canvas material in its wooden frame. The result was a soft, painted fabric I could roll up into a tube for easy transportation.

Now all I had to do was locate Scarlett, deliver the painting, and instruct her on how to use it. I had my doubts about whether the process would work again, but I consoled myself with the memory of Iris, and how easy that had been. The entire problem of where Scarlett could actually be when she transported herself, and how she would keep her rucksack and belongings safe whilst she was away, were dilemmas I had yet to find an answer to. I hoped she might come up with a solution of her own for those issues.

Finding Scarlett was quite a challenge in itself. I drove over to the railway bridge several evenings in a row, but there was no sign of her. Eventually, I tracked her down, but she was reticent to even talk to me at first.

"I didn't imagine I'd ever see you again. I went away and thought about everything you'd said to me, and none of it made any sense." She stuffed her hands into her pockets and scowled at me. Her coat was buttoned right up, despite the balmy evening sunshine and warm temperature.

"I didn't come looking for you for any dubious reason. Believe me. It was Jack who sent me. He was the one who wanted me to find you. To tell you not to worry."

"Yeah, well, you understand how psycho that sounds, don't you? From my point of view. I mean—you—talking to my dog. After he's dead."

"I know. But you have to believe me. It's really true. As crazy as that might seem. Here, why don't you look at your painting? Tell me what you think."

I handed her the tube, and she slowly unravelled the canvas, laying it down on the pavement in front of her. She stood staring at it for a long moment, not saying anything, as tears streamed down her face. She made no attempt to wipe them away, letting them fall onto the painting.

"How did you know?" She glared at me, swiping her sleeve across her face, and sniffing loudly.

"How did I know what?" I was confused. *Did she like the painting? Had I done them both justice? What else was wrong now?*

"Jack's eyes. How did you know he had different coloured eyes?"

"Oh that! I was amazed when I saw them. They're spectacular, aren't they?"

Scarlett rubbed her hand over her forehead. "I can't take all this in. You really have seen him, haven't you? Over there, on this other rainbow side?"

"Let's sit down. Take a minute. Talk it through. I appreciate it's a lot to take in. But yes, I have met him. Twice now, in fact. And I'm hoping you will see him soon as well." I gathered up the painting, held her elbow, and steered her over to the nearby park, sitting beside her on a wooden bench. The pine trees behind us smelt sweet, almost like ice cream, as the wind wafted the woody fragrance across the grounds. I took a deep breath, inhaling the distinct scent, and tried to stay calm. *I need to reassure Scarlett that everything's going to be fine. That she can see her Jack again.*

It was a good half hour before she perked up. I explained it all to her one more time as she sat fingering the edge of the canvas material. The painting appeared to glow in her lap, and I knew I needed to convince her it was real before she upped and left me. It was hard work, as she seemed distracted. *I guess she's just wary of trusting people. It must be tough living rough on the streets.* I estimated her age to be about twenty-five, but she had a world-weariness about her that made her seem much older. More cynical.

"Alright. Let's say it's true. I can visit Jack. What do I need to do?" Scarlett leant forward, resting her hands on her knees.

I ran through the basics with her. "There are a couple of things that have been bothering me, though. Your rucksack and sleeping bag. I don't think you can take them with you to Archaven, the rainbow land. You've got to hold on to the painting. Not let it go. Guard it with your life when you're over there. It's your only way back."

"I could leave my stuff at the café. The one we went to the first time I met you. The owner there is good as gold. He often lets me dump my gear in the storeroom during the day. He wouldn't mind."

I nodded. "That's great. But the other issue is a bit more complicated. You see, when you're over there visiting Jack, the painting goes with you. But wherever you are standing when you travel, it leaves a kind of window behind that someone else can look through. You must be in a safe, private location away from everyone before you touch the painting."

"That's okay. I have a secret place, a sort of cave behind the railway bridge where I sleep sometimes. If I hear anyone coming, I slip away and hide. You wouldn't believe some of the drunks and druggies that stagger down there. They've never found me. I'm good at concealing myself away, making myself invisible. You don't need to fret about that."

"And you have to promise me you won't stay there too long? You must stay alert. Keep yourself safe. And you can only go there once."

"Yeah, yeah, you told me. There's a scary little lion guy. I shouldn't wind him up. And I can't fall asleep. I've got it." Scarlett shrugged, her face a picture of amusement. "You sound just like my mum, you know? Don't worry about me; I'll be fine."

"Alright, I get the message. Right, there's one more thing you need to know. The butterfly. That's the crucial part. If this is going to work, the butterfly will be glowing." I pointed over to the painting. "Yes, there it is. Do you see that? It's sort of shimmering? That's what needs to happen. Then, you simply touch the canvas with your fingertip and the magic begins."

Scarlett still looked cynically at me, but she ran her hand slowly over the painting. A gasp escaped her lips as she jerked backward, her eyes widening.

"Wow, did you feel that?" She frowned at me, tapping on the canvas.

"Nope, nothing. Did something happen?" I tried not to smile as she leapt to her feet, waving her arms in the air. "Do I take it you're now a bit more convinced that I'm telling you the truth, then?"

"That was freaky. Just for a second, my head started spinning, and the world went dark. Is that how it goes?"

I patted the seat beside me. "It's alright. Come and sit down. Yes, that's what happens. And then the next thing you know, you'll be over there. With Jack. And you can tell him everything you need to. And give him the biggest hug ever."

"This is insane, you know. Like, totally mental. But you seem so calm about it all."

"Well, I can assure you I wasn't the first time it happened. It freaked me out. I thought I was actually going mad. But seeing my dog, Molly, made it all worthwhile. And now I can help other folks see their pets too. That's pretty special." I gave her a nudge. "So, when are you going to do this, then? Would you like me to be there with you when you get set up?"

"Yep, definitely. How about tomorrow morning? Say, ten o'clock? Does that work for you? That would give me time to go over to the café and dump my stuff. Meet you at the bridge?"

I jumped up, looking at my watch in horror. It had almost gone dark; we'd been chatting so long. "Yes, that's fine. Sorry, I must dash. Are you sure you'll be okay?"

Scarlett nodded. "Yes. Stop worrying. See you tomorrow."

CHAPTER TWENTY

This time, I knew Scarlett would be there waiting for me. She was hopping from foot to foot as I approached the railway bridge and clambered down the steep footpath the next morning.

"Let's do this. I hardly slept last night. I was so excited at the prospect of seeing Jack." She waved the portrait painting in front of me and grabbed my arm, pulling me down further under the bridge. It was almost dark as we stepped into a type of tunnel behind a large rock jutting out from the side wall of the embankment.

"No-one will find us here. Now, what do I do again? Just stroke the butterfly and think of my boy?"

The canvas seemed to glow brighter in the gloomy shadows as Scarlett lifted it up and stretched out her fingertips. I gasped, even though I knew what would happen, as she disappeared in a flash of light, leaving me standing alone. Where the painting had been, a window appeared, exactly like it had with Iris, and I leant forward, eager to see what was happening.

Scarlett was in a field, but different from the one I always met Molly in. This one was more barren, with outcrops of rocks and a steep bank on one side. A lone owl flew overhead, and I caught a fleeting glimpse of a fox before it scurried into the undergrowth.

Although I couldn't hear anything, there was no mistaking the joy on Scarlett's face as Jack bounded over the field towards her and she fell onto the ground, gathering him in her arms. I stared harder as a second dog appeared in the distance. A small white poodle. *Poppy. That's brilliant. Jack must have found her.*

Scarlett reached over and showed Jack the painting, then rolled up the canvas. As she did so, the window on my side shrunk until it was only a sliver of shining blue light floating in the air. If I turned to view it from the side, it was nearly invisible. *At least I don't have to worry about anyone being able to see into the rainbow world while Scarlett is over there now. And that's not a bad idea for any future paintings. Much safer.*

I went back out of the tunnel, settling myself down on a rock in the sunshine, and pulled out my sketchbook and pens. *I think I might be waiting here for quite a while before Scarlett returns.*

The time actually passed quickly until I heard a sudden crashing sound behind me, and Scarlett clambered up the path to join me. She was breathless, brushing leaves and twigs from her clothes, her face flushed with excitement.

"It was incredible. I saw him. My boy. You were right. He's okay. Better than okay. He looks wonderful. Happy. Safe." She whirled past me and gasped as she tried to catch her breath.

I smiled at her, tears filling my eyes as a whole gamut of emotions spilled across her face. Joy, pride, happiness, and relief were all etched on her features.

This is what it's all about. This is why I risk everything with The Keeper and his silly rules. So that people like Scarlett can experience this wonderful opportunity to see their beloved pets again.

"I know. It's amazing, isn't it?" I felt emotional myself as she skipped and danced around.

"I can't wait to go back there and see him again."

"You know that's not possible, don't you? I told you what The Keeper said to me, didn't I? That you can't return. You can only go over there once?"

"Oh him. Pah! I saw that little lion creature staring at me. He didn't scare me." Scarlett flapped her hand in the air. "I'm not bothered about him. Look, I've got to dash. Thank you so much for everything you've done for me. I'll never forget this."

She was gone in an instant, the rolled-up canvas tucked under her arm. *Well, that didn't end quite how I expected. Now what am I going to do about Scarlett if she's determined to revisit Jack? How can I stop her, though? It's not as if I don't understand where she's coming from. I couldn't bear it if someone told me I couldn't go back and see Molly. And why didn't I tell her she had to keep this a secret before she raced off? What if she goes round telling people about Archaven?*

I had to hope she would be sensible and not rile up The Keeper. I didn't fancy coming up against him when he was angry again.

I couldn't spend too much time worrying about Scarlett, as I still had the set of paintings to finish for Anna before her big move down to the cottage. I completed the last one literally the day before her removal day. She had sent me a text inviting me round that weekend, and I squeezed all five paintings into the boot of my little car before driving over there.

Her husband, Geoff, was busy sorting out boxes in the garage as I pulled up outside the cottage. Anna raced over to me, enveloping me in an enormous hug that almost knocked the wind flat out of me. She tossed back her head, her trendy high ponytail swishing from side to side. Not a hair out of place, as usual. Anna had perfectly coiffed long auburn hair, and her elegant painted fingernails and designer clothes seemed incongruous for the traditional old Devon cottage they were moving into. She had never conformed to the stereotypical teacher ensemble, always looking more like a London financial expert or magazine editor. The warmth of her smile and embrace was, however, totally genuine.

"You're here! Come and see what we've already done. It's still a bit of a mess, but the furniture all arrived yesterday, and we're slowly getting there." She called over to Geoff, "Hun, can you get the paintings out of Laura's car for us?"

I walked over to help him, but Anna gripped my arm and pulled me towards the front door. "Oh, leave him to it. He'll manage. Come inside. I've got a bottle of bubbly open."

"But it's only midday. I can't possibly drink anything. And I have to drive home, anyway." I knew what Anna was like when she started drinking that early.

"Spoilsport."

She practically dragged me through each room, chattering away about the plans she had, all of which seemed to involve spending a lot of money. We walked into the kitchen, and Anna put the kettle on. Bayley, their cocker spaniel, wagged his tail but barely moved from his fluffy cushioned bed. His muzzle was white, and he looked up at me with watery, wise old eyes.

"Hello, boy." I sat down on the floor beside him and gently stroked his head. "How old is he now, Anna?"

"Oh, don't sit down there. He's getting on for about thirteen now. I think the move got to him a bit. But he's fine." Anna dismissed my concerned expression with a wave of her hand. "Have a cup of tea if you won't join me for a glass of something nicer." She topped up her bubbly and plonked herself on a carved wooden chair at the kitchen table.

"You'll come over next Saturday, won't you? We're having a housewarming barbecue. Nothing special. Just some old—and new—friends. You're welcome to bring someone with you."

Chance would be a fine thing. Perhaps I should invite Enid. Or Iris. Or Scarlett. That would go down nicely.

I suddenly realised that most of my friends were retired grannies. Or homeless. *That's a point. I haven't heard from Scarlett since the day she crossed over to see Jack. I hope she's alright. And I haven't seen Molly for several days. She must be wondering where I am. I'd better pop over there tomorrow and check up on her.*

"Earth to Laura. What are you daydreaming about?"

Anna prodding me in the ribs brought me back to reality with a jolt. "Sorry, I was miles away." I tried to fasten my attention on Anna, who was looking at me with a sceptical expression on her face.

"Really? I've seen that look before. You're up to something, and I want to know what it is. I'll get it out of you, eventually. As long as it doesn't have anything to do with that ridiculous story you made up last time about the rainbow land." She huffed, wagging her index finger at me. "Honestly. You had me almost believing you that night. Ludicrous nonsense."

Well, that told me, didn't it? Remind me not to share anything else with Anna about that, then. I couldn't imagine what she would say if she knew about Scarlett.

"No, right, better get going then." I drank the last of my tea and shot up, shoving my bag onto my shoulder. "Have fun getting everything organised. And I hope you like the paintings." I scurried out of the door and exhaled deeply as I sank into the driver's seat of my car and started the engine. I could feel a tension headache beginning to throb in my temples as I kneaded the muscles at the back of my neck. *Maybe Anna moving down here isn't such a great idea after all.*

> Love, love, love the paintings! I'm getting Geoff to drill holes in the walls for them as we speak. Sorry I was sharp with you. See you next Saturday. Don't be late xx

The text message pinged as I arrived home and sank down onto the sofa. Kicking off my trainers, I curled my legs under my body and reached for the thousandth time over to the space beside me. *Molly's spot. It always would be.*

Who cares what Anna or anyone else thinks? I know it's real, and that's all that matters.

I fell asleep, dreaming of my darling girl running across the field alongside me, the sun glittering in the evening sky.

CHAPTER TWENTY-ONE

The day of the barbecue dawned bright and sunny. I had some time free before I needed to pop to the supermarket to pick up a few things. It would never do to turn up at Anna's housewarming party empty-handed.

Maybe just a quick trip over to see Molly. It had been too long, and I was missing her. I landed in my usual spot on the meadow, the vibrant colours of the flowers creating a carpet of blossom. I walked towards her favourite magnolia tree, hoping she was there. It was eerily silent as I glanced around. The smell of freshly mown grass over by the river filled the air as I idly wondered who maintained all the trees and plants.

There was no sign of Molly. *That's strange. She's always here. Almost as if she knows when I'm about to visit her.*

I sat for a while, hoping she would appear, as the sun dipped behind an ominously dark cloud. *Great. I've never needed a coat over here before, but it sure looks like it's going to rain soon.*

I didn't know what to do. *Should I go looking for her or stay here?* I'd never travelled far from Molly's tree, as I was always content to be with her wherever she was. But something made me pick up her painting and start walking. *If I keep the river on my left, I can't really get lost.*

With each step, an icy dread tightened its grip on my stomach. It was a persistent, nagging feeling that Molly was in danger, and I had to find her. I quickened my pace, my heart pounding in my chest.

Soon her meadow was far behind me as I trudged on, tramping across mossy banks and muddy river paths. My trousers and trainers were filthy, covered in mud splatters and leaves, as I traipsed on, not knowing where I was going. Only that, somehow, I knew I was travelling in the right direction. Now and then, a rainbow appeared in the distance, flickering above the river, before disappearing again from view.

I stopped, gasping for breath, after climbing up a particularly steep path, the river now far below me. The water was spilling and tumbling along, white tufts of waves swirling across the surface. The heady, fragrant scent of a tropical flower made me pause. It conjured up images of mango fruit, ripe and bursting with flavour, and reminded me I had eaten nothing since breakfast. And that was hours ago.

I rifled through my pockets, hoping to find something to eat, but came up empty. My throat was parched, and I longed for a drink of water too. Perching on the edge of a rock, I exhaled slowly as a blackbird hopped along the path in front of me.

Now what do I do? How much farther can I go? And how will I ever find Molly? What if something dreadful has happened to her?

The blackbird bobbed right up to my feet, head on one side, one beady eye staring at me. I marvelled at how beautiful he was, with his yellow beak and shiny black feathers, as he dipped his head up and down.

It's almost as if he's trying to talk to me. Now I know I'm going mad. A talking blackbird. Whatever next? Although... why not?

He hopped away a few feet, then stopped and looked back at me.

He wants me to follow him.

I figured I had little to lose as I gathered up the painting under my arm and set off. Every so often, the blackbird would fly ahead and check back to make sure I was still behind him. After about an hour, he came to a stop, circling round a gap in a fence that led to an old ramshackle shed. Only a few broken rafters remained of the roof, allowing the wind to whistle through. Waist-high weeds hid the battered wooden front door, their dry stalks scratching against my legs as I forced my way through them. My hands were soon scraped and bleeding as I grabbed hold of the door and tried to force it open, dragging a pile of rocks out of the way. The screeching sound as the door finally gave way made me jump, and I looked around, fearful that someone would have heard the noise.

I peered inside the dark interior, my eyes taking a few seconds to adjust to the light. A solitary white butterfly swept past me, and then I saw her, huddled in the corner, her eyes wide and scared.

"Molly. My darling girl. Whatever happened to you? Why are you in here?"

She staggered to her feet, then wagged her tail and raced up to me, almost knocking me over in her excitement.

"You're here. You found me. I can't believe it."

"But what are you doing here, so far away from your meadow? Who did this to you?" I nuzzled her neck, showering her with kisses as I clung to her. "Come on, let's get out of here. It's so dark and creepy."

I stepped back outside, and the blackbird swooped down and looped around me, its wings fluttering.

"Thank you, little one," I whispered, as it flew away. "I will never forget you."

"Who are you talking to?" Molly asked as she padded out beside me and looked up at the sky.

"Someone who helped me to find you," I replied. "I would never have managed it without them."

Molly stretched her back legs and shook her head. "Boy, am I glad to be out of there."

"But how did you end up inside that shed? Those rocks in front of the door looked like they had been placed there recently. After someone had shut you in there. Is that what happened? Did someone, or something, lock you in there?"

Before Molly could answer, there was a deep rumbling in the field below us. It sounded as if the very earth itself was being torn apart as a flash of lightning seared across the sky. A golden bronze figure strode towards us, mane gleaming as if on fire. Flames shot from his mouth as he seemed to fly over the land, until he stood right before us, clothes billowing in the wind. The Keeper.

"It was I who trapped her inside there. To teach you something vitally important that you seem unable to grasp thus far. I am in charge here. Not you. And when I give you a command, I expect you to obey it. Without question." He glared at me, his fur glowing.

Fury filled my heart as I faced him, my emotions raging. I struggled to keep my anger at bay as I replied. "You. You did this? To my sweet Molly. She's done nothing wrong. How dare you treat her like that?"

"I knew you would be concerned if she was not under her tree. That you would search for her. But you were not supposed to locate her so easily." He stroked his beard; eyes fixated on me as I squirmed under his gaze. Molly scuttled behind me, cowering down, her entire body shivering.

"Look what you've done to her," I said, pointing at Molly. "You had no right to do that to my dog."

He rebuffed me and carried on speaking, like a Victorian headteacher berating a small child. "I am impressed that you found her. Bravo," he sneered. "However, that does not alter the fact that you have blatantly ignored my instructions, showing a complete lack of respect for my authority. I say it again. I am in charge here."

"I don't know what you're talking about."

"The girl you led over here. The one with the collie dog, Jack. That is what I am talking about."

"What has she done?" My heart sank as I feared the worst.

"I explicitly told you that other people may only visit here once. Although I am now beginning to regret that decision, considering what has happened."

Unsure how to react, I stuffed my hands in my pockets, the weight of his statement hanging heavy in the air.

"That girl has been here five times in the last week alone. And several times before that. Riling up the others and causing trouble. Promising other dogs all sorts of things she cannot provide. It's not right. And I explained that to you from the start. I couldn't have been clearer. Only one visit. Perhaps I shouldn't have allowed you to keep coming back, either."

"Oh please, no, don't say that. I'll sort it out. I promise I will. Please let me continue to see my Molly. She means everything to me."

In truth, I had no idea how I would do that. I hadn't seen Scarlett since the day she'd visited Archaven and then disappeared with the painting under her arm. But I wasn't about to let The Keeper know that.

"You certainly seem to have an unusually strong bond with your dog. I was not expecting you to find her by yourself. But this cannot continue forever."

I almost cried as I pleaded with him, but he seemed oblivious to my requests.

Molly stepped in front of me and lifted a paw in submission. "We will not go against you. Just give us more time." She bowed down as The Keeper threw back his head and roared. A thunderous echo rolled around the hills, the sound booming and reverberating, making me stumble backwards, my ears ringing from the fierce noise. But Molly stayed calm, motionless, as The Keeper fired out a blast of flames into the air above us, then turned tail and stormed away.

I sank down to my knees and hugged Molly. "I'm so sorry, my darling. This is all my fault."

"No, it's not your fault. What you're doing is a good thing. You don't see the other side of it, like I do. How happy little Poppy was to be reunited with her owner again. And the transformation in Jack is nothing short of amazing. He was so depressed before, worrying about that girl. Knowing that she was blaming herself for what happened. And now, he's like a different dog. Strong. Confident. With a future to look forward to. Don't blame yourself. And for now, don't stop doing what you're doing. We'll sort out The Keeper. He'll come round when he sees how much better we all are."

My heart overflowed with love and pride. "You always were such a brave and wise girl. I have so much to go away and think about. But never doubt one thing. And that is my love for you. I would have travelled this entire land looking for you, and I wouldn't have given up until I found you. Nothing can keep us apart. Nothing."

CHAPTER TWENTY-TWO

The party was in full swing when I arrived, with people chatting and laughing. In the garden, strings of coloured lanterns cast a magical glow across the trees, their delicate paper rustling in the breeze. Geoff bustled around behind an enormous gas barbecue, the aroma of grilled meat wafting across the lawn. Anna was busy talking to a group of people as I reached for a soft drink, then wandered over to her.

"Laura, meet my new colleagues. Everyone, this is Laura, my best friend since uni." Anna chinked her glass against mine.

It was too much for me after everything that had happened that afternoon. There I was, enduring inane small talk with a bunch of people I didn't know. And inside I was a churned-up mess of emotions.

I made my excuses to the group and disappeared into the kitchen, sinking into a chair, which was where Anna found me.

"There you are. I've been looking for you. Gosh, it's busy, isn't it? Geoff's rushed off his feet, and I think we're about to run out of sausages."

"How can you possibly have so many guests? You've lived here for less than two weeks, and you already know more people than I do."

"Oh, I came down here for an inset day at the end of last term. It was a chance to meet all the staff, and I mentioned we'd be having a little party. I wasn't expecting them all to come, though! I guess not much happens around here in the summer."

Anna scurried around the kitchen, loading her arms up with more plates of food. "Are you sure you're okay? You seem kinda frazzled tonight?"

"Yes, I'm fine. Just a bit tired. Here, let me help you with that." I grabbed a Styrofoam box from the fridge, lifting the lid to peer inside. "I reckon you've got enough food for a while." There were at least thirty sausages in there, along with another wrapped package labelled 'ribs'.

"Come on then, let's go feed the masses." Anna marched outside, and I traipsed behind her, wishing I could stay hidden in the kitchen.

I grabbed another drink and wandered round, eventually finding a quiet spot on a bench in the front garden. Everyone else seemed to be in the back garden, dancing to an 80s Greatest Hits album streaming through an outside speaker.

"That's a peaceful corner. Mind if I join you?"

I turned around, annoyed at being disturbed, until I saw who it was.

"Our friendly estate agent. Hello, Tom. What are you doing here?"

"Oh, Anna invited me. In fact, I think she invited most of the village, by the looks of things. She's certainly settling in well." He waved a bottle of beer in the air. "Can I get you another drink?"

"No, I'm good, thanks. But feel free to take a seat if you want to." I shuffled along the bench to make some room, and Tom flopped down beside me. I couldn't help but notice the crisp scent of aftershave he was wearing. Almost tangy, like freshly cut lemons. I glanced over at him as he took a long swig of beer and briefly closed his eyes.

"Oh, that tastes good. I've been looking forward to that all day."

"Busy day, huh?"

"You could say that. I almost didn't come tonight. I was so tired, but Anna insisted. She can be quite persistent when she wants to be.

And it's only a five-minute stroll away from my house, so I couldn't really say no."

"You live here in the village?" I shuffled round a bit to face him, trying not to look too interested.

"Yes, I'm a Devon boy. Lived here all my life. My dad was the local butcher, so everyone knew him. He died a couple of years ago. It's been tough for my mum."

"I'm sorry. That must be hard for you. My dad died when I was only a child. I hardly remember him. It was just me and Mum growing up. She passed away fifteen years ago now. I still miss her."

"We've got quite a lot in common, haven't we?" Tom patted my arm as I nodded in agreement.

We chatted for a while longer, then sat in companionable silence, listening to the other partygoers enjoying themselves.

"Maybe we could go out one night together. Actually plan something, rather than just keep bumping into each other. What do you think?" Tom's declaration startled me. *Is he asking me out? On a date? Or just as friends?*

The answer came as he leant forward and gently touched my cheek. I squirmed away, then regretted it, as Tom instantly drew back and shot up off the bench.

"I'm sorry. I didn't mean anything by that. Sorry." He looked flustered as he glanced down at his feet. "Let's pretend that never happened, shall we?"

"No, it's fine, honestly. You took me by surprise, that's all." I stood up, longing to take him in my arms, but my feet felt like lead. "It's just not a good time for me right now. I'm still trying to get over losing Molly, and I have lots of work to do." My voice tailed off. I knew I sounded pathetic, but I couldn't help myself.

"No, no, that's okay. I understand. I'd better get going. Busy day ahead tomorrow." Tom spun round and was out of the gate and halfway down the road before I could even fashion a reply.

Well done! You certainly blew that one, didn't you?

I sat on the bench watching as the guests started to leave, full of cheerful laughter, hugs and promises to meet up again soon. Anna found me there some time later and offered to make me a coffee.

"That sounds like a good idea before I drive home. I'll help you tidy up first, now that almost everyone's gone." There were still a few stragglers chatting, but the music had died down, and Geoff was carrying plates and cups inside. I picked up a few cushions and followed him and Anna into the kitchen, which was strewn with dirty crockery and half-full bin bags.

"Don't worry about all this. We'll sort it out in the morning. Come into the lounge and chat with me for a while. I've hardly seen you all evening. Geoff, darling, would you make us both a coffee?"

Anna patted the space on the sofa beside her, and I sank down, grateful for how comfortable it was. *I'd better watch out. I'm in danger of falling asleep here.*

"So, I saw you talking to our handsome estate agent." Anna grinned at me. "When's the first date, then?"

"There is no first date planned. You won't let up, will you? We're just friends. That's all."

"Mmm... yeah, right? I saw the way he was looking at you."

"Honestly, give it a rest, please. I've got enough on my plate without you nagging me." As soon as I said it, I knew I'd made a mistake.

"What do you mean? What is going on with you?" Anna leant towards me as I cringed inside. "You're up to something, and it's not good. I can tell. You forget I've known you for a long while now. It's that rainbow land twaddle again, isn't it?"

I squirmed under her gaze, feeling my temper rise as my face flushed.

"I'm right, aren't I? You're still dabbling in all that nonsense. It's time for a reality check, Laura. What are you playing at? I know you miss Molly, but you've got to move on with your life. Grow up. Stop making up this silly rainbow land in your head."

I couldn't help it. I clenched my fists as the words rushed out of my mouth before I could stop them.

"It's not nonsense. It's real. As real as you and I are sitting here now. I get to see my girl again. I'm sorry if you can't believe me, but it's true. And it's really helping me, knowing Molly is okay. And it's helping others, too. It's not just me. Other folks have been there. Thanks to my paintings."

I sat glaring at Anna, daring her to challenge me further. *Well, I've done it now.* I wasn't sorry. I knew I was telling the truth, however absurd it might sound. And I had Iris and Scarlett to back me up as well. *Scarlett. Now there's a problem for me to sort out tomorrow. How am I going to find her?*

Anna stared at me, not speaking, but her eyes said everything I needed to know.

"You don't believe me, and I don't blame you." My words hung heavy in the air. "I think it sounds crazy, too. But I'm not making this up. Honestly."

The tension in the room was almost palpable as I grabbed my coat and bag and got to my feet.

"I don't want to fall out with you. You've been my best friend for so long. But you don't get to tell me to grow up like that. I'm not some naughty schoolkid in your class that you can admonish."

Anna didn't even get up off the sofa as she turned to face me. "Maybe it's best if we have a break from each other for a while." Her voice faltered as she swept her hand over her skirt. "I'm going to be busy with my new job soon, and well, I just think it might be better..."

"Fine. If that's what you want. I won't stay where I'm not welcome." I stormed out, hitching my arms into my coat, and slammed the front door shut behind me.

CHAPTER TWENTY-THREE

I slept badly, tossing and turning and reliving everything that had happened with Molly, The Keeper and then Anna. *This is developing into a nightmare. And I still have to find Scarlett and stop her from visiting Jack again. How on earth am I going to do that?*

As I munched my breakfast, I resolved not to invite anyone else to visit Archaven. I was still reeling from the kidnapping of Molly. Finding her trapped in the shed had really frightened me, and I was determined not to do anything to put her in danger again.

I've got more than enough on my plate dealing with Scarlett; I don't need to add any more complications by involving other people. And that includes keeping the whole thing a secret from everyone. No more talking about it. To anyone.

Satisfied with my decision, I wandered down into my studio and logged on to my laptop. The usual emails were waiting for me, and I deleted them all. Except one. It was simply titled 'Can you help me?'

Dear Laura,
  I know you are a local artist who paints pets. I would love you to paint our beloved cat as a memory piece. Bella was only five years old

when we recently lost her. It was a tragic accident, and we all miss her so much.

Best wishes, Sarah and family.

Okay, so I can paint her cat for her. Easy. No need to do any more than that. No rainbow stories or butterflies. Just a regular client.

I replied, offering to meet her the following day, and then sped out in my car, driving around for hours, hoping to find Scarlett. I gave up once it got dark and headed home again.

Sarah breezed into my studio the next morning, and I liked her straight away. She was bright and friendly, exclaiming over my studio layout and flicking through my art brochures.

"Tell me all about Bella." I handed Sarah a mug of tea. "It helps me if I know something about the subject I'm painting."

"Oh, she was so special. A beautiful girl. We got her as a tiny kitten when my girls were still small, and she was part of the family. I've two daughters, Amber and Lola, both at school now. Bella slept in their room every night with them. She was more like a dog than a cat. Loved to follow us everywhere around the house. Here, I've brought some photos of her to show you."

Sarah handed me an envelope, and as I slid out the photos, I gasped at the sight of a gorgeous white-haired cat staring back at me. She was a delightful soft bundle of fur with startling blue eyes.

"Bella was a beauty, wasn't she? A Ragdoll. She was so affectionate. Such a character, too." Sarah's eyes filled with tears, and I reached over and passed her a paper tissue.

"Sorry, it's silly of me to get so emotional. I can't stop crying when I think about her. The girls were distraught when they found out she had died."

"Not at all. I understand what you're going through. I lost my own girl not that long ago. Molly. A golden retriever. She was my world."

"Oh, then you know how much it hurts. Bella was only five. She had so many more years ahead of her. I blame myself every day for what happened. I left the front door open, only for a moment. She was an indoor cat, you see. Didn't enjoy going outside much. But something spooked her, and she ran out the door. Our neighbour's dog saw her and chased after her. Poor Bella must have been so scared. She clambered up a telegraph pole, desperately trying to escape the dog's jaws. But she'd never had to climb anything like that before, and I guess her claws were too soft. I couldn't bear to watch as she slipped and slithered her way up that wooden mast. And then she lost her balance and fell to the ground. She died instantly."

Sarah's lips quivered as she continued, the tissue crumpled in her hand. "It's my fault. If I hadn't opened the door. She'd still be with us. I had to deal with it all before the girls came home from school. Didn't want them to see anything. I can still picture her lying there on the pavement, her beautiful soft white fur covered in blood."

Sarah burst into tears, and I wrapped my arms around her as she broke down, grieving for her Bella.

"I am sorry. That must have been so terrible for you. Are you sure you want me to paint her portrait now for you? You wouldn't rather wait a while?"

"No, I think it will help to see her face every day. We'll hang the painting in the lounge on the wall above where her bed used to be. That way, she'll always be with us." Sarah blew her nose and let out a long sigh. "I just wish the last image I have of Bella wasn't her lying there like that. It was terrible. I held her in my arms and wailed. I knew straightaway she was dead. My poor Bella."

I wonder if I could find Bella? Perhaps if she saw her again—just once—and knew she was alright? No, stop it. No more visitors to Archaven. It's too dangerous. For Molly—and for me.

"What sort of portrait were you thinking of? And is it solely of Bella, or would you like me to feature any of the family as well?" I waited anxiously, silently praying she wouldn't want everyone included.

"No, only Bella. Front and centre. A nice big painting of our girl. About this size, if that's possible?" Sarah lifted one arm above her head, the other hovering near her knees.

"About a metre high. Yes, I can do that. A portrait format would work well." I studied the photographs again.

Phew. No people. Just the cat. Should be alright then. All my other rainbow paintings have had a person in the design as well. I'm sure this one will be fine. A normal pet portrait. And not a butterfly in sight.

"Oh, and I'd love you to put this in the painting, too." Sarah reached into her bag and lifted out a fluffy blanket. "Bella's favourite comforter. I really want this to be featured. Perhaps she could sit on it, or it could be in the background?"

My heart sank as I took hold of the pale grey blanket. A whimsical pattern of pink flowers and yellow butterflies covered the entire surface.

Butterflies. Loads of them. Brilliant. Just what I need.

"That's fine. I can incorporate it into the design. No problem." I named a price Sarah was happy with and promised to contact her when the painting was ready for collection.

As soon as she left, I picked up my pencils, dug out a suitable canvas from my storage rack, and started work.

It'll be cool. Nothing to worry about. No need to mention Archaven to Sarah. It's not like I have to say anything at all. She doesn't need to know.

But all the time I was drawing and painting Bella, all I could think about was her lying dead on the ground. Her intense blue eyes seemed to follow me round the room as soon as I had painted them into her portrait, tormenting and challenging me with a tenacious, fixed glare. It was even worse when I added all the butterflies on the blanket. It was as if they were all alive, refusing to sit still on the surface of the canvas, flitting around underneath the bristles of my paintbrush.

This is insane. I'm imagining things now. Maybe Anna's right, and I am going crazy.

I threw down my brush and stomped up to my flat, promising to give myself a day off to relax.

There's only one thing for it. A quick trip over to see Molly. Purely to reassure myself that she's really there. And that I'm not going mad.

She was waiting for me when I landed. I ran over to her, feeling the comfort of her warm body snuggled into mine. "Everything is alright when I'm with you. You're okay, no more trouble from The Keeper?"

"No, it's been really quiet here. All fine."

I settled down and told her about all the things that had been happening. I was expecting her to reassure me I was doing the right thing, not getting involved in another episode like the one with Scarlett. Instead of answering, Molly glanced up at me, her eyes betraying the uncertainty she felt.

"What is it? What's wrong? You're not telling me something, aren't you?"

"Well," she hesitated, pawing the ground. "I was hoping not to mention it. But now you've told me about Bella, I don't think I have any choice."

"What do you mean?"

"Bella. The cat. I'm almost certain I've seen her over here. She's a pretty white thing with amazing blue eyes? Bit spoilt?"

I fumbled around in my pockets. "Hang on a minute. I might have a photo of her with me. Yes, here it is." I showed Molly the photo of Bella I'd been working from.

"Yes, that's her. She's been a bit of a pain, to be honest. Very clingy. I can't get rid of her some days; she keeps hanging around here. I'm not sure she's even used to being outside. She doesn't seem interested in any of the wildlife or walks round here. I hear her yowling some nights. She's down by the river, in a little hut that has suddenly appeared."

"That would make sense. She was an indoor cat. Her family was everything to her. She must be missing them." I puffed out my cheeks. "That certainly hasn't helped me. In fact, knowing all that has only made things worse. What am I going to do?"

"I've no idea. But whatever you do, please don't agitate The Keeper. Being trapped in that building was terrifying. I'm not sure I could cope with that again. I'm content to sit here and wait for you. As I said before, time has no meaning here. Not like where you are. But I guess for Bella, she's really struggling with it all. Maybe seeing her owner might settle her down. Reassure her everything will be fine in the end."

"I'll have to go away and think about all of this. I swear I won't put you in any danger, though. That's a promise. I'd never let anything or anyone harm you. You will always come first for me."

Arriving back home that evening, I paced around my flat, trying to decide what to do. *I wish I weren't so alone with all of this. If only I had someone else I could talk to. And why me? What makes me the chosen one? Just because I painted a butterfly on Molly's portrait. Now I'm up to my neck in this, whether I like it or not.*

I turned off the light as I went to bed, knowing I wouldn't get a wink of sleep all night.

CHAPTER TWENTY-FOUR

I decided to pay Iris a visit, hoping to find a kindred spirit I could confide in. I went via the local supermarket, where I bought a cake and some biscuits for her, then rang the doorbell to her flat.

"You're not too busy, are you?" I hesitated on the doorstep.

"Always got time for you, my dear," she said, as she ushered me inside and hung my coat up near the door. In the lounge, I stopped in my tracks. My painting of Poppy had pride of place on the main wall.

"She really was a pretty little poodle, wasn't she?" I smiled as Iris came into the room, carrying a tray loaded with tea and cake. "And I guess I should have known better than to bring you shop-bought baked goods, eh?"

"Oh, one can never have too many cakes. That's what I always say." Iris poured our tea into delicate bone china teacups from an ornate, patterned teapot. "It tastes nicer like this. I can't abide tea bags. But I'm sure you didn't come here to talk to me about tea. So come on, what's been happening? Tell me everything."

She settled back in her armchair, and I set my teacup down on the table before launching into an update on the Land of the Rainbow Bridge, as Iris liked to call it. Her eyebrows shot up as I explained about Scarlett, and she looked visibly worried when I mentioned how The Keeper had kidnapped Molly, but she didn't interrupt me. Once I'd finished speaking, she leant over and patted me on the arm.

"Well, no wonder you're looking fraught. That's a lot to carry on your own. I'm guessing you haven't talked to anyone else about this?"

"I tried to tell my friend Anna, but she didn't believe me, and now we've fallen out. She's my best friend, and we haven't spoken in days. She told me she thought I was going mad."

"Oh dear, that isn't good. We don't want you losing your friends over this, do we?"

"It's so hard. It's different with you. I can talk to you about it, and you won't laugh at me. Or worse. You've been there, you know it's real. It's so nice being able to open up to you." I reached for a slice of cake, placing it carefully on a plate. My hands were trembling so much, I was worried I would drop the pretty china crockery. It looked like it was part of one of those vintage tea sets you see on television. The ones that go for a mint in the auction room.

"Oh, and I've seen Poppy since as well. She's fine." *Better not tell her Jack bullied her, and she ran away. No point worrying Iris. She's back now and safe.*

"I'm so pleased she's alright. So, have you got any more customers lined up?"

I told her about Sarah and her cat, omitting the gory details about the accident.

"And?" Iris prodded me. "What are you not telling me?"

"You're too perceptive. That's your trouble." I laughed. "I don't know what to do now. Do I tell her about Archaven? Molly has already told me they have a new cat on the block. It has to be hers. But am I storing up more trouble for myself—and Molly—if I let Sarah go over there?"

Iris wheezed, and her teacup rattled against the saucer beneath it. "You don't exactly make things easy for yourself, do you?"

"I know. I never asked for any of this to happen. Some days, I wake up and wish I'd never painted that butterfly. Then none of this would have happened." I stared up at Poppy's painting. "But then I would never have seen Molly again. And you wouldn't have been able to visit Poppy. But why me? I'm nothing special. I'm just a girl who missed her dog."

"Have you always had dogs, or was Molly your first?"

"We had a Labrador at home with us when I was a child. But Molly was my soulmate. She was the first pet I could finally call my own. My mum had a way with dogs. They would invariably come over to her for some attention. She'd always keep a few biscuits in her bag in case she met a stray dog when we were out and about. She knew all the local dogs by name, and they would come racing up to her in the street. Usually with their owner still attached to the other end of the lead." I smiled at the memory. "I miss my mum. She died fifteen years ago. She would have loved Molly."

Iris nodded. "I've had dogs and cats all my life. They used to arrive at my door, and I could never turn them away. Your mum sounds like she was a gentle soul. Animals have a way of knowing whom to trust. Sometimes I think they are far more intelligent than us humans."

Suddenly, Iris had a coughing fit, and I panicked. She was holding the side of her chair with one hand, her other hand hovering over her mouth as she rasped and croaked, gasping for air. I knelt in front of her, stroking her back as she puffed and panted.

"Are you okay? Can I get you anything? A glass of water?"

She shook her head as she finally calmed down. "No, I'm alright. A little shortness of breath. That's all. Nothing to worry about." Beads of sweat had gathered on her forehead, and I reached over and handed her a tissue from a box on the table.

"Didn't seem like nothing to me, Iris. Are you sure you're okay?"

"Yes, yes, dear, don't worry. You sound like Sadie, fussing and flapping. It's just old age catching up with me."

"Well, if you insist. But if it carries on, I think you should see your doctor. Just to be sure."

"Of course. I will. Now, how about another piece of cake? Unless you have to rush off anywhere?"

I knew she was changing the subject, but I let it pass. "Okay. One more quick slice, then I have a painting to finish."

We spent another half an hour chatting, then I bade her goodbye, promising to visit her again soon.

Sarah's painting took an entire week to complete. A week when I picked up my phone at least once every day, hoping to see a message from Anna. But there was nothing. The sensible part of me said I could always pick up the phone and call her, but my stubborn side refused to give in. *I've not done anything wrong. It's not my fault she doesn't believe me.*

I emailed Sarah, letting her know that her portrait of Bella was ready to be collected. She was at the door of my studio within the hour.

"I'm so excited. I can't wait to see it." She shrieked when she saw the canvas propped up on my easel. "Oh, my goodness! That's my Bella. You've captured her perfectly. She almost looks real. You are so clever."

"I'm glad you like it." I started wrapping it up for her as she pulled out her purse.

"Like it? I love it. Wait until I show the girls when they get home from school. They're going to be so thrilled. Dan too. My husband always made out that he wasn't too fond of cats, but I would often catch him giving her a cuddle when he thought no-one was looking. This is going straight up on the wall in the lounge. Thank you so much."

Sarah left, promising to send me a photo of the painting in its new home. I tidied up the studio and went for a quick walk to the local park. *Some fresh air will do me good.* I passed a group of youngsters rushing home from school, their uniforms in complete disarray. *Of course, the schools have started back. Maybe that's why I haven't heard from Anna. She'll be busy with her new job.*

I sauntered along, enjoying the early autumn late afternoon

sunshine. The trees were already turning, their leaves dancing in the breeze as they fluttered to the ground, and in the distance I could hear the delighted squeals from the children in the play area. The path was dusty underfoot, with strands of grass lying dormant and parched on the ground. A few weeds had crept through the paving slabs, their tender stems defiantly nodding their intention to survive. I said hello to a couple sauntering past me as I turned a corner, looking for a bench to settle down on for a few minutes, and almost collided with Tom, who was walking in the opposite direction. He had a golden retriever on a long lead, and the dog bounded up to me as soon as it saw me. He licked my hand, then sat patiently at Tom's command.

"Impressive. Hi Tom." Instantly I recognised the dog. *It's the same one that Tom had that day at the deli. The one that looks like Molly.* "So, is this another dog from the rescue you're taking for a walk, then?"

"Hello Laura. No, this is Cooper." Tom wound the dog lead around his hand as Cooper sniffed the ground, his tail wagging. "I'm fostering him for a while. He's had a pretty rough start to his life. So, I'm giving him a temporary home. Just to get him house-trained and ready for a permanent adoption."

"He's a beauty. How old is he?"

"Almost two years old. But he came from a hoarder. She had loads of dogs all trapped in a room together. Poor lad hasn't had it easy, and he's pretty scared of new people. Or of being locked up or left for long periods on his own. Obviously. I think the previous owner hit him too. But he's coming on in leaps and bounds."

"He's lovely." I bent down, and Cooper gave me his paw.

"Hey, he's never done that before. He must really like you."

"He reminds me a lot of my Molly." I looked away, embarrassed to discover I had tears in my eyes.

"I'm sorry, I never thought. Of course. Molly was a retriever too, wasn't she? They're a wonderful breed of dog, so intelligent and affectionate. I'm enjoying having him around. There's never a dull moment with him." Tom patted Cooper's head. "Well, better get on. I promised this boy a long walk before we go home. It was lovely to see you again, Laura." He hesitated. "Perhaps you'd like to come on a little hike with Cooper and me sometime? Take a picnic and make a day of it?"

"That would be nice. You know where to find me. I'm in my studio most days."

They walked away, leaving me missing Molly even more than usual. *Maybe I can just sneak over there and see her again?*

CHAPTER TWENTY-FIVE

I knew I'd been neglecting my work when I received a plaintive message from Mrs Thomas at the art gallery, asking me when I was going to bring in some more paintings. She also cryptically suggested that it might be worth my popping in to see her. I raced over there as soon as they opened the next day, and she greeted me with a wide smile.

"There you are. I was getting worried about you."

The calm interior of the gallery, with its white walls and cleverly placed display areas, was full of enticing art and local crafts. Soft music was playing, and two customers were wandering around, exclaiming at how beautiful the artwork was. I wondered where my paintings were and spotted a couple tucked away on a back wall. *Well, that's only to be expected. I can't hog the spotlight all the time.*

"If you're looking for your paintings, you won't find many here. Just those two over there." Mrs Thomas looked rather pleased with herself as she handed me a piece of paper. "You'll see that I've sold seven more original Laura Adams paintings since we last met. How's that for a result? I'll transfer the money to your bank account at the end of the month. I hope you're happy."

"Happy? Wow! That doesn't even begin to describe it. I'm absolutely thrilled. Thank you so much."

"No need to thank me, young lady. Just promise me you'll bring in some more paintings for me to sell soon. We get busy with sales for Christmas from mid-October. So, that gives you a few weeks to create some new work for me. I'm assuming you still want us to represent you. You haven't had any better offers, have you?"

"Oh gosh, no. I'm delighted to be here."

"Good," she said, bustling around behind the sales counter. "I was worried you'd gone with a different gallery. As I hadn't heard from you for so long."

I apologised and promised to get straight to work on a new series of paintings, and left the gallery, my head spinning.

Maybe I can actually make a real living out of this now. Instead of barely surviving each month. I have to take this more seriously. No more pet portraits or trips to Archaven. But then a vision of Molly, sat patiently under her tree waiting for me, leapt into my mind. *But how can I abandon her?*

I drove home full of ideas for new paintings, and as I approached the Thread and Needle store, hoping to see Enid, I spotted Sarah perched on the bonnet of her car, parked right outside the shop.

"Oh good, you're back." She dashed over towards me, her hands shaking as she put her car keys into her handbag. "Have you got five minutes? I really need to speak to you."

"Of course, let me sort out something with Enid inside here, and I'll be right with you." Sarah followed me into the store. "Why don't you go through to my studio and I'll be there in a minute?"

Enid raised her eyebrows, but I flapped my hand at her and signalled for her to be quiet.

Once Sarah had disappeared from view, Enid shot a glance towards my studio. "Everything alright?"

"I don't know. Sarah's a recent client. She seemed fine when she took her painting home with her the other day. I hope nothing has happened to it. I'm not really sure why she's here."

"Well, I think you'd better go and find out, don't you?" Enid winked at me.

I smiled and headed for my studio.

Sarah was pacing up and down as I entered the room, her stiletto heels clacking on the tiled floor.

"Thank goodness you're here. I need to talk to you. It's about the painting."

"Is something wrong with it?" Her staccato manner completely floored me as she marched around the studio. "Come and sit down and talk to me."

"My girls. They've been having these dreams. It's all very weird. I don't know what to do."

I tried to stay calm as she finally sank down onto my sofa and gazed up at me. "You have to help me."

"Okay. Start at the beginning. Tell me what's happened. Take your time. No rush."

"It's my daughters, Amber and Lola. Amber is ten. Lola is just six; it was her birthday last week. Dan, my husband, hung your portrait of Bella up in our lounge the minute I arrived home. And the girls were so thrilled to see it. There were a few tears though, I don't mind admitting. You captured her expression so perfectly. Well, when it came to bedtime, Lola clambered onto our footstool in the lounge and stretched up to kiss the painting. She was very gentle, whispering, 'Night, night, Bella' as she touched her face. Amber looked surprised, but Lola begged her to do the same. I think she did it just to please her sister. Off they went to bed, and in the morning I crept into Lola's bedroom to wake her. But she was already wide awake, which is most unusual. She's almost impossible to rouse normally, but she was sitting up in bed, her eyes shining as she grinned at me. She's missing one of her front teeth at the moment, which makes her look even more cute than usual."

Sarah stopped and looked sideways at me as I sat down.

I think this is going to take a while. Better get comfy.

"Would you like a drink? Tea, coffee? I might have some juice in the fridge?"

Sarah shook her head. "No, I'm good, thanks. Sorry, where was I? Oh yes, Lola. She told me all about a dream she'd had during the night. It was about Bella, and it was obviously a vivid dream. She could remember everything about the field she saw Bella in, how happy she was. I thought little of it until we were all sat having breakfast together and Amber recited the exact same dream. Almost word for word. Lola was so excited, but I just put it down to a coincidence. That kissing Bella's painting goodnight had triggered them both into thinking about her as they slept."

"Dreams can be funny things," I said, trying to make light of it. But inside, my heart sank. *Here we go again.*

"I know. I still didn't think much about it until the next day. They'd insisted on kissing the painting goodnight again the previous evening. It's become a 'thing' they do every night now. Well, they both came downstairs telling me they'd dreamt about Bella again. In the same field, only they could now add much more detail to the illusion. They described everything so clearly, as if they'd both actually seen her. And then yesterday morning, for the third day in a row, Lola was almost in a trance as she recounted her latest dream to me. She painted this graphic picture of a river with rainbows sparkling in the sky. And she described a strange lion figure, half man, half lion. I figured she must have read a book at school about that, but then the room went quiet, as Amber turned to me and said, 'I saw that figure, too. And the rainbows over the river. With Bella sat patiently waiting for us.' I was a bit taken aback, I can tell you."

"So, what did you do?" I hoped she had simply quashed it all as happenstance. Merely the over-active imagination of two young girls.

"I sat them down and talked to them both. I wanted to make sure they hadn't concocted their stories together as a bit of a joke. But they were adamant they hadn't made it up. Lola even turned round and said, 'It's the painting, Mum. Every time I kiss the painting, I can feel the butterflies tickling my chin.' Amber then chimed in, talking about a strange 'energy' that came off the painting when she touched it. So I waited until the girls had gone to bed last night, when Dan was busy in the kitchen clearing away our supper things, and I walked up to the painting."

Sarah paused and looked over at me. "You'll never believe what happened?"

Oh dear. I think I can. Let me guess... you felt something shiver inside you? The room went dark? The ground fell away beneath you? My expression must have given me away.

"You already know what I'm going to say, don't you?" Her voice was low, a sombre challenge in the sudden silence of the room.

"Well, possibly."

"You're keeping something from me, aren't you? About the painting? I felt the same tingling my daughters described when I touched the canvas. Just for a second or two. A dizzying sensation came over me as the room tilted, and the floor seemed to rush up to meet me. What exactly is going on? These are my girls we're talking about here. I would never put them in any danger or harm's way. So you'd better come clean with me. And quickly."

I confessed everything to Sarah and reassured her that her daughters were safe. She sat wide-eyed as I told her all I knew about Archaven and what had happened to Bella. Sarah occasionally asked me a question, but mostly she let me do all the talking.

"The strange part of it all is that Amber and Lola are both dreaming about the rainbow land without actually visiting it. It's as if they are being protected from it. Maybe they're simply too young to go there. No-one has ever had dreams or visions like that before." I explained about the others that had travelled there and described The Keeper as a lion man without going into too much detail. *No point scaring her.*

Sarah pursed her lips. "I'd like to forget this ever happened. But I can't. And my girls won't let me, anyway. The strange thing is, they were both so desperately upset when they found out Bella was dead. Heartbroken. They both sobbed themselves to sleep the day she died. We were all devastated. I've tried to put a brave face on it for the girls' sake. But after they're in bed each night, I reach for a glass of wine. A big glass. And I let the tears fall. But now, since Amber and Lola have been having these dreams, they both seem so content. No more tears at bedtime." She pulled a handkerchief from her pocket and wound it around her manicured fingers.

"My girls have told me they're convinced Bella is well. That she's fit and healthy. Happy. And that they'll see her again one day. That she's waiting for them. Exactly like you've described."

"That must be some comfort to you?" I asked, tilting forward in my chair. "Surely knowing she's there, not in any more pain, is a good thing?"

"I wish I could be so certain. That's the trouble, you see. The last picture I have in my mind of Bella is of her lying on the pavement. Dead. I can't shake off that awful image. It's all I see when I close my eyes and think of her. The girls can visualise her in a beautiful meadow basking in the sunshine. All I have is the memory of her accident. Her body, all shattered, blood everywhere."

Sarah sobbed, and I leant over to comfort her. "It's just so horrible, picturing her like that."

"Well, if you wanted to…" I started to speak, then faltered. *What am I doing? Telling someone else they should go over there. Am I mad? After what happened to Molly?* And yet, seeing Sarah collapsed in a heap, shoulders racked with pain as she wept, I couldn't think of anything else that would console her.

"What?" she hiccupped as she wiped the tears from her eyes. "Are you suggesting I travel over there? To see Bella? Could I do that? Is it dangerous?"

"It might help you. If you saw her—just one more time. Without all her injuries. It may give you some closure. Help you move forward and start to heal. But you can only go there once. You must promise me that."

"Fine. Okay. I want to see her again. Would that be possible? I'd like to go there tomorrow morning while Dan's at work. I'm not sure I could even begin to explain all this to him." She smiled through her tears. "Tell me what I need to do."

CHAPTER TWENTY-SIX

"You didn't tell me she could talk!"

I chuckled as I turned up the volume on my phone.

"Afternoon, Sarah. I take it Bella is well?"

"Better than that. She's thriving. And so happy. She's made lots of new friends. There's a clowder of them."

"A what?"

"I know. I had to look it up. That's the name for a group of cats. So much nicer than a colony, I thought. Anyway, they've all banded together, and they're teaching her how to be a proper outdoor cat. She climbed her first tree yesterday."

I smiled as Sarah told me all about her trip over to see Bella. The pride was evident in her voice. And something else too. Relief.

"I can never thank you enough for this. It was like a miracle when she ran up to me. She wrapped herself around my legs, purring contentedly, and I just started sobbing. She looked amazing, with no injuries. No scars. It's as if the accident never happened. She's absolutely fine."

"And you were alright over there too?"

"Oh yes. It was weird. I felt perfectly safe over there. Protected. It all seemed instinctive to me somehow. Like I'd been there before.

Perhaps the vivid descriptions my girls had recounted of their dreams made the place feel strangely familiar. I didn't see the lion creature you mentioned. Mind you, if he's anything like the character my girls described, I'm glad he wasn't there."

"I'm so pleased everything went well. You must be so relieved."

"I'll rest easy now I can picture her over there. Thank you so much. Although you could have warned me about the talking bit. That really freaked me out when she started chatting away. It's funny. Her voice was exactly how I'd always imagined it in my head. Except she's much brighter than I gave her credit for. She's a wise girl."

"So what's next?" I had to make sure Sarah wouldn't be hopping back over there like Scarlett.

Which reminds me. I still haven't located Scarlett.

"Oh, I'm not going back there, if that's what you're asking me. I've said my goodbyes to Bella, and I'm content. Knowing that she's happy and protected is enough for me. But I think I'll call a halt to the girls kissing the painting goodnight each evening. Just in case."

"That might be wise. Well, you know where I am if you need anything else or simply want to talk. I know how hard it is to lose a beloved pet. And then the whole Archaven rainbow land takes some getting your head round."

"It'll be our secret. And I will forever be grateful to you for persuading me to do this. Thank you."

I dragged out a canvas and perched it on my easel after Sarah's phone call, and tried to focus on my work.

A picture of The Keeper, steam coming out of his nostrils, slithered into my mind. *I'm sure he won't be happy when he finds out what I've done. Well, one-nil to me. That'll teach him.* Just hearing the joy in Sarah's voice had made it worthwhile. *So what if he's angry with me? I'll sort it out the next time I'm there. I've got to stop being so scared of him. Although... what if he tries to kidnap Molly again? He wouldn't do that—would he?*

My visit over to Archaven later that day initially bolstered then challenged my resolve. Hearing all about Bella had made me long to see Molly's sweet face and make sure she was safe, and I rushed to finish my work so I could be with her.

I arrived amid a spectacle of noise and splendour. On the far side of the field, an enormous rainbow covered the sky, hovering above the river. It was the largest bridge I'd ever seen there; its immense size dwarfed everything around it. I couldn't take my eyes off the prism of colours gleaming and sparkling against the misty backdrop of the evening sky. I stood almost hypnotised by the display unfolding before me.

Molly trotted over to me as a cascade of silent fireworks filled the sky, shooting a dazzling array of stars into the air. A host of animals had lined up facing the river, forming a guard of honour as a lady walked slowly towards the rainbow. She stopped to pat the heads of several dogs and cats as she strolled along, obviously not in a hurry. She stepped onto the bridge, and a long procession of animals followed her. The scent of roses hovered in the air, heady and sweet, reminding me instantly of my childhood garden.

Even from my distant vantage point, the lady's face was clearly visible as she turned, her eyes scanning the field one last time before she disappeared from view. I could almost feel the wind ruffling her blonde hair. She looked angelic. Peaceful. Ageless and content.

"That's someone important crossing over. Someone who dedicated their life to helping animals." The Keeper had sidled up behind me. "Tell me, what have all the people you keep sending over here ever done for our wider animal family? Nothing, I am sure." He snarled at me, his teeth gleaming white and sharp against his mouth. I shivered.

Now's not the time to buckle. Remember how you felt after talking to Sarah?

I raised my chin and stared straight at him. "They all loved their pets very much. The same way that I love Molly."

I stooped down to wrap my arms around her, protecting her. Molly's fur tickled my arm as she gazed up at me. The devotion in her eyes was clear for all to see. I kissed her nose, then stood up, bracing myself for a verbal exchange.

The Keeper stepped back and raised his arms in the air. A dark cloud appeared, and a fork of lightning screamed out of the sky, rocketing towards the earth. It hit Molly's blossom tree like a guided missile, shattering the trunk and scorching the ground. Flames leapt along the branches, and within seconds the entire structure was alight.

I staggered backwards, losing my footing and ended up sprawled on the grass. Molly barked and wheeled around as The Keeper clapped his hands. Instantly, the cloud released a torrent of water over the tree, leaving it steaming and sizzling. The stench of burnt wood was unbearable as I leant forward and retched.

I looked up, ready to say something to The Keeper, but he was already walking away from us. He glanced back over his shoulder and pointed his finger menacingly at Molly, his tail swishing behind him.

"Oh Molly. Your gorgeous tree. It's all gone." I stared over at the place where her magnolia tree had stood, majestic and imposing. All that remained was a smouldering mass of charred wood and branches, the ground still simmering with the heat.

"He means business, doesn't he? This is getting serious now. I need to keep you safe. If anything ever happened to you, I'd never forgive myself." My heart was pounding. Molly settled down beside me, and I hugged her tightly.

"I'll be alright. He's just angry. He'll calm down again. Everything will be fine." Molly looked across the field. "I'll just find another tree to settle under."

I spent some time with Molly nestled in my arms, waiting for the tremors in my body to subside. My hands were still shaking as I finally gathered her painting up and said goodbye to her. Back in my lounge, I sat for ages in the dark reliving everything that had happened. One thing I was certain of: my priority had to be Molly's safety. Whatever the cost.

The next morning, my phone rang just as I was heading into town to do some shopping.

"Hello Laura, it's Tom here. Anna gave me your number. I hope you don't mind."

I stored away that snippet of information about Anna. "No, of course not. It's nice to hear from you."

"I've got some news I thought you might be interested in. Do you remember Pam, the lady who founded the Second Chance animal sanctuary and rescue shelter? I think it's the place you adopted Molly from?"

"Yes, that's the one. I'd forgotten her name, though. She's been there for ages, hasn't she?"

"Almost thirty years. Goodness knows how many animals she rescued over that time. Well, she died last week after a long illness. I think it was a relief for her in the end. She struggled to do much for the charity after her diagnosis, but she always kept in touch with everyone. It was her funeral yesterday."

"I'm sorry to hear that. She's left behind quite a legacy." *I bet that's who I saw yesterday. Crossing the Rainbow Bridge. How wonderful for her. I wish I could tell Tom all about it.*

"Yes, she was some lady. She really inspired me. Anyway, that's not why I'm calling you. I wanted to let you know that the charity has asked me to take over running the place. At least temporarily. I'll be there three days a week, and there's another lady, Karen, who's going to step in as well and help."

"Wow, that's great news. But are you sure you'll be able to manage it all? What about your work for the estate agency?"

"I've got some savings put by. And I can still do my property job when I'm not at the shelter, so it shouldn't be a problem. But I finally get to follow my dream of working in animal rescue."

"That's fantastic, Tom. I'm so pleased for you. And I know you'll be brilliant there."

"I've got lots of ideas to raise the profile of the shelter and increase the fundraising. The budget has really taken a hit recently, so I'm hoping to get things back on an even keel. And I need to update the entire adoption process, too."

"Phew. Sounds like you're going to be busy."

"Yes, you could be right. Well, the real reason I rang you was to ask you a favour. Would you come out and celebrate with me? Please?" Tom's voice wavered, and I hesitated.

Was he asking me out again? On a date?

"Just as friends," he interjected. "Not a date or anything."

"Oh, that's okay then." I tried to hide the disappointment in my voice.

"Great. Does that mean you'll say yes? If you're free? Tonight?"

"Of course. Yes. Absolutely."

He rang off, then sent me a text with directions to a little bistro restaurant he'd discovered. I set down my phone and stared at myself in the mirror in my bedroom. *What on earth am I going to wear?*

CHAPTER TWENTY-SEVEN

The drive over to the harbour village of Axmouth was a pleasant thirty-minute trip through open countryside. I reduced my speed, rolled down my window, and let the evening breeze swirl through the car. The air was fresh with the scent of honeysuckle, the hay bales stacked perilously high in the fields beside the road, and the sky teeming with a flickering horde of birds swooping and diving across the setting sun. I glanced in the mirror for the tenth time, checking my hair and make-up as I parked in the only public car park on the map, and brushed my hands over my cotton trousers as I alighted from the car. My patterned top hung loosely as I grappled with the long necklace I'd hastily added to my outfit at the last minute. *Might be a bit too much? Too late now. Tom said it was a bistro, didn't he?*

I threw on my coat and grabbed my handbag, shoved my keys inside and tried to figure out which direction to walk.

The village seemed far too quiet and rural to have a trendy bistro nestled amongst the cottages and bric-à-brac shops that lined the main street. I tramped along, checking the map on my phone, and hoped I wasn't late. A flurry of homemade posters twirled in the wind, each one attached to a lamppost. I stopped to read one and unfurled the edges to get a better look at the text.

>MISSING DOG. Reward Offered.
>Have you seen my beagle called Hazel?
>She's white, black and tan coloured with adorable floppy ears.
>Last seen 20th September in Axmouth.
>£500 reward.

The poster had a photograph of a gorgeous-looking dog, complete with contact information. *The poor owner. She must be distraught.* I checked my phone. *Almost a week since the dog went missing. And heck, I'd better get a move on, else I'll be late.*

The bistro was small and welcoming as I pushed the door open, dead on seven thirty. Tom was already at the bar, soft drink in hand, as he rose out of his seat to greet me.

"You found it okay, then? They haven't been open long. I discovered this little gem during my travels for work one afternoon. The menu is excellent." He gave me an unexpected kiss on the cheek, then offered to take my coat for me and gestured to the seat opposite him. "What would you like to drink? I thought we could start here before we move into the restaurant."

"Just a Diet Coke, please. That would be lovely."

I looked around. It was still early, and the place was quiet. Soft lighting caressed the corners of the room, with leather chairs and sofas lining the walls of the bar area. Beyond, I could see a glimpse of the main seating area, tables laid out with fancy napkins and glassware. *Glad I didn't wear my jeans.*

"So, how are you? How's things? Busy as ever?" Tom settled back in his armchair as he folded his fingers together and smiled at me.

"Yes, all good, thanks. And wow! This place is certainly posher than going on a picnic with Cooper."

Tom chuckled. "Ah yes, sorry about that. Cooper sends his apologies. He checked, but apparently this particular bistro doesn't allow hairy, slobbering, greedy golden retrievers to dine here. Next time, a picnic. I promise."

"It sounds like Cooper's settling in well, then?" I raised my eyebrows and grinned. "Pretty soon he'll be a permanent fixture, I bet."

"No, he's definitely a temp." Tom shook his head. "He needs someone to give him a forever home. But that won't be me. He's a lovely boy, though. No trouble at all."

We chatted easily for a while, updating each other on our latest news and work.

"I saw those posters on the way here. The missing dog. The owner must be beside herself. I can't imagine how that must feel." I took another sip of my drink.

"Yes, I know her. Audrey. She's a lovely lady. Recently widowed, I think. She got Hazel, her beagle, from our rescue centre. I remember her clearly, as it's unusual to have a pure-bred dog up for adoption. Most of them get snapped up really quickly, but Hazel was in the kennels for quite some time before Audrey adopted her. Hazel was quite a noisy thing and liked to bark a lot. But very sweet and affectionate. I hope Audrey finds her."

We moved into the restaurant area, the server seating us at a private corner table overlooking the gardens. The trees were lit with lanterns, casting a golden glow over the grass. "How pretty!" I exclaimed, taking it all in. It was hard to decide what to order. The menu was so enticing, but I eventually settled on a simple salad for a starter, followed by salmon and smoked cod fishcakes. I was determined to save some room for dessert, as they had a baked vanilla cheesecake on the menu that sounded divine.

"I was sorry to hear about Pam from the rescue centre. Everyone there must be so upset at her passing." I handed the bowl of bread rolls across to Tom as he shook his head.

"Yes, it was so sad. The funeral was lovely, though. If you can say that about a funeral. It was a proper celebration of her life and work. The staff had filled the church with red roses. The smell was incredible. And so many people who had adopted dogs through her attended the service. Lots of them brought their dogs with them too. It was pretty crowded in there!"

I pictured the pile of unopened envelopes stacked up beside my front door in the flat. Perhaps I'd actually received an invitation to her funeral without realising it. *How embarrassing. And roses. Of course. I remember that scent; it was the sweet smell that accompanied that lady across the Rainbow Bridge. It must have been Pam then. Now what do I do? Should I tell Tom or keep quiet? Do I want to potentially spoil an enjoyable evening? And our friendship?*

"You're looking pensive. Is something wrong?" Tom looked concerned as I brushed a tendril of hair away from my face and took a deep breath.

"I've not been completely honest with you. There's a lot about me you don't know." I grimaced, trying to decide how to word it all.

"Let me guess. You're actually married, with seven children, and your husband runs a rival estate agency?"

I giggled, despite the feeling of despair that was creeping into my bones.

"No, nothing that sinister, I promise you. It's…" I tailed off, uncertain of whether to proceed, just as the main courses arrived at the table.

"Saved by the food," I joked, trying to make light of the way the conversation was heading. The meal was beautifully presented, but I hardly tasted a thing as I toyed with the food on my plate.

Tom set his knife and fork down on his empty plate, made his apologies, and got up to visit the bathroom. I watched him as he walked away.

Just tell him and get it over with. Then at least I'll know where I stand with him. Whether he'll even want to have anything else to do with me after tonight. He might think I'm mad. Or maybe he'll believe me. Maybe.

I thought back to Molly and how wonderful it felt each time I saw her, and remembered Tom telling me about his beloved dog, Max. *What if I could find him for Tom? Wouldn't that be brilliant? And I can tell him about Pam, too.*

Tom returned to the table, holding a dessert menu. "Why don't you order a nice big pudding and then you can tell me what's on your mind? I know you're keeping something from me. It's okay. I'm a big boy. I can take it. Whatever it is. Just spill it out."

That was the signal I needed to open the floodgates, and I bared my soul, telling him everything. Molly and her painting, the butterfly, visiting Archaven, and the excitement of seeing other people reunite with their beloved pets.

"But that's incredible. No wonder you've been acting strangely. Carrying all of that inside you."

"You don't think I'm crazy, then?"

"No, why? Should I?" Tom quipped, then stared at me. "You've not told many people, have you?"

"No. And the ones I have told were, well, let's just say I've had a mixed response. My best friend, Anna? She hasn't spoken to me in weeks. She's made it perfectly clear she doesn't believe me. I'm surprised you've taken it so well."

"To be honest, your story reminded me so much of a recurring dream I kept having after Max died. You could have been describing the exact same field that I saw him resting in. As if he was waiting for me. Just like you portrayed Molly. I haven't thought about that dream for years, and your explanation sent a shiver down my spine. But it all made sense to me when you started talking."

Tom swept his hand across his forehead. "It's quite a lot to take in, isn't it? You said you've instigated other people visiting their pets too? How's that been?"

I folded up my napkin and placed it on the table. "The others I've encouraged over there have mostly been fine. Except one. Scarlett. She's proved to be a bit of a problem." I described the issues I'd had with The Keeper, and Tom's expression grew serious.

"Crikey, Laura. It sounds as if you need to be careful over there. It's not like anyone can race over there and rescue you if you get into trouble. Right?"

"Yes. I know. But I can't stop going. I miss my Molly so much, and it's so wonderful being able to see her again."

"I get that. But promise me you won't take any risks over there?

We need you over here too, you know?" Tom's face softened as he reached over and squeezed my hand.

"I won't. I'll be careful. But, oh, it's so special being there. I wish you could have seen the reception they gave Pam when she arrived. All the dogs and cats that lined up to greet her. She was glowing with pride and love."

"It certainly sounds incredible. Who knows, maybe one day I might even join you and visit it for myself. See if it's really as magical as you say it is."

"So I'm not going mad then?"

"Oh yes, I definitely think you're insane. But then again, all the best people are."

We gathered up our things, and Tom insisted on paying.

"I'm sorry. We were supposed to be celebrating your new job, and instead all we did was talk about me all night." We strolled back to my car, Tom reaching over to rest his arm around my shoulder as we walked. The sky overhead was clear, stars twinkling in the distance, as the church clock chimed ten.

"Well, that's not a problem. It just gives us an excuse to go out to dinner again." Tom opened my car door for me, then stepped back and bowed gently.

"To my new friend and time traveller. Thank you for a wonderful evening. Take care driving home and navigating the worlds beyond what we can see. I'll be in touch soon."

I drove home with a smile on my face and a lightness in my heart I hadn't felt for a long while.

CHAPTER TWENTY-EIGHT

It was almost inevitable that the lost beagle would be waiting for me the next time I visited Archaven. She was sitting beside Molly, hunched up into a ball. I nearly didn't recognise her; she looked so frail and helpless.

"This is Hazel," Molly said as she sprung up to greet me.

"I know. I've seen the posters where she lives. Her mum is advertising a reward for her safe return."

"Really? Audrey, my mummy, is looking for me?" Hazel looked up at me, and I saw pain etched across her face. "She's going to be so sad when she finds out what happened to me."

"You'd better sit down," Molly said. "You need to hear Hazel's story. A few of us have been helping piece things together for her, and it makes for a pretty tragic tale."

"I've not had much of a life," Hazel said, her brow wrinkling. "But it's not my fault."

"It never is your fault, my dear. It's always us humans who are to blame." I held out my hand to her as she checked me out. Her touch was so delicate, her nose barely glancing across my skin as she sniffed my fingertips.

My reply seemed to pave the way for her, though, as she recounted her life story to me.

"I used to live with a family. But they were always at work. Being left home alone, I was bored. I'd chew things. Just for fun. And bark. I enjoyed barking. It made me feel safe. But they'd come home and see the mess I'd made and beat me. I could never wait all day for the toilet, so I'd end up peeing on the carpet. I didn't mean to do that, but I couldn't help it. That made them even more angry."

She paused, and I waited quietly. It was obviously painful for her, remembering all that had happened.

"They beat me a lot. Usually with a stick. I'd run and hide under the sofa, but the man would drag me out and hit me. I'd bark at him, and he'd hit me again. Harder."

She flinched, licked her lips, and continued.

"Eventually, they got rid of me. Dumped me at a shelter. I was happier there, to be honest. Although it was cold at night, and there were lots of bigger dogs in cages around me, I actually felt safer there. At least no-one hit me. The staff were nice, but they kept telling me nobody wanted to adopt me. They said it was because I barked a lot. But I can't help that. I'm just a noisy dog, I guess. Even if it does get me into trouble. I'd sit in my cage some nights and howl. That always made me feel better."

Molly bowed her head. She plainly recognised Hazel's predicament.

"One day a lady came to the shelter, and she stopped outside my cage. I can still remember what she said to the member of staff. It was the best thing I'd ever heard. 'A beagle. I love beagles. What's her name?' I didn't know I was a beagle until that day. I fluffed out my chest and tried to look important as I woofed at her with excitement. 'She's gorgeous. I'll take her', the lady said, and that's how I came to be living with Audrey. My new mummy."

Hazel's eyes rimmed over with tears as she described her new home.

"Audrey had a husband, too. He was called Frank. But he died not long after I arrived. I don't think that was my fault. Although I did bark at him a lot when I first met him. I don't like most men. They've always hurt me. Frank wasn't too bad, and he never hit me, though. He would stay home with me when Audrey went to work. That was nice, because if I went to the back door, Frank would open it for me. So I could go outside to do my business, if you know what I mean?" She squirmed, and I patted her leg.

"But then Frank died, and Audrey was sad. But she still had to go to work each day. She tried to leave me inside the house, but, well, I'm not too good at waiting. So she'd come home to a mess. She told me I was naughty, and so she left me outside in the garden instead. There was a shed I could shelter in if it was raining. And anyway, the garden was fun. There were so many birds to bark at and chase."

Hazel rolled over onto her back and stretched her legs out. I pictured her racing around, yapping at the local birds, and smiled. I felt my eyes growing heavy, and I jumped to my feet and shook myself.

"Give me a minute. I need to go for a quick walk. Keep myself alert." I marched around, waving my arms in wide circles, fighting off a series of yawns. *I must stay awake. Don't fall asleep. Has The Keeper put a curse on me? I always feel so tired when I'm here.*

"That's better." I sat down beside Molly. "Sorry about that. Carry on, Hazel. Tell me what happened."

"It was the neighbour. Bill. He was friends with Frank, but Audrey never liked him. She said he was 'shady', whatever that means. I kept my distance whenever he was around. He used to sit in the shed with Frank, drinking beer and smoking. Audrey never let Frank smoke inside the house. I was grateful for that. Bill even had a key to our back gate. He would often let himself into the garden, waiting for Frank to join him."

Hazel's body trembled as she stared at the ground.

"But after Frank died, I never saw Bill in the shed again. But I could hear him in his garden next door. He was forever moaning and shouting. 'Shut up! Stop barking. Will someone shut that blasted dog up?' But it wasn't my fault. The birds drove me crazy, and I had to chase them. And I was bored. Woofing at the birds was just how I liked to pass the time, I guess."

"So Bill didn't like your barking, is that it?" I wanted to check I'd got her story right.

"Yes. And then one day, it was really strange. He crept into the garden when Audrey was at work. He had a big, juicy piece of chicken in his hand. I was wary of him, but he called me over. And the chicken smelt so good. I couldn't resist. I chomped it all up and licked my paws, making sure I hadn't missed any tiny morsel of the tasty meat. Bill sat on a bench, watching me. And then a savage tremor vibrated through my body, and my legs shuddered. I felt sick, and I tasted foam in my mouth. Bill sauntered over to me as the trees and plants swirled in front of me. My head was spinning. He picked me up and carried me back to his house. The last thing I remember is his garage door closing behind us and everything went dark."

Molly moved closer to Hazel and licked her face as if to comfort her.

"And then I woke up here. On the grass. With Molly looming over me. I can't tell you how frightened I was. But she's been such a good friend. Helped me to settle in. I miss my mummy, though. She won't know what happened. What Bill did to me."

Molly nudged my leg with her nose. "That's where I thought you could help. Can you find Audrey and tell her what Hazel has said? It's not right that Bill gets away with this. It's obvious he must have poisoned Hazel."

"But I can't prove it, can I? Bill would simply deny it all, and there are no witnesses. Just your word against his. And it's not as if I can explain to anyone how I know all of this. I can't risk telling Audrey. What if she goes to the police?" I shook my head. "How can I make such a speculative allegation against Bill? I can hardly quote Hazel and what she's told me here, can I?" I couldn't see a way forward.

"What if you found some evidence to support it? I don't know what happened to my body, but I'm sure I was wearing my favourite dog collar when Bill grabbed me. And I'm not wearing it now?" Hazel's brown eyes locked onto mine as her face pleaded with me.

"It was a pink leather collar with fancy rhinestones all the way round it. And it had a tag with my name on it and Audrey's phone number. A red tag shaped like a paw print. She was most insistent that I had a posh collar to wear. What if you found that in his garage?"

"I don't know. I'm going to have to go away and think about this. But I promise you I won't let it rest. I'll do everything I can for you. I'm just not sure how to approach Audrey and explain this. She's already so upset, thinking you are missing. How do I tell her that her neighbour poisoned you and that you're no longer alive?" I tried to come up with a solution that would satisfy Hazel. It seemed like an impossible task.

The setting sun reminded me it was time for me to depart. I repeated my promise to Hazel that I would try my best to put things right for her and hugged Molly tightly before saying goodbye to both of them.

Back home, in the quiet of my flat, I warmed up a tin of soup and sat at the kitchen table, staring into space. *You've really gone and done it now. What a nightmare situation to sort out.* Hazel's face haunted me as I tried to eat my supper. I threw down my spoon in despair. *It's no good. I've got to do something. Somehow, I have to tell Audrey. If it were me, and it were my dog that was missing, I'd want to know. No matter how painful it might be.*

I wished I had never set foot on the grassy meadow of Archaven.

CHAPTER TWENTY-NINE

I woke up late after a poor night's sleep, Hazel's wretched face haunting my dreams.
I need to contact Audrey. Tell her what happened. Even if she doesn't believe me. I have to try.

The weather suited my mood as I made my breakfast; the rain was lashing down the kitchen window. *It's not worth going back over to Axmouth yet. Not in this downpour.*

My studio was dark and dreary, and even the overhead lights didn't seem to make much difference. I huddled over my easel, trying to muster up some enthusiasm for the painted canvas in front of me. But I couldn't stop thinking about Hazel. It was lunchtime before the rain eased up, as I sat and munched a sandwich. *It's no good. Might as well get this over with. I can't paint in this mood, anyway.* I grabbed my coat and bag and jumped into my car.

All the way to Axmouth, I kept telling myself it was a waste of time. *You probably won't find any of the posters. The rain will have washed them all away.*

I was right. I trudged up and down the main street, looking for one of the black and white printed posters. *All gone. They were attached to the lampposts. Now what do I do?*

I was about to give up when I spotted one stuck on the wall inside the bus stop. I unfurled the paper and could just make out the details. Audrey Sampson. With a mobile number to call.

My hands shook as I dialled the number, but it went straight to her answering machine. *Great. Now what?*

I sat down at the bus stop and typed a text message. Then deleted it. And re-worded it. Three times. *Keep it simple. Just arrange to meet her.*

> Hello. My name is Laura. I'm in Axmouth today. I have some news about Hazel. Could we meet up?

I wandered around the village, waiting for my phone to ping. Eventually, a message appeared.

> I'm still at work. Could meet at 4.30? There's a coffee shop beside the mini market. See you there?

I checked my watch. I had an hour to kill and went for a drive through the local countryside. It wasn't an area I knew well, and I was hoping to find inspiration for some new paintings. And it helped to take my mind off the impending meeting, which I had a horrible feeling about in the pit of my stomach. I arrived back in plenty of time, parked up, and made my way to the coffee shop.

It was gloomy inside as I pushed open the door and looked for a quiet table. Everyone stared at me as I wriggled my way through to the furthest corner and sat down. *Why did I sit here? I should have sat near the door. And what am I doing here, anyway? I have absolutely no idea what Audrey even looks like.* I toyed with the menu and ordered a latte, my head shooting up every time the door opened. Finally, a woman walked in and looked around, and I knew instinctively it had to be her. I waved my hand, and she marched over.

"You're Laura?" she said, standing in front of me.

"Yes. Audrey. Take a seat. Please." I gestured to her as she continued to size me up, then perched on the edge of a chair.

"Sorry, I haven't got long. I've just come from work. I'm a teacher at The Park Primary School, with a ton of lesson planning for tomorrow to catch up on. So tell me, what do you know about Hazel?"

My heart sank. The Park Primary. That's where Anna works. Brilliant. What are the chances of that?

Audrey's attitude had unnerved me, and I struggled to get started.

"Well, it's a bit of a long story. I'm not sure you're going to believe me. But I had to come here today to talk to you. For Hazel's sake."

Audrey's eyes narrowed as she flapped away the server approaching our table. "No thanks. Not today. I don't think I'll be staying long enough for a drink."

"I've seen her, you see. But not here. In another place. Where pets go when…" I faltered as Audrey fixed her steely gaze on me. I could tell she didn't believe me and was on the verge of leaving, and my words tumbled out as I tried to explain everything.

How can I tell her that Hazel is dead? And that her neighbour killed her?

The further my speech unravelled, the more I realised how ridiculous it all sounded. Even to me. *I should never have come here.*

"I've seen her. Honestly. She's really upset and worried about you."

How am I going to convince her? I know. The collar. I'll tell her about that.

"She's wearing a pretty decorative collar. With a name tag." I couldn't for the life of me remember what colour Hazel had said the collar was.

Audrey glared at me. "Yes, well, that's not difficult. As she's wearing that collar in the photo on all the posters I placed around the village. You'll have to do better than that."

It was obvious I was losing her. I tried once more to explain things, but I felt like I was simply digging a bigger hole for myself the entire time I talked.

"So what you're trying to tell me is that my dear Hazel is dead? And you've met her in some dream fantasy land? You seriously expect me to believe that?" Audrey's voice rose in volume, and several people turned around to stare at us.

"I'm guessing you're just here for the reward money, eh? You've got a nerve, young lady. Well, you're not getting a penny. Not for that ridiculous made-up story. You ought to be ashamed of yourself, coming here and upsetting me like this. I never want to hear from you again. Do I make myself clear?" She stormed out, leaving me sat in tears. I pushed my cup away, placed a five-pound note on the table, and walked back to my car in despair.

Well, that didn't exactly go according to plan, did it?

After another sleepless night, I gave up at around five in the morning and got up. I shuffled out to the kitchen in my pyjamas and put the kettle on. My favourite photo of Molly, pinned to the fridge, made my eyes well up, and I rested my hand across my forehead.

I felt physically sick. The relentless thoughts in my brain pounded against my head like waves crashing against rocks. *I was only trying to help. I can't believe how rude she was. That was such a nightmare.*

I slurped my coffee and thought about the day ahead. *I've got to talk to Hazel. Explain what happened with Audrey.* I knew she was going to be upset. *Might as well go over there now. No point waiting.* I showered quickly, got dressed and propped Molly's portrait on the kitchen table in front of me.

It was quiet as I landed on the ground and brushed my hands over the soft grass. A solitary bird was soaring overhead, chirruping with the dawn, as the first fingers of light spread over the distant hills. *I wish I could stay here. It's so calm—no drama, no problems to sort out. Just a tranquil, idyllic land. And Molly. My dearest Molly.*

I strolled over towards her, smiling as I watched her stretch out her front paws and yawn extravagantly before bounding up to me. She'd found a new tree to settle under, an imposing poplar tree with a deeply furrowed bark. I glanced across the field at the blackened, charred skeleton of her old magnolia tree, its branches reaching into the sky like disfigured arms clawing upwards. A constant reminder of the ferocious anger of The Keeper that day. I shuddered. *Maybe it's not so peaceful and safe here after all.*

"You're early. Is everything alright? Have you got news for Hazel?" Molly looked hopeful as I sank down on the grass and sighed.

"Sorry. Not good news, I'm afraid."

Hazel appeared across the field and raced up to us. "Have you seen her? What did she say? What's happening?"

"I'm really sorry, Hazel. I promise you I tried. But Audrey didn't believe a word of what I said to her." I left out the part about her storming away. I couldn't see the point of upsetting Hazel any further.

"But you have to make her understand. You can't let that man get away with what he did to me. It's not right. And what if he does it to another dog? Please go back and try again. I beg you." Hazel's eyes filled with tears as she prowled around us in a circle, her teeth bared.

Molly stared up at me, her brown eyes melting like chocolate on a hot summer's day, as I inhaled a lungful of air and then expelled it slowly.

"Don't give me those eyes, my girl. You know I could never resist you when you looked at me like that."

Hazel slumped down to the ground, as if she had a giant weight attached to her back, and I buckled. "Okay, okay. I'll try again. But I can't promise you anything."

"Thank you," said Hazel, her lips trembling. "I just want her to know what happened. For justice to be served. And so that I can finally rest here in peace."

CHAPTER THIRTY

How can I convince Audrey that I'm telling the truth? I paced around my studio, flinging paint in all directions as I attacked the canvas in front of me.

It's no good. I doubt she'd let me approach her again, even if I knew where she lived. No point trying to call her either. So how do I get in touch with her?

My phone ringing burst across my thoughts, and my stomach plummeted when I saw the caller ID displayed. *Anna. Great. Somehow, I don't think this is going to be a friendly call. I bet Audrey said something at school today.*

I deliberated about not answering, as the ringtone kept jingling and buzzing in my hand, but I knew that would be futile. Anna on the warpath was a sight to behold. I'd seen grown men quake in her presence. She wouldn't rest until she'd spoken to me. *I'm sure this has something to do with Audrey.* I wasn't wrong.

"You're unbelievable, do you know that? I've had a member of my staff today in floods of tears. Telling everyone about a crazy woman who approached her yesterday. About her missing dog, Hazel. Some drivel about a rainbow land, and how Hazel was dead. And apparently, the woman had then seen Hazel in this fantasy land. I knew it was you straight away. I'm right, aren't I?"

I couldn't get a word in, even if I'd wanted to. I just sat there, my body trembling, a cold sweat breaking out on my face, as I listened to Anna's torrent of words assaulting me.

"She's had to go home. She was too upset to stay here. You really are a piece of work, aren't you?"

I tried to interject, but gave up. *What's the point of trying to defend myself?*

"She doesn't know I'm ringing you. But if I were you, I'd stay well away from her. And me as well."

The phone went dead, and I stared at the blank screen for ages. It was strange. The longer I remained there motionless, the more determined I was to put things right. To speak to Audrey again. Make her listen to me. Tell her what really happened to Hazel. I felt the blood boiling in my veins as I sat there steaming with anger, thinking about the neighbour. What he'd done to poor Hazel. *Justice. That's what she asked for. And I'm determined to get it for her.*

I just had to come up with a plan for contacting Audrey. *And this time I'll have it all mapped out beforehand. I'll know exactly what I'm going to say to her to convince her it's true.*

Anna's phone call had done the opposite of what she, I'm sure, intended to happen. It had fired me up, set me alight, and made me staunchly committed to defending Hazel. And revealing the truth to Audrey. Whatever the cost.

The answer came to me in a blinding flash. *Of course. Tom. He said he knew Audrey. She'd adopted Hazel from his rescue centre. Would he be willing to help me?*

There was only one way to find out, as I dialled his number with trembling fingers.

"Laura. How lovely to hear from you. How are you?"

"Are you busy? Have you got time to talk?" I dodged the welfare question, as I hadn't a clue how to answer it.

"Yes, I'm good. Fire away."

I wavered. How to explain this over the phone?

"Any chance we could meet for a coffee? Anywhere. Name your spot." *Better to do this in person, I think.*

Tom suggested a local café in town, and I hurried over there, meeting him at the door. We grabbed a table outside, ordered coffees, and Tom leant back in his seat.

"I'm all yours. Tell me what's up."

Tom sat quietly as I recounted the entire story of Hazel and Audrey. I told him everything, leaving nothing out, hoping he would want to get involved.

"That's quite some dilemma you're in there. I'm guessing you're telling me because you need my support?"

"Yes," I replied, my gaze unwavering as I looked into his eyes. "You know Audrey. She might listen to you. Could you at least convince her to put some feelers out? Investigate this. See if what Hazel said is true. Although I've no reason to doubt what Hazel has told me. I've met her. You should see her, Tom. She's petrified it could happen to another dog. And so distraught, as she knows Audrey is still looking for her. She just wants to put her mind at rest. And get some justice."

"It's a tough call. You're asking Audrey to believe in something that, quite frankly, most people would struggle to accept. It's not going to be easy."

"I know. But I have to try. For Hazel's sake. And Audrey's too. If it were your dog, wouldn't you want to know what had happened?"

"Yes. You've got me there. And especially as she was one of our own rescue dogs. I can try to contact Audrey and find out if she'll meet us. But I can't promise anything, okay? I'll go over to the office later today and look up her details. I'll call her and see what she says."

"Thanks, Tom. I owe you one for this."

"Well, you can start by paying for the coffees," he said, and delivered a cheeky smile as he got up. "And then, when we've sorted it all out, I think the least you can do is take me out to dinner."

"It's a deal. And thank you again."

"Save your thanks for later. I haven't done anything yet. Leave it with me. I'll be in touch."

He waved as he strode away, and I made my way back to my car.

It was the following afternoon before Tom called me. He told me he'd spoken to Audrey, and she'd agreed to meet him that weekend at her house.

"But there's a problem. I explained I knew you, but she clammed up. Wouldn't let me talk about it, and almost refused to meet me. So, she doesn't actually know you're going to be there. I guess we'll just have to play that one by ear, see how it goes."

"Well, it's better than nothing. Thank you. I'll spend some time beforehand thinking it through. I can only try my best. But at least this gives me another chance to talk to her."

Tom arrived bright and early on Saturday morning to pick me up, and we drove over to Axmouth in almost complete silence. I kept running sentences through my head in readiness for meeting Audrey, but everything I considered sounded hollow and forced. Like an actor reading their lines whilst holding the script in their hands. *I'll have to improvise as I go along. It'll be better if it doesn't sound too contrived.*

I rang the doorbell and held my breath as footsteps approached. The door opened, and Audrey stood there; her expression changing from surprise to unveiled annoyance in a split second.

"You again. I thought I'd made it perfectly clear I didn't want to see you again. Ever. And how on earth did you get my address?"

Tom stepped forward and held out his hand.

"I'm Tom. From the Second Chance Animal Rescue Centre. We spoke on the phone. I'm the one who arranged to meet with you. And this is Laura. I'm sorry I didn't tell you she'd be with me. But we really need to talk to you about Hazel. Please, just give us ten minutes of your time and we can explain everything."

Audrey folded her arms and glared at me. My stomach churned, and I wanted to run away, but I stood firm, twisting my hands together behind my back.

"I don't mean to hurt or upset you. But if you'll give me a chance, I think I can help you." I waited as Audrey assessed me, her eyes boring into me like sharp daggers.

"Very well. Ten minutes. No more. Come inside." She opened the door wider and ushered us into her living room. I perched on the edge of the sofa as Tom sat beside me and gave my knee a gentle squeeze.

I breathed in a long, calming breath and started from the beginning, telling Audrey about Molly and what happened after she had died. My voice fluttered as I described the first time I travelled to Archaven and saw her again. I couldn't tell what Audrey was thinking, but I sensed she was giving me her full attention, and I carried on with my story. When I reached the part about Hazel, Audrey leant forward, her eyes filling with tears.

"I'm still not convinced about what you're saying. But let me ask you one question. Something you would only know if you'd actually seen her in your rainbow land, as you call it. You mentioned last time Hazel talked about her collar. But my posters were all printed in black and white. Did Hazel tell you what colour it was?"

I was suddenly grateful I'd memorised everything Hazel had told me. Including the details of her distinctive collar that I'd forgotten the last time I spoke to Audrey.

"It was a pink leather collar with rhinestones. And it had a red paw print shaped name tag."

It was as if someone had opened the window and let in a freezing cold burst of air as I sat in silence, waiting for a response. I shivered and pulled my coat tighter around my shoulders as Tom gave me a reassuring slight nod of his head.

"She's really gone then?" Audrey reached up her sleeve for a tissue and blew her nose. "If I'm honest, I knew in my heart she'd died. There was no other real explanation for her disappearance. She'd never run away from me. And who would want to take her? But I just kept hoping." Her voice tailed off as she sniffed loudly, then smacked her hand on the table in front of her.

"But you're not telling me everything, are you? How did she die?"

Tom interjected. "Are you sure you want to know?" Audrey

nodded, and Tom looked at me, his eyes full of concern. "Okay, Laura. Go ahead."

"Hazel told me what happened. But I must prepare you. It's not a pretty tale. And it involves your neighbour." I tried to lead into things gently, but it was obvious Audrey was impatient to know.

"Bill? Do you mean Bill?"

I nodded.

"I've never liked him. Couldn't see what my Frank saw in him. But they were friends for years, so I just put up with him. Are you saying Bill was involved in all of this?"

"Yes. I'm so sorry." As I explained about the poisoned meat and Hazel's last memory of Bill carrying her into his garage, Audrey shrieked in pain.

"My little poppet. Oh, this is too terrible for words. I have to do something. I can't let him get away with this."

"That's why we wanted to come and talk to you." Tom's voice was calm and measured, and I was so grateful for his presence beside me.

"The problem is, how do we prove any of this? I can hardly go to the police and tell them what you've told me. They'd just laugh at me." Audrey looked over at us, her eyes wide and filled with a desperate plea, her face etched with pain.

"I'm so sorry to have hurt you. There was no easy way to tell you all of this." I could feel her anguish as she sat opposite me, her hands fluttering as she clutched her handkerchief.

"No, that's okay. You were brave to come here today. Especially after everything I said to you the last time we met. I only wish I could think of a way forward."

"There is one thing that might move things on." Tom squeezed his chin with his hand, his face pensive. "I'm not sure if it'll work, but it's worth a shot. We need the police to investigate this, don't we?" he asked as I nodded in agreement. "So, what if they had an anonymous tip-off that someone had seen Bill carrying a dog similar to Hazel into his house the day she went missing? Just to get the ball rolling? Get them to at least visit his house and talk to him? Would that work?"

"It's got to be worth a try." I turned to Audrey. "What do you think?"

"You'd do that for me?" she said, tears collecting in her eyes again.

"Yes, why not? We've got nothing to lose. I'm game. I'll call them, no sweat. It's the least I can do." I leant forward and patted Audrey's arm.

"I can do one better than that," said Tom. "I have a cousin in the police down here. Let me call him. He'll know what to do."

CHAPTER THIRTY-ONE

"You didn't tell me you had a relative in the police?"

I walked outside with Tom, having left Audrey tidying up her lounge and promising to call her as soon as we had more news.

"Ah, there's lots you don't know about me," Tom said as we climbed into his car. "Got time for a quick coffee back at my place?"

"Yeah, sure, why not?"

I was excited at the thought of seeing his home until I remembered he lived near Anna.

He turned right along a country lane, and we were soon far out of town, heading towards their village. As we drove past Anna's cottage, I slid down in my seat.

"I hope I don't bump into Anna. We're not exactly friends at the moment." I regaled him with the recent phone conversation I'd had with her, as he slowed down and parked outside a quaint country house set back from the road.

"Relax. She doesn't know where I live. I've hardly seen her at all since that barbecue." He got out of the car, and I looked left and right before even undoing my seatbelt, expecting Anna to appear at any second.

"Wow. She really got to you, didn't she?" Tom said as he opened the front gate, and I followed him down a pretty cobbled pathway lined with a profusion of flowerpots bursting with orange and yellow chrysanthemums. "My mum. She loves these. She's always popping round with more plants for me. Can't stop her. It keeps her busy, though, so I don't mind."

I stopped and admired a beautiful display of roses and lavender beside the front door. I closed my eyes and breathed in the exhilarating sweet scent, trailing my fingers through the purple stems.

Tom's house was a surprising mix of a traditional old stone structure outside, but inside it was all modern furniture. As soon as he opened the front door, a golden retriever bounded up to us, wagging its tail and spinning around in a frenzied burst of excitement.

"Hello Cooper. Okay, boy, calm down. Do you want to go outside?" The dog raced after Tom as he walked to the back door and opened it. A flash of amber shot through the door as Cooper bolted into the garden, only to return a few seconds later, clutching a soft fluffy toy in his mouth.

"He'll settle down in a few minutes. Won't you, daft boy?" Tom ruffled Cooper's head.

"I'd forgotten you were fostering him."

Cooper rolled over and stretched his legs up in the air, a wide grin splitting his face in two.

"I think he's after a tummy rub," Tom laughed at us. "Now, tea or coffee? Or something stronger?"

"Tea would be lovely, thanks."

Cooper had the same goofy expression that Molly had displayed whenever I rubbed her tummy, and the memory made me wince. *Not over you yet, girl. But I'm getting there slowly.*

"You'll never forget your girl. It doesn't matter how long it's been. You'll always miss her. I understand. I still miss Max."

"How did you know what I was thinking?"

"I could see it in your eyes. It's so tough, isn't it? And now Audrey will be feeling exactly the same way. My heart went out to her today. Hearing all that about her Hazel. It was horrible, wasn't it?"

Cooper twirled around, his tail pummelling my legs. His adorable eyes begged me to play with him as I bent down and picked up a tennis ball. "I'm just so glad you were with me. I'm not sure she'd have even invited me in, let alone listened to me, if you hadn't been there. Do you really think your cousin can help us?"

"Oh, he's a big animal lover. Had dogs all his life. He'll be up for it, don't worry. And he owes me several favours."

"I don't think I want to know the details. But thank you. You were great today."

"My pleasure." Tom stuttered, and I thought he was about to say something else, but he turned away and started tidying up the kitchen. I didn't push him as I finished my cup of tea and placed the empty cup on the draining board.

"Time to go, if that's alright. I've got a few things to do at home."

"Of course. Let me get my keys, and I'll drive you back." He whistled to Cooper, who trotted over and sat at his feet, as Tom looped a collar round his neck and picked up his lead. "I'll take the boy with us and give him a walk once I've dropped you off."

The return journey seemed to be over in minutes. Seeing Cooper sprawled on the back seat as I got out of the car gave me a sharp pang of nostalgia. *I wish I could take him for a walk.*

I waved goodbye as Tom shot away and I climbed up the stairs to my flat, opening the door into a cold and gloomy hallway. The profound silence was deafening.

I waited impatiently for more than a week, constantly wondering if Tom's cousin had uncovered any information, before finally hearing from Tom again.

His voice was restrained when I answered his call, and he launched straight into an update.

"So, it's good news on one level. But desperately sad as well. My cousin did some uniform house-to-house enquiries and knocked on several doors, so as not to look too suspicious. By the time he arrived at Bill's house, the man was already distraught when he opened the door. It didn't take long for Bill to break down and confess to stealing Hazel. He swore he didn't mean to kill her. He was just at his wit's end, hearing her barking in the garden. But he admitted to poisoning her, and he handed over her pink leather collar that he'd hidden in the back of his garage."

"Oh no, poor Audrey. She's going to be so distressed."

"My cousin went there in person to speak to her and tell her the news. He said she took it pretty well, and she telephoned her sister straightaway to come round to be with her."

"So, what happened to Hazel's body?" My voice cracked. I dreaded hearing the answer, but needed to know.

"He buried her in a field a few miles away. My cousin called for assistance, and his colleagues escorted Bill to the location to retrieve the body. They took it to the local vet's, apparently, and left Audrey to make arrangements from there."

"And Bill? What happens to him?"

"Oh, my cousin said he will definitely be prosecuted. It's an offence under the Animal Welfare Act, and he could face a fine or even imprisonment. It's up to the court to decide."

"Good," I said, my temperature rising. "What he did to Hazel is unforgivable. She was just a poor, innocent dog that was lonely."

"I know. To be honest, I don't envy my cousin having to deal with things like that. I couldn't be a police officer, that's for sure. All that upset. I'm far too soft. So they say." I detected an edge to Tom's voice that I hadn't heard before.

"Nonsense. You were brave enough to step in and help with this. It was all your idea to involve your cousin, and that turned out to be an excellent decision. However hard it is for Audrey at the moment, and she must be so distraught, at least she can gain some closure now. But it's such a ghastly ending. I can't stop picturing little Hazel. It's awful. Do you think Audrey would like some company? I'd be happy to visit her?"

"Funnily enough, I was about to suggest the same thing. How about we meet up at mine, say, in an hour's time, and then go over there together? It's the least we can do after everything that's happened."

"That sounds like a plan." I raced round after our phone call, gathering my things together, and dashed out to my car. I arrived at Tom's place just as he was opening his front door and pulling on his coat, and we jumped into his car and drove over to Audrey's.

She answered the doorbell, her face pale, and her eyes ringed with red. Her whole body trembled as she hugged me.

"I'm dreadfully sorry. I don't even know what to say to you. You must be feeling so awful." I tried to muster up the right words to console Audrey, but I gave up and just held her as she cried onto my shoulder.

"I'll put the kettle on." Tom squeezed past us both and walked into the kitchen.

"Come on, let's sit down, shall we?" I held Audrey's arm as I led her into the lounge. She collapsed onto the sofa, and I sat beside her, rubbing her shoulder and listening to her sobs, her grief hanging like a dark, damp curtain in the room.

Eventually she calmed down, her tears spent, as she took a few shuddering deep breaths and was still. She looked at me and then across to Tom, her eyes still red and puffy, as she blew her nose and took a sip of tea.

"This is going to sound strange, but thank you. To both of you. As painful as this is now, and boy, does it hurt, I'm glad I've found out what happened to my Hazel. You were right. About everything. I can't believe my own neighbour would do this to me. To my little Hazel. Not after all the years of friendship he shared with my late husband. I'm not sure I can ever forgive him." She hesitated, then continued, looking straight at me. "It's what you told me that's giving me the strength to get through this. That you have seen her, since…" She paused. "Since, well, you know… what transpired. I can't bring myself to say it out loud. But you've talked to her, seen that she's okay. Not in pain or in danger anymore. That's enough for me."

"Maybe I could arrange for you to visit her? Over there. If you wanted to…"

"No," Audrey interrupted me, her voice cutting through the air like a sword slicing through a ribbon. "I know what you're going to say. And that's really nice of you. But I don't think I could do that. I wouldn't have a clue what to say to her; after all she's been through. I feel partly responsible, you see. And I have to live with that. Knowing that you've seen her is enough for me. Next time you're with her, give her a big kiss from me. Tell her I love her and I'll be beside her again one day."

"I understand. But if you change your mind…"

"I won't. But thank you. What I will be doing, though," she said, looking at Tom, "is donating the reward money to your rescue centre. Second Chance Animal Rescue, isn't it? You can expect a bank transfer from me in the next few days. As my way of saying thank you."

"That's very generous of you. Thank you. Are you sure you're going to be okay? Can I do anything to help you?" Tom's concern was evident as he looked at Audrey.

"Yes, I think so. I know one thing. I can't stay here. Not with that man next door. I'm going to move in with my sister and put this place on the market. I should have done that when Frank died. But I kept putting it off. So, there is something you can help me with. You're an estate agent, aren't you? You can come round and value this place and put it up for sale for me."

We spent another hour sat with Audrey, letting her talk about Hazel, until she seemed calmer. More composed. We said goodbye, with Tom promising to be in touch again the next day.

The drive back to Tom's for me to collect my car was a quiet one, as we both sat processing everything. *Poor Audrey. And dear Hazel. I must go over to Archaven and update her. Tell her that Bill has confessed. And that Audrey loves her. So much.*

Thinking about Hazel made me long to visit Molly and wrap my arms around her. *I don't know what I'd do if I couldn't see her again.*

I only hoped I never had to find out.

CHAPTER THIRTY-TWO

Life quietened down a little after all the drama with Audrey. I balanced my time between working on new paintings and visiting Molly whenever I had a free hour. I found Hazel and updated her on the news, and she seemed calm, accepting what I told her with a nod of her head. She didn't ask about Audrey visiting her the way I could with Molly, and I didn't press the issue. It was as if Hazel knew it would be too difficult for Audrey without anything being said.

After that, it was always just Molly and me. I never saw Hazel again, and Molly seemed content for life to return to normal. Although I had to smile as I said the word normal to myself, sat on the meadow beneath Molly's golden-yellow poplar tree, cradling her head on my lap. *There's nothing 'normal' about visiting Molly in this rainbow land.*

The other strange thing was the complete absence of The Keeper. I hadn't seen him at all for many weeks. His lack of presence in Archaven unnerved me and kept me on edge. I jumped at every twig cracking or unexplained loud noise. Molly told me not to worry, that things were fine, but I couldn't relax completely.

Several times I observed a bright rainbow exploding in the distance across the river, and I always took a moment to stand respectfully. *Another special person reuniting with their beloved pet and crossing over. Into what, though?* The mystery of what lay beyond the Rainbow Bridge captivated my imagination, and I spent hours fantasising about what this mist-shrouded afterworld held in store. That the animals crossed over so eagerly surely meant that whatever was waiting for them was a good thing. Beyond that assumption, my creative inventiveness dried up, leaving me utterly enthralled and bewitched by the entire concept.

I was busy in my studio one afternoon when Sadie appeared at the door.

"Hello, remember me?" she trilled as she came in, holding a trendy hessian bag.

"Of course I do. How are you? And how's Iris? I must pop round to see her again soon. It's been ages…" My voice tailed off as I noticed Sadie's expression. "Is everything alright?"

Sadie gulped. "That's why I'm here, actually. I'm sorry. It's bad news. Iris passed away last week. She'd been ill for quite some time, but didn't tell anyone. She collapsed at home and died before the ambulance crew could even take her to the hospital."

"Oh no, Sadie, I'm so sorry to hear that. Your gran was such a lovely person."

"I know. She was. And I'm going to miss her a lot. But that's not the only reason I'm here. She wanted you to have something. She was most particular about it. Told me several times, 'If anything happens to me, I want you to give this to Laura. The lady that painted my Poppy for me.' Even made me write it down so that I wouldn't forget."

It must have been obvious from my bewildered expression that I had no idea what she was talking about.

"It's alright. Nothing to worry about. Here," she said, unravelling a velvet pouch from inside her bag. "Gran told me to give you this. She was most insistent."

She handed me the pouch, and I opened it slowly.

"Oh, it's the butterfly brooch she wore in the painting. It's beautiful." I spun it round, letting the light catch the diamonds on each wing. Miniature waves of colour flickered around the room, shades of blue, green, and yellow dancing across the walls, spiralling and twirling like a ballerina in full flight.

"Are you sure? Iris really wanted me to have this?" I was stunned as I held the beautiful antique item in my hands.

"Yes. Absolutely. It meant a lot to her. In fact, when she died, she had the brooch in her hands, clutched to her chest. I don't understand what the significance was, but she certainly treasured it."

"She explained to me that her late husband, Arthur, had handed it to her when they were courting. It was his mother's. Apparently, he couldn't afford an engagement ring, but he gave her the brooch instead. I guess it was like a promise that one day he would marry her." I smiled as I remembered Iris recounting the story to me, her face radiant, full of love and joy.

Sadie's eyebrows arched upwards. "She never told me that. I always assumed it was just an old piece of jewellery she liked. Now I know why it was so special."

There was a quizzical expression on her face. "Which explains why it meant so much to her. But why you? I don't mean to be rude, but the whole family was a bit taken aback when I told them what she'd made me promise. That I would deliver this to you."

I looked down at the brooch, wondering what to say in response.

"Hang on a minute. I'm remembering something." Sadie nodded. "That day at the café. When we first met up. You talked about that rainbow nonsense. You mentioned a butterfly then. I'm sure you did. Yes, you said you touched the butterfly on the painting of your dog and then you ended up visiting her. In some fantasy land. Yes, that's it."

I could almost see the cogs whirring round in her brain as Sadie started piecing things together.

"Gran went there too, didn't she? Your portrait of her with Poppy. Gran was wearing a butterfly brooch. That brooch. The one you're holding in your hands. Oh, my goodness. She visited Poppy after she'd died. I'm right, aren't I? And she kept it a secret, didn't she?"

"Yes. She did. And I'm not sure why she didn't tell you. I think she didn't want to worry you. She just went over there once, to see Poppy.

To give her one last hug and tell her she loved her." I glanced over at Sadie, trying to read her expression, but she turned away from me.

"So, what happens next?" Sadie asked, spinning back round to face me. "You must know. Now Iris has died? Does she get to be with Poppy again?"

I told her about Archaven and what I'd witnessed when other people arrived there. The wonderful moment when they reunited with their pets. "But I'm completely in the dark about what comes next. Once someone has crossed the Rainbow Bridge. That part is shrouded in mist and secrecy. But it's always a joyous occasion, and I don't think we have anything to fear. I'm sure Iris is there with Poppy, and all the other animals she'd adopted over the years of her life. I hope that is a comforting thought for you. It is for me."

Sadie nodded, her eyes filling with tears. "It all makes sense now. Thank you for being honest with me. We can lay her to rest, safe in the knowledge that she's in a better place. With her darling Poppy. Thank you."

Sadie left, and I sank down in my chair, suddenly exhausted by all the recent events that had occurred. *Who knew that all this would be so emotionally draining?*

CHAPTER THIRTY-THREE

My next surprise guest arrived the following morning as I was setting up in my studio. A hesitant knock on the door, and in walked Enid.

"I've got a visitor for you." She stepped aside and ushered Scarlett into the room. "I found her outside the shop, looking lost. Well, I'll leave you to it," she said with a wave of her hand.

I almost didn't recognise Scarlett. Her long hair had been cut into a trendy, layered style, and she was wearing clean jeans, white trainers, and a fluffy light-blue wool jumper. She looked healthy and happy.

"Scarlett? Is that really you?"

"Yes, it's me. The new me." She spun around with a flourish, then collapsed onto my sofa.

"Nice studio you've got here. Very nice. I used to enjoy art at school, especially sketching. It always made me feel calm when I had a pencil nestled in my hand. You know what I mean?"

I felt anything but calm as I stood there, watching her take everything in.

"So, where have you been? I've tried to find you several times with no luck."

"Oh, I'm back up in Manchester, where I'm from. I'm staying with my aunt while I get back on my feet. I hitched a ride with a guy one day who was driving up there, and it just seemed like fate." She twirled a finger through her hair, her foot tapping on the floor. "I've got a job working in a supermarket. It's not much, but it's a start. And I've been saving up enough money for the coach fare to come back down here. To say thank you to you. And to give you this."

She reached into her bag and handed me a rolled-up piece of canvas. It was frayed around the edges, dirty and tatty, but I knew what it was before I even opened it.

"Are you sure?" I asked, searching her face for an answer.

"Yes. Definitely. I've thought long and hard about it, but I have to get on with my life. I'll miss seeing Jack, but if I'm honest, I got a bit obsessed with it all. My aunt noticed it first. How many times I was absent. She said I'd disappear for hours on end. And I kept missing work. They threatened to sack me. That's when I knew it had to stop."

Her words sent an icy shiver down my spine. *Am I that obsessed with it, too?*

"My aunt sat me down, and I told her everything. She helped me to see how all my trips over to visit Jack were affecting every other part of my life. So I went there yesterday morning for the last time. To say goodbye to my Jackaroo. It was the hardest thing I've ever had to do. But now it's done. It's over. No more journeys across to the rainbow land." She let out a protracted sigh. "And then I caught the National Express coach down here to see you. So here I am, giving you back the painting."

"I understand. I think you've made the right decision, if that helps?" My mind darted over to the last time The Keeper had threatened me. I knew the sheer number of trips Scarlett had made was like pouring petrol on a dry pile of tinder. And The Keeper's vehement fury was the spark that ignited the entire stack of wood. Inside, I breathed a sigh of relief. *One more problem solved.*

"Yeah, well, anyway, it's done now. No going back. That's why I had to come and see you. So that I could return to you my only method of visiting Jack. It didn't seem right to just destroy the painting. I wanted you to have it." Scarlett stood up. "And thank you. What you gave me was magical, and I'll never forget it. If you're ever over there and you see Jack, tell him I love him. And I'll be with him again one day." She hoisted her bag onto her shoulder and smiled at me.

"You're welcome. And best of luck with everything. You know, you should try drawing again. Maybe it will lead to something. Here, hang on a minute," I said, scrabbling through my storage boxes. "Take this, and these." I handed her a new sketch pad and some pens. "For you. Here's to a fresh start. And good luck."

As soon as she'd gone, I packed up my art materials and raced over to see Molly. Scarlett's words were ringing in my ears as I landed in the field and looked around. *Am I neglecting my work too? Am I coming over here too much? Is this affecting me in the same way?*

I brushed away my concerns as Molly scampered over to me. Her beautiful face was full of joy as she raced around in a wide circle, her tail wagging her whole body.

"You'll never guess what?" Molly collapsed in a panting heap on the ground. "We watched Poppy reunited with her owner. The old lady—remember her? It was wonderful. Poppy looked overwhelmed with it all at first, but Jack escorted her to the bridge, just in time to see the lady arrive. Their reunion was something else. And there were so many other dogs and cats there too—even a majestic dappled grey horse who led the way over the Rainbow Bridge. All the animals surrounded her as she held Poppy in her arms and strode across the shimmering bridge, getting younger and younger with every step. We all cheered as she disappeared from view. It was a very special moment."

"That's wonderful. I'm so pleased for her." *I wish I could have been here to see that. It sounded like quite a spectacle.* I perked up by thinking about how I could now tell Sadie all about her gran and the send-off she'd received.

I sat in companionable silence with Molly, occasionally stroking her fur as she slept beside me, her head resting on my leg. The view was even more spectacular than normal as the sun glinted over the water. The trees that lined the riverbank were swaying in the breeze, and the smell of the lush grass and wild herbs was intoxicating. Rosemary and thyme combined in a heady blend of a fresh green pine scent with a hint of spice. My mind wandered as my eyes grew heavy, and I felt myself nodding off.

A sudden harsh bang, like a shotgun being fired, startled me. Molly shot up, her ears alert, and barked once. A loud, threatening bark, which was immediately answered by a roar that vibrated the very ground beneath me. Molly lay down again, her tail stiff, eyes unmoving. The sky darkened as if someone had pulled a blind down and shut off all the lights. Everything went silent. The birds stopped chirping. Even the trees seemed to freeze, motionless. Expectant.

His stride echoed around the field as he marched in our direction. Steam soared from his back as he stomped along, placing one foot in front of the other like a soldier marching forward towards adversity. Bold. Confident. Unafraid. The Keeper. He halted in front of me, and I rose to my feet, determined to at least be standing tall as he spoke to me.

"I thought I made it perfectly clear. One trip. That girl was here again yesterday. I have lost count of how many times she has visited us. Even sleeping here at night. It's not right. And you don't seem to be taking this seriously enough. It has to stop."

"It's alright. I've spoken to her today. Yesterday was the last time. She promised me." My throat was dry as sandpaper as I stood before him, the haughty stare of his amber eyes drilling into mine.

"And you believe her? What's stopping her from returning here again? I don't trust her."

"No, I promise you, she won't be back." I didn't want to mention how I knew she wouldn't be able to visit Jack in the future. About the painting. How it was once more in my possession.

"You seem very certain of that. Would you care to enlighten me on how you are so convinced of that fact? I have chased her away so many times, and she always reappears. She has taken absolutely no notice of my threats."

I realised I was treading on dangerous ground. *Remember, The Keeper seems to know what I'm thinking. Be careful.* I tried to conjure up a suitable answer that would placate him, but before I could reply, he hissed another question into my face.

"Would it have anything to do with a painting, perhaps? And a butterfly?" He leant forward until he was so close to me I could smell his hot, cinnamon-scented breath. I recoiled backwards and tried not to lose my footing.

"How did you know about that?" I stammered, then realised I had just confirmed his suspicions with my response.

"Oh, I have my ways of finding out what I need to know. And your friend was most accommodating in answering my questions. Particularly once she thought her beloved dog was in danger."

I kicked myself. I should have known there was more to Scarlett's story than she was letting on. And that explained why she was suddenly so keen to give up the painting.

"It would appear that you have quite a talent there. Your paintings can apparently transcend time and space. All by adding a little butterfly. That is most interesting." The Keeper stroked his beard, his face deep in thought. "It would be such a shame if I were to remove all the butterflies from this land, wouldn't it?" His tone was chilling as he paced back and forth, his hands locked behind his back. "Mmm, yes, that might make it very difficult for you over in your world, I would imagine."

I gasped. It felt as if he had punched me in the stomach as I listened to him.

"I warned you what would happen if you persisted with all of this. Obviously, the prospect of your dog going, shall we say, *missing* again, wasn't enough of a threat for you. Any more nonsense like this, and you will pay the price."

"It won't happen again. I promise. She returned the painting to me. And I will destroy it. You have my word."

"Make sure you do." The Keeper growled at me. "And just in case you don't think I am serious about all of this…"

A dark and menacing cloud appeared overhead. The Keeper clapped his hands, and torrential rain cascaded down, soaking Molly and me in an instant. She shook herself as I ran my hands over my arms, trying to repel the worst of the water. Soaked to the bone, my clothes clung to me, heavy and freezing cold, as a pool of water engulfed my feet and ankles. My teeth were chattering as I stomped around, sploshing more water into the air. The rain ended as suddenly as it had begun, the cloud stealthily disappearing from the sky.

"I control everything here. Even the weather. So, do I make myself clear? No. More. Visitors."

I nodded, unable to speak, as The Keeper roared, flames firing from his mouth like a volcano exploding, then turned and stormed away.

I fell to the ground as Molly huddled at my side, whimpering and shaking.

CHAPTER THIRTY-FOUR

I was still soaking wet when I landed in my bedroom, which freaked me out more than anything else. That something happening over there would affect me back home had never really occurred to me. In the early days, I had worried about getting injured or lost in Archaven, but so much had transpired since then I'd hardly given it another thought. But as I took a long hot shower and then dried myself, panic set in. My stomach was on fire, and my head was pounding, making me feel sick and dizzy.

No more visitors. That's what he said. Does that include me? I'd kissed Molly goodbye, leaving her stretched out on a patch of grass to dry off. *No, he can't mean that. He's always accepted me and my trips to see Molly. He won't take that away from me. I rescued him from that well. That must mean something. That can't be the last time I will see my girl. But is she even safe over there anymore?*

It was late afternoon. I glanced at my phone, noticing I had three missed calls and a text message. The calls were all from Anna. *I'm not sure I can cope with her right now.*

The text message was from Tom.

> Got some news! Call me when you get a chance.

He answered on the second ring, his voice sending a jolt across my body. The realisation I had missed him made me catch my breath.

"Hot off the press! Remember Audrey? And how she said she'd donate the reward money for Hazel to the rescue centre? It was five hundred pounds, I think she was offering? Well, she doubled it! A bank transfer for one thousand pounds arrived today."

"That's incredible. Really generous of her."

"It's all thanks to you. We could certainly use that money as well. It's perfect timing. So what about that meal you promised me? Tomorrow night, are you free? And do you like pizza?"

"Yes. And yes. To answer both your questions. Pizza sounds great."

"Good. I'll send you the directions. Meet you there at eight?"

My heart leapt as I ended the call, then sank down to the pit of my stomach as I remembered the missed calls from Anna. *Now what do I do?* I thought about ignoring them, but I knew if she wanted to get hold of me, she would persist until she tracked me down. *Might as well get it over and done with.*

Inside, I was praying she didn't pick up, but she answered straight away.

"Laura. Thanks for getting back to me. I wasn't sure if you'd want to speak to me again. After what I said to you last time." Her voice sounded different. Hesitant. Meek. Not exactly words I would normally use to describe Anna. And there was something else in there, too. She was upset. I knew her too well.

"What do you want?" I gave up any pretence of feigning interest in how she was doing. *Cut to the chase. If you're going to be mean to me again, get on with it.*

"I owe you a huge apology. I need to begin by saying that. And the rest. Well, life's been tough lately. Really tough."

She was rambling, and not really making sense as I weighed up whether to end the call.

"Don't hang up. I know. I deserve that, but please don't. Look, I need to see you. Say all of this in person. It's not right on the phone like this. Please, can we meet up?"

The catch in her voice told me she was genuinely upset. I paused, searching for the right words to say.

"Okay. You can come here if you like. Tomorrow's Saturday. In the morning?"

I gave her directions and arranged to meet at eleven.

"I'm so sorry. That's the first thing I must say to you. Before anything else."

Anna crept into my studio, her face full of apology, as she held out her hands to me. I eased into the hug with some trepidation, but her response was sincere as she gripped me tightly and let out a deep sigh. I stepped back, gazing at my friend of so many years as she wiped away tears from her cheeks.

"It's okay." I tried to make light of it all, but her face scared me. She was apologetic; that much was obvious, but her eyes, red and blotchy, told another story. There was a deeper layer of grief and sorrow there, barely hidden, although she attempted to conceal it, but I could see straight through her.

"Audrey told me everything. Said you were the reason she found her dog. It sounded dreadful, the neighbour doing that to her."

"Yes, it was tragic. So, what did she actually say to you?" I hoped she hadn't told her too much. I knew what Anna thought of my fantasy rainbow land, as she called it.

"Only that you'd heard a rumour about the neighbour carrying a dog into his house. Somehow, the police got involved. She was a bit vague about how that happened. And they located her dog buried some miles away. That must have been so awful for her." Anna had a faraway look in her eyes as she talked to me. A sadness that went far beyond the events in question. *There's something she's not telling me.*

"You did more than that, though, didn't you? You didn't just hear a rumour, did you?" Anna stared at me, her gaze like a flashlight searching my face for clues. As if she sensed there was more to my story than Audrey had let on. Her piercing glare reminded me instantly of one particular teacher at my primary school who had always picked on me in class.

Here we go. Wait for it. Any minute now, she's going to have a go at me.

With a surge of anger, I folded my arms across my chest, my fists clenched.

"What makes you say that?"

"Because I desperately need it to be true." Her answer caught me off guard.

"What? Do you mean my 'twaddle about a rainbow land' that you spat at me the last time we talked?" I hadn't forgotten her conversation with me. I had etched it, word for word, onto my heart.

"Yes, that. I'm so sorry I said that." Anna's voice broke as she sobbed.

I reached over and held her in my arms. "What is it? What's happened?"

"The rainbow land you talked about. Please tell me it's real."

Anna plunged forward, a high-pitched wail escaping her lips as she collapsed onto my sofa. The sound echoed around my studio, a keening howl that was borderline animalistic.

"Why? Has someone died?"

"Yes. It's Bayley. My dearest Bayley. He's gone. He almost made it to his thirteenth birthday. But he's gone."

She broke down again, her breath coming in enormous gasps as I held her hand, trying to comfort her.

I didn't know what to say to her. I understood the sharp, gut-wrenching pain of losing a beloved pet, the kind that leaves an irreparable crater in your heart. *Yes, I know all about that.* But I had no idea how to console someone else.

In fits and starts, Anna told me what had befallen Bayley. As she talked, I sat picturing his cute little cocker spaniel face, remembering how old and grey he was the last time I'd seen him.

"He was off his food. I didn't think much of it at first. I was rushing around trying to get ready for school. Geoff was away at another of his blasted conferences. I promised Bayley I would pop home at lunchtime to check up on him. He had the run of the garden and the house, so I wasn't too worried about him. And then I was busy at work with a last-minute staff meeting arranged for our lunch break, and I never got home until the end of the day."

Anna gripped my arm. "Oh, Laura, it was awful. As soon as I walked through the door, I knew something was wrong. Bayley was listless, his head rolling from side to side. I scooped him up and rushed him to the vet. He died in my arms while the vet was examining him. They haven't found out what was wrong with him yet, but that doesn't really matter now, does it? He's gone. My baby has gone. And if only I'd returned home at lunchtime, I might have been able to save him."

"You don't know that, Anna. And it's no good thinking like that. It's not your fault. He was old; it was just his time. He died in your arms. Exactly how he would have wanted to go, I'm sure. But it's awful, isn't it?"

"I knew you'd understand. The pain. It's unbearable. I keep picturing him lying there. In my arms. Every time I look at his bed in the kitchen, I cry. I miss him so much. I just want to hold him again. Kiss his nose. Tell him I love him."

"I don't have a magic wand. There's no easy way through this. But you will survive it. One day at a time."

Anna looked straight at me. "But that's just it. You *do* have a magic wand. Don't you? A way for me to see him again? Your rainbow land? Please. Tell me how I can go there?"

"You've got to be joking! After everything you said to me before…" I couldn't believe what I was hearing.

"Laura. I beg you. I need to see Bayley again. And I know you can make that happen. If you want to."

I looked over at Anna, her face beseeching me to help her. I felt so conflicted, my emotions involved in a two-way sparring match that left my head spinning. *No way. No chance. And yet—this is my best friend. In pain. Asking me for help.*

"I'm sorry I was so mean to you before. I hope you can forgive me."

Anna blew her nose. "I've always been jealous of you, if I'm being totally honest."

"What? You? Jealous of me? What do you mean? You're the one with the career. The nice husband. Flashy car. Lovely house." I shook my head.

"I know. I've been incredibly lucky. But you had such a special relationship with Molly. Anyone could see that. An unbreakable bond. I was so jealous of that. I never felt that with Bayley, you see. Well, not until he died, and then I realised how much I actually loved him. But by then it was too late."

I was speechless as Anna continued. "And then you started talking about your rainbow land. How you could visit Molly after she'd died. Your love for her is so strong, even now, that you appear to have been able to defy the grave. Do you know how incredible—and impossible—that sounds? I didn't know what to say to you when you first told me. But now I really need it to be true."

She reached into her bag. "I've got a photo here of Bayley and me. I know you need that. For the painting. Please, Laura. Please work your magic for me. For us." She fingered the photograph, stroking the image of Bayley, and my resolve faltered.

"I'll have to think about it. I'll let you know. Don't pester me, though. I'll call you when I've made my decision."

She pressed the photograph into my hand and whispered, "Thank you," as she gathered up her things and left.

I held the image in my hands for ages, staring at the goofy, cheerful face of Bayley, remembering all the fun times he'd shared with Molly over the years.

I had no idea what I was going to do.

CHAPTER THIRTY-FIVE

Anna's my oldest friend. And she needs me. I know I can help her. But... the hurtful things she said to me. They're difficult to forgive.

The chilling image of The Keeper crept into my thoughts. Cold. Calculating. Threatening. *He said no more visitors.*

This is impossible. How on earth am I supposed to decide what to do?

I grabbed my jumper and raced upstairs to my flat, almost knocking Enid over in the process, as she stood in her shop doorway.

"Sorry. Can't stop. Talk later."

I knew from the expression on Enid's face I was pushing things with her. *I've got some explaining to do afterwards. But first, I need to see Molly. She'll know what to do for the best.*

I held my breath as I brushed my fingers over the butterfly in her painting.

I'll never tire of this magic. Being able to visit my girl. I clung to the canvas as the world spun around, and I alighted in her meadow. The birds were chirping and cheeping in the trees; the river glistening in the distance. *All is well. And there she is. My Molly.* I ran over to her, caressing her fur as I landed soft kisses on her nose and head.

"Every minute I spend with you is precious, my darling." I kissed her again, my heart swelling with love.

And how can you deny this to Anna? She permeated all of my thoughts, as I angrily swept away the image of her in my overwrought mind. *Not here. This is my special time. With Molly.*

"And who's that over there?" I watched as a dog bounded over from a distant field towards us.

"That's Bayley. Remember him? I loved playing with him. And now he's here. We've been having such fun chasing each other. I let him catch me now. Sometimes." Molly gave me her distinctive, mischievous half smile, her eyes sparkling.

I chuckled as I remembered all the times Anna and I had laughed, watching Bayley try to keep up with Molly, his little legs spinning around in excitement. Often he would tumble over, only to get up, woofing and shaking himself, before racing after her again.

Bayley hesitated, his nose twitching as he kept his distance.

"It's okay, Bayley. It's my mum. Laura. You remember her? Your mum's best friend." Molly placed her paw gently on my leg.

Anna's dog scampered up to me then, his face a picture of wonder and disbelief.

"It's really you? Molly said you could visit us here, but I didn't believe her."

"Yes, it's me. And your mum sends her love. She misses you." I bent down to stroke him as he panted, his mouth agape.

"You've spoken to her? My mum? She's... alright?" He paused.

I nodded. "Yes. I was with her yesterday."

I continued patting Bayley's chest as he huffed and puffed. He stared up at me, his eyes wide and nervous.

"Could she..." He stopped.

"I think I know what you're going to ask me." I tilted my head as I considered how to respond. "You want to know if she can visit you here? Is that it?"

"Yes. But Molly told me it could be dangerous. For you. And for us."

"It won't be easy. That's for sure. I really don't know what to say to you. Whether to risk it. But you'd like to see her? If it's possible?"

"Of course. Just to console her. Convince her I'm fine. Molly explained everything to me. How we stay here, safe from harm, waiting for the day we're reunited. It's lovely here. Peaceful. Calm. I'd love my mum to see it all. I'm sure she'll be upset that I've gone, and I'm positive this would help to reassure her. If she could see me here, like this."

"I understand. And you're probably right. But I must think this through carefully. You'll have to trust me on this one. Let me weigh it all up. I don't want to put you—or Molly—in any danger. I'm sure she's told you about The Keeper, if you haven't already met him?"

Bayley shook his head. "No, but I've heard stories about him. I'd rather not bump into him unless I have to. He sounds scary."

Molly tucked herself in closer to me as I fondled her ears, taking pleasure in how safe and content I felt beside her. Her warm breath tickled my arm as she softly licked me. *I can't do anything to risk this.*

"Leave it with me, Bayley. I'll try to make the right decision. But I will go back and tell your mum that I've seen you today. She'll be relieved to know you're here with Molly. And you look so well, too. Don't worry. We'll work something out."

Bayley thanked me and settled down comfortably beside Molly, as I gave her one last, gentle kiss on her nose before departing.

The assortment of tops and trousers scattered across my bed spoke volumes.

It's just pizza. I struggled to decide what to wear every time I met Tom. *It's not like you're going on a date or anything.* I tossed another gaudy printed jumper onto the bed. *Or is it a date?* I glanced at myself in the mirror, running my brush through my hair for the hundredth time. *That'll have to do. Time to get going.*

Tom certainly looked as if he were on a date when I arrived. He was standing outside the restaurant, waiting for me, wearing a smart shirt, unbuttoned at the neck. No tie, thank goodness. That would have been too much. Jacket looped over his arm. Dark cotton trousers and a pair of shiny brown shoes completed his ensemble.

It's not a date. Yeah, right? So why's he holding a bunch of flowers? Oh heck.

I smoothed down the skirt I was wearing, suddenly feeling self-conscious.

"Laura! You look lovely." Tom reached over and kissed my cheek. His citrus cologne enveloped me as he smiled and handed me the hand-tied bunch of roses and lavender blooms.

"Here, these are for you. I remembered you liked them."

Of course. They're the same flowers that were growing in his garden.

"Thank you so much." I inhaled deeply. The heady scent was wonderful. Intoxicating. "You shouldn't have. But that was very sweet of you. Thank you."

I touched his cheek but withdrew my hand quickly, leaving Tom looking a tad uncomfortable as he opened the door to the restaurant.

"Shall we?" he said, gesturing to me.

The restaurant was almost empty as we stepped inside, and the server directed us to a quiet table in the window. Old LPs covered every inch of wall space, and modern country music was playing softly in the background. With pizza and drinks ordered, the conversation naturally shifted into a discussion about our favourite music and bands we'd seen live.

"Another thing we have in common, then. We enjoy the same music." I fell silent, toying with the napkin in my lap. *Why am I so tongue-tied and nervous around this man?*

"You seem a little preoccupied. Is everything alright?" Tom topped up our water glasses as the server arrived with our food.

"I'm okay. Just hungry. Is that pineapple on top of your pizza? Yuk!" I tried to deflect the conversation away from my problems. *Time enough for that later, after we've eaten, perhaps.* In truth, I had no idea what to say to Tom. *Do I tell him about Anna? Should I ask for his advice or not?*

It felt as if every time we met, all I talked about was Archaven. *I don't want to bore him. Or frighten him away. This is actually really nice tonight. Just sat here, chatting, enjoying a pizza. He's good company. I hope I don't spoil things.*

"Come on, Laura, I know something's up. You've been staring at that last slice of pizza on your plate for at least five minutes. Is it something I said?"

Tom jolted me back to reality as he touched my hand across the table. "It's about Molly, isn't it? You can tell me. I don't mind."

I took a deep breath, then spilled out what had happened since I last saw him.

"So you see, I don't know what to do. Anna is my best friend, and she misses Bayley so much."

I finished talking as our coffees arrived, and I waited for the server to finish at the table before I looked up at Tom.

"Well, what's the problem? Why can't you help her? Create one of your wonderful paintings and give her the chance to see Bayley again. What's the harm in that?"

I hesitated. I'd omitted to mention the crucial part about The Keeper and his sinister warnings. *And now it's too late. You idiot, Laura. Why didn't you tell him everything?*

"You're right. I should help her. Now, I insist on paying tonight. It's my way of saying thank you for what you did for Audrey. As we agreed."

I signalled over to the server for the bill as Tom leant back in his chair.

"Fair enough. I still think you're not telling me everything. But that was one delicious pizza." He patted his stomach and smiled. "I really enjoyed this evening, Laura. Perhaps we can do this again sometime soon."

"Yes, definitely," I said, as he helped me on with my coat. We walked back to the car park as I clutched the bunch of flowers to my chest. "And thank you again for the lovely flowers."

"My pleasure. Right, I'd better be off. Early start tomorrow. Night, Laura." He strode off towards his car, leaving me standing in the middle of the car park. He hadn't tried to kiss me goodnight, and I drove all the way home wondering if it had been a date or not.

I guess I'll be doing a portrait of Bayley then. I kicked myself. *Why didn't I tell him what The Keeper had threatened? Now I have to do the painting, else it will look like I don't care about Anna. Brilliant. I'm such a fool. Well, I'll have to hope it all turns out alright.*

I shuddered. I couldn't bear to think about Molly and what might happen to her.

It's going to be fine. It has to be.

CHAPTER THIRTY-SIX

Anna was thrilled when I rang to tell her my decision, but I felt a gnawing sense of regret as I ended the call. *I hope I've made the right choice.*

The painting seemed to take ages to come together, which didn't help my mood. I kept making mistakes, and I couldn't get the expression on Bayley's face right. His eyes looked like they were scowling at me as I threw down my paintbrush in disgust.

Right on cue, Enid tapped on my door and came into my studio. She wandered over to my easel and broke into a broad smile.

"Is that Bayley and Anna you're painting? How lovely. Is everything alright with them?" She took one look at my face and said, "I'll put the kettle on," before disappearing into the kitchen.

I knew that was her way of saying, 'Shall we chat?' and as she returned, balancing two mugs of tea in her hands, I sighed.

Here we go again. I can't keep going over this with everyone. It's exhausting.

We sat together as I explained about Bayley's passing, and how upset Anna was. But I chose not to tell Enid the real reason I was painting Bayley and Anna's portrait. Although it was obvious she had guessed, especially given the knowing smile she gave me while gathering up our mugs before she left.

After Enid had gone, I sat in quiet contemplation, trying to process everything. *Am I getting carried away with this? Is Archaven taking over my life? Is that why Tom hurried away last night? Because I can't seem to talk about anything else. And whenever I mention it, there's a problem in there somewhere. And now I feel like I'm lying to Enid, too. The one person who has always been here for me.*

I thought back to Scarlett and the last time I'd seen her. The haunted look in her eyes as she talked about Jack and being with him. And how hard it had been for her to leave him. I shuddered. *I can't do that. Say goodbye to Molly? Impossible. I can't risk it anymore. Just Anna. One last visitor, then I'm going to keep this all to myself. No-one else needs to hear about this ever again.*

I picked up my paintbrush and carried on daubing paint onto the canvas in front of me.

It took me an entire week to finish the painting, but finally it was complete, and Anna rushed round to view it.

She was delighted with it. I had added a simple white butterfly in the background, identical to the one in Molly's portrait, and as I explained how it worked, Anna's eyes lit up.

"I can't believe it. I'm actually going to see my boy again." She clapped her hands together. "Can we do it today?"

"There's something else you need to know. Before you decide."

Her face dropped as I told her about The Keeper.

"And you can't come with me? I have to go over there alone?" The hesitation in her voice was obvious.

"Yes, but there's a way I can watch you. It will be alright. There's a window that opens over here once you arrive in Archaven. It lets me observe what's happening. Don't worry, I won't go anywhere. I'll stay right here the whole time you're over there."

"Okay! Let's do it!" she exclaimed, her voice bubbling over with unrestrained excitement.

It was Enid's half-day closing, and I knew it would be quiet in my studio.

"Why not? Yes, let's get you over there and into Bayley's arms."

I had a sudden blinding flash of inspiration. "There's just one more thing I must tell you, though. You can only visit Archaven once. That's the rule. You need to say everything you want to and then say goodbye to Bayley. Once you return, I'll have to paint over the butterfly. You won't be able to repeat the trip. And you must keep it a secret, too."

I breathed a sigh of relief, the weight on my chest lifting like a hot-air balloon launching into the sky. *Why hadn't I thought of that before? It's a simple solution that should help things run more smoothly. And give me less to worry about. With a bit of luck, Anna will travel there and back without any problems. Maybe The Keeper will be busy and he won't even notice her.*

"That's okay. Once will be enough for me. I'm quite scared, though. Are you sure it's safe for me to do this?" Anna stammered as she scrunched her hands up under her chin.

"Perfectly safe. You'll be fine. Now go over there and be with your boy. And say hi to Molly from me if you see her."

Anna closed her eyes, touched the butterfly with her palm, and was gone in a flash of orange flames.

I settled down to watch her through the window as it appeared in front of me. She was beaming as she spun Bayley round in her arms and held him close. I tried to spot Molly in the background, but all I could see was a spectacular waterfall cascading down the side of a mountain.

It's a different location from Molly's. That's why I can't see her. It's strange, though; she was with Bayley the last time I was there.

I could just make out another dog sat quietly in the distance, but it definitely wasn't Molly.

I followed Anna as she walked beside Bayley. His joy at seeing her was so obvious as he trotted along, his tail spinning. All too soon, it was evident that Anna was saying goodbye, and I turned my gaze away, wanting to give her some privacy, even though she couldn't see me.

She reappeared in the studio abruptly, collapsing onto the sofa with a soft thump that startled me.

"Oh, Laura. I can't put into words how much that meant to me. I'm so sorry I doubted you. Dear Bayley, it was so wonderful to see him again. And talk to him too. That was incredible." Anna was positively glowing, her face flushed and animated as she danced around the studio. "Thank you so much."

"I'm so relieved everything went smoothly. Did you see Molly while you were there? I could only watch snippets of the world you were in."

"I didn't spot her. But I was so wrapped up in savouring every moment with Bayley, if I'm honest. Why? Are you worried about her? I'm sure she's fine."

"No, not a problem. She was probably busy playing with something in another part of the field. Right, I need to sort out your painting now."

Anna reluctantly handed over the canvas, her hand stroking the butterfly one last time. "If you must…"

"Yes, I have to do this. Why don't you have a look round Enid's shop while I get my paints out? She won't mind. It shouldn't take long to dry."

I deftly painted over the butterfly and cleared up my palette and brushes as Anna came back into the studio.

"I know it's for the best. Covering up the butterfly. I do understand. And thank you again."

I checked the canvas was dry and handed it back to her.

"This will have pride of place on our bedroom wall. And every time I look at Bayley's portrait, it'll remind me of today. I'm not going to tell Geoff. I don't think he'd believe me, anyway. Thank you. You're a good friend." She kissed my cheek and left in a whirl of promises to meet up for lunch the following week.

As soon as she'd gone, I gathered up my things and raced up to my bedroom.

I need to check that Molly is okay. I had a sinking sensation in my stomach that something was wrong. *She should have been there. What if The Keeper has captured her again?* I felt physically sick as I grabbed her painting and hurtled over to Archaven, my heart racing.

The meadow was silent. Too silent. I looked around, my pulse pounding in my ears. *Calm down. She'll be here.*

It was eerie. No birds were singing. The sky was full of clouds, hunkered in layers, obliterating the habitual blue sky. The river was as still as a Gothic shrine, its surface a ghostly mirror reflecting the grey clouds and silent trees, and even the gentle breeze that normally caressed my face was absent.

I padded around, looking in all our usual haunts. Twigs snapped beneath my trainers as I walked through the woodland, making me jump. Every tiny noise seemed to be amplified, reverberating through the undergrowth as I stood still, hoping to hear Molly's husky bark announcing her arrival. Nothing. There was no sign of her.

This is ridiculous. She has to be somewhere. Unless...

I shook off the memory of the first time she went missing. When The Keeper had trapped her in that shed. *Molly could be anywhere. How on earth am I going to find her?*

I sank to the ground, my breath coming in rasping gasps as I tried to focus and stem the rising panic spinning inside me.

A sudden pattering of paws scuffling through the leaves made me shoot up, desperately hoping it was Molly approaching. A set of pale blue eyes surrounded by dark grey fur stared over at me. *Amazing eyes. A cute dog with a white beard. But not Molly.*

"You're Laura, aren't you?"

"Yes. How did you know that?"

"Molly talks about you constantly. I'm Max." He held out his paw, and I sensed instinctively that he was no threat to me.

"My Molly. I can't find her. Do you know where she is?"

"No. But I saw what happened to her. The Keeper came and dragged her away. Her bark was a high-pitched scream, and I ran over to help her. But it was hopeless. He was just too strong for me. It was as if he had cast a spell over me. I felt weak and sluggish. The last thing I saw was Molly; her face constricted in pain. She shouted over to me, 'Wait here for my mum. Laura. She'll come back, and she'll know what to do. She'll find me. Like before.' I didn't understand what Molly meant, but she was so insistent. So I've been sitting here waiting for you ever since."

"You were the dog in the background? When Anna was over here?" It was as if I had asked myself the question, rather than the dog sat in front of me as I tried to clear my head.

"I thought it was you at first, but then another dog raced up to that lady, and I settled down again." Max's eyes were downcast, and I reached out to stroke his head.

"It's okay. It's not your fault. But I've no idea where Molly is, or how I'll find her." I choked back a sob. "This is all my fault. The Keeper warned me what would happen if I sent anyone else over here."

"I can try to help you if you like. Molly has always been so kind to me. She's special. Everyone says that about her. You as well. What you have done here is a miracle."

A crazy idea whizzed through my mind. "You said your name was Max?"

It couldn't be? Could it? Surely that's just too much of a coincidence?

"Yes, I'm Max. Why?"

"You didn't know…" I paused. This is too outrageous to be possible. I thought back to my conversations with Tom. *Light blue eyes. Crossbreed. Wiry fur? Max?*

"Did you have a family before? When you were… alive? Was there a boy called Tom?"

Max's entire face lit up. "Yes. I did. I worshipped him. He was everything to me."

"I know him. He's my friend. And he still talks about you."

"You really know him? That's amazing." Max seemed pensive. "It's been so long. He'd be a grown man now. What's he like? Could I meet him?"

Max's questions gave me an idea. *Hunting for Molly on my own would be an impossible task. But what if I had some help?*

"Max, can you do me a favour? Could you round up as many dogs, cats, animals… anyone that wants to support me? If we create a big search party, maybe we can find Molly? Would you do that for me?"

"Yes, of course. Great idea. I'm sure lots of us will get involved. We all love Molly."

I arranged to meet him at the same place in exactly twenty-four hours' time. Max sniffed my hand as I studied his face for a long moment, trying to memorise his features.

I've got a lot to do. And I don't know if Tom will even help me. But I have to try. For Molly's sake. I must find her.

I shot back into my bedroom, sprawling on all fours in my haste to get things moving.

But first, I've got a portrait of a dog with pale blue eyes to paint.

CHAPTER THIRTY-SEVEN

I spent virtually the whole night on the portrait of Max, only finishing it in the early hours of the morning, when I crept into bed and tried to get some rest. It had taken me almost an hour trawling the internet, looking for images of a dog that resembled the picture I had in my head of Max. I eventually found a shot that was good enough for me to work from. The final touch was adding his startling light blue eyes. I'd even struggled to come up with a suitable background until I remembered the flowers Tom had given me the other night at the restaurant. I'd shoved them into an old jam jar, but the combination of roses and lavender seemed ideal as a backdrop to Max's complexion and colouring. And a light blue butterfly sat on a flower complemented his eyes perfectly.

I tossed and turned in bed, knowing that I needed to get at least a few hours' rest before the day ahead, but sleep evaded me. Frustrated, I sat up and grabbed my phone.

I wonder what a blue butterfly signifies? I cast my mind back to that day when I had Googled a white butterfly, feeling comforted by the reassuring message of safety from a departed loved one that it conveyed.

Blue butterflies symbolise the powerful emotions of joy and hope. Their presence denotes a positive omen and good fortune. If a blue butterfly comes across your path, consider yourself very lucky.

Well, we're certainly going to need some luck today.

I was up, showered, and dressed by eight, champing at the bit to call Tom and see if he would help me, but I didn't want to contact him too early. Finally, at eight thirty, I could wait no longer. He answered on the third ring, sounding dishevelled and barely awake.

"Sorry, did I wake you?"

"No, you're okay. I'm just rushing out the door. Is everything alright?"

"I'm after a favour. But if you're busy…" My heart plummeted. I hadn't thought about what I would do if he were unavailable, as a lump rose in my throat.

"Never too busy for you. Look, I've got a house viewing at nine. It's near your studio. Why don't I pop by afterwards?"

"That would be great. Thank you."

I paced up and down as the minutes dragged themselves around the clock face on my studio wall.

4 pm. That's the time I said I'd meet Max. What if Tom can't come? Or if Max hasn't found anyone to help us? Well, I'll just have to go it alone if that's the case. I couldn't stop thinking about Molly, wondering if she was in pain or hurt. *Or worse.* I shivered, despite the warmth of the room. *She can't be.* I couldn't even bring myself to say the word. *She has to be alright.*

Tom arrived at eleven. He walked into my studio and straight up to the painting I'd propped up on my easel.

"You know, that looks just like my Max. That's uncanny. Who's this one for then? Another new client?"

Maybe this is going to work after all. Take it steady.

"Funny you should say that. It is Max. Well, I hope it is. I've tried my best to represent him."

Tom leant in closer. "Those are his eyes. That's exactly how I remember him." He looked puzzled. "But how did you know? And why are you painting him now?"

"Come and sit down." I tried to pacify him, but he continued to stare at the canvas.

"Those flowers in the background. They're the same as the blooms we had in our garden when I was growing up. My mum loved that garden. She still plants roses and lavender everywhere she lives."

"And they're the same flowers you gave to me. They were from your garden then?"

Tom nodded and pointed to a spot on the painting. "And that's a butterfly right there, isn't it? I know what that means. Archaven. Your rainbow land. What's going on?"

I sat on the edge of my seat, my heart thumping as I explained about Molly and Max.

"And you've painted this portrait of Max because you want me to go over there with you to help you find Molly? And the only way I can travel there is via this butterfly? That's right, isn't it?"

I nodded, unable to speak. I was on the verge of tears as I waited anxiously for his reply.

"Well, what time do we leave?"

I leapt up and hugged him, kissed his cheek, then pulled back in embarrassment.

"Sorry. Thank you. I've dreaded asking you. I worked all night on the painting, not knowing if you would help. But I have to find her. Put things right. It's all my fault, you see."

"I think you'd better tell me more about this Keeper character. So that we can prepare ourselves. No good going over there without a plan of some sort. How dangerous is he anyway?"

My idea had worked. Tom was on board, and a wave of relief washed over me. I sat mulling over how I would ensure we could travel in unison and land in the same place in Archaven. *I've never crossed over*

there with anyone else. *What if I joined our two paintings together? Would that work?*

I carefully unhooked both paintings from their wooden frames, the same as I'd done with Scarlett's painting. I laid the two pieces of limp canvas material on my worktable while I racked my brain for a solution. *Why don't I clip them both side by side onto a large sheet of backing paper? That way, our paintings will hopefully connect us both as one unit?*

When it was time to depart, Tom and I stood beside each other, one hand each clinging to the sheet of paper, the other touching our respective butterflies simultaneously.

We landed together, feet and knees bumping onto a patch of freshly mown lawn filled with the scent of lavender. Tom's shocked expression amused me as he looked around, unable to contain his surprise at the scene before us. We were in a well-tended garden with pots of flowers scattered along a path that led to a small potting shed. Beside it was a vegetable plot, with rows of healthy plants neatly lined up, leaves nodding in the breeze. A tatty homemade scarecrow, his head bobbing on a wooden pole, made me smile. But it was the lavender that captured my attention, as small bees flitted from stalk to stalk, greedily devouring the morsels of pollen. I stopped to listen to a bird perched high in an apple tree. It sounded like an owl at first, but then I recognised the 'coo-coo' sound as that of a dove, singing its heart out in the afternoon sunshine.

"This is incredible," Tom said, his face ablaze.

"I know. Amazing, isn't it?" I spun around, trying to check where we were. I spotted the gnarled and blackened skeletal remains of Molly's magnolia tree in the distance and relaxed.

"No. Not that. Well, no, obviously that. But this place. This is my childhood garden. Precisely how I remember it. And that scarecrow over there? I made him with my dad."

Just at that instant, a dog came racing round the corner and hurtled towards us.

"Max. It's you! My boy," Tom sobbed as he held Max in his arms. "I never, ever thought I would see you again. I still miss you, even after all these years."

"Do you like it? Did I do it justice? Our garden?" Max bounded round and round, his tail spinning like a Ferris wheel.

"Yes, it's incredible. Even down to the same old broken flowerpots that Mum refused to throw away." Tom replied. "But how did you do it?"

"What do you mean by 'do it justice', Max?" I asked. "Did you create this garden?"

"Well, sort of. The Keeper approached me when I arrived here, and he told me I could stay in any place I wanted from my imagination. The garden from our old house was always my favourite spot, so I closed my eyes, pictured it in my mind, just like he instructed, and when I opened my eyes, I was standing on our lawn. Everything precisely as I had recalled from memory."

So that's how each animal gets its own special setting over here. It's magical.

I stepped away, leaving them to embrace, as I savoured the moment. The joy on their faces was unmistakable. I felt a surge of love for them both, but then I remembered Molly was still missing, and with a hideous lurch, my heart plunged into my stomach.

I stared over at her poplar tree, willing her to appear. *She should be there, lying peacefully, warming her tummy in the sun. Instead, who knows where she is? And it's all my fault.*

I tried not to rush Tom. I knew he would want some time with Max, but he must have sensed my unease as he walked over to me.

"Right. Max and I are ready. And Max has a surprise for you. Look over there."

I shaded my eyes against the sun as I gazed over to where he was pointing. At first, I couldn't see anything, then a long line of animals slowly came into view, all walking towards us. Dogs, cats, horses, even some pigeons, all led by Jack, walking majestically at the front of the line. I recognised a couple of other dogs, including Bayley, but there must have been at least fifty animals surrounding us.

Max silenced them all with a wave of his paw and turned to me.

"We're all here and ready to search for Molly. We all know and love her and want to bring her safely back home. Don't worry, we'll find her. We've already divided ourselves up into teams, and the plan is to meet back here at sundown. We'll all go off in different directions, and if we spot her, we'll howl until others come to help."

Max pulled something out from behind the shed. "This should help track her. Line up, everyone, and take a good sniff of this scent before you depart." He dropped a cuddly toy on the ground, and I uttered a cry of pain. It was Toffee, the old, battered teddy bear Molly loved so much.

I held my head in my hands and wept. I couldn't help myself. It was all suddenly too painful.

"We'll find her. We will. And look at all the support we have. Trust me. We'll get her back." Tom's presence helped calm my fears as I wiped away the tears from my face.

"I know. I'm sorry. It's seeing her toy again. We have to find her. I just hope…" My voice tailed off as Tom gave me a fierce stare.

"No thinking like that. Come on, everyone's eager to move off. Let's stay together with Max. I'm sure he's going to locate her. He's always had a fantastic nose. Could rummage around and spot even the smallest morsel of food under the table. He's a wonder dog. We'll take the route along the river. I've got a hunch that's where we'll find Molly."

He rolled up our paintings, stashing them in the rucksack he was carrying, and we set off.

CHAPTER THIRTY-EIGHT

We'd only been walking for a few minutes, Max leaping ahead then racing back to loop around us in a wide circle, when the sky suddenly darkened. A radiant shaft of light spun above the river as a broad rainbow of colour shimmered and settled across the water.

Tom leapt backward and grabbed hold of my arm. "What on earth is that over there?"

The arc of the bridge came into view as the animals nearby started cheering. A lone white Samoyed dog elegantly stepped forward as a young boy appeared in the distance. A hush fell over the assembled crowd as the boy and dog embraced, then turned and walked onto the bridge. They were gone in an instant, the spectrum of colours fading as the river beneath them roared.

"Is that what I think it was? The Rainbow Bridge you've talked about? Is that what happens to us when we die?" A look of utter disbelief washed over Tom's face as he gaped at the water.

"Will that be you and me one day, lad?" Tom bent down to hug Max, his face buried in the dog's grey fur. When he lifted his head up there were tears in his eyes as he gathered himself together and said, "I think it's time we found Molly, don't you?"

We marched along the river path for what seemed like hours, only stopping to drink from a flask of water Tom had in his rucksack. Soon the landscape changed, becoming more rocky and isolated. The trees lining the path looked as if they had been there for centuries, standing tall and majestic. The route appeared familiar to me as I desperately tried to recall where I'd found Molly last time.

"Tom, I think we might be getting closer. I don't know why. I just sense Molly's somewhere nearby."

At that moment, something caught my eye. Above me was a blackbird perched on a branch of a tree. His song was both tender and haunting as he warbled and chirped, capturing my attention. *Of course. Last time a blackbird helped me to find Molly. This can't be the same bird, can it?*

He hopped from tree to tree, his shrill call an invitation to follow him as I sped up, Max darting forward.

We descended into a valley, the river rushing below us, as the bird flew away. I stopped in my tracks. Ahead lay a field, the edges of which were bordered by enormous mirrors, reflecting the view back towards us. And stood in the centre of the grassland was The Keeper. Arms folded. His expression unreadable. But I could almost reach out and touch the tension in the air around us, as Tom dropped his rucksack to the ground.

"No need to tell me who that is," he said, as he rummaged inside the bag, drawing out a large dog whistle. "Time for some backup." He gave three sharp blasts on the whistle, and Max howled in support, as The Keeper looked on.

The Keeper stamped his foot, and the ground beneath me shuddered and rolled, as if an earthquake was about to occur. The tremors lasted for several seconds, then all was silent.

"So, you have dared to challenge me again." He raised his arms above his head as flames flared out from his body, shooting up into the sky. "You seem to think you can do whatever you like here. But I warned you there would be consequences."

The mirrors lifted, and for an instant I could see across into another field. In the centre was a magnolia tree, identical to the one

Molly had loved. And beneath it sat Molly. She looked unharmed, but she made no movement towards me. It was as if she were in a trance.

My heart leapt into my throat as I struggled to breathe. *My darling girl. Trapped.*

Molly's gaze remained fixed on The Keeper as the mirrors descended, blocking her from my sight.

I raced across the field and screamed at the top of my voice. "No! Give her back to me."

I didn't care about The Keeper or my own safety as he stepped towards me, one arm raised in fury. Thunder and lightning spun across the sky, illuminating the mirrors with sinister flashes of light that circled the field.

"Molly. I'm coming. Don't worry, I'll rescue you." I shrieked in pain as flames of scorching fire shot up from the ground, a wall of searing heat that cut me off from the vast wall of mirrors.

"Halt. You cannot go through there. No-one can." The Keeper's voice echoed around me.

"But that's my dog. You can't do this to her." My voice sounded so feeble as I choked back hot tears of rage, and my legs buckled as the gravity of the situation hit me. "This is hopeless. How will I ever save her?"

Tom stepped up beside me and rested his hand on my shoulder. "Look behind you. You're not alone."

A line of animals had crept into the field, each one standing calmly and assertively, facing The Keeper. I recognised every one of them.

Bayley stepped forward first, his tone deferential as he addressed The Keeper.

"Sir, please do not punish this girl. Laura meant no harm. It was so wonderful seeing my mum again. Laura merely gave us the chance to be reunited with our loved ones. Even if only for a few moments."

Toby the cat spoke next. "It's true. I've watched others arrive here and meet up with their pets. They're not trying to hurt anyone. Simply looking for closure. Comfort. I'm looking forward to the day my owner comes. It will be a magical day when we cross that bridge together."

Bella stepped tentatively in front of the group. "My mum came over. Just to see me. I could reassure her I was fine. After that terrible accident. And she could go back and tell the girls I was alright, too. Imagine how amazing that was for me. How can you be angry about that?"

Hazel marched forward. "My turn now. I had an awful end to my life. A man murdered me. But you already know that, don't you?" She spoke straight to The Keeper, her head held high. He shuffled his feet, but remained silent. "I could tell my mummy what had happened. They arrested the man who killed me. That's a good thing. He won't be able to hurt another animal again. All thanks to Laura and her bravery. Don't punish her for that. Let Molly go. You can't keep her trapped like that. It's not right."

Finally, Jack spoke, his voice halting but clear. "This is a miracle. Nothing short of a miracle, what Laura has done. I know you were angry with me and my Scarlett. All the times she kept coming over here, to be with me. She was so lonely. I was her only friend out there, sleeping rough on the streets. And Laura healed Scarlett through her magical painting. She gave her hope and a reason to live. Knowing that I was over here, safely waiting for the day when I'd be with my girl again. You see, it's different for us. When we arrive here, we watch others reunited with their loved ones as they cross the Rainbow Bridge. You've told us all about it, too. How we just have to be patient, to wait. And time doesn't matter over here, anyway. Yesterday, a thousand days, a hundred years. They're all as nothing to us. Meaningless. But for our loved ones, those still alive, they have no way of knowing what will happen after we die. Whether they'll ever see us again. Wouldn't it be amazing if Laura's actions meant the entire world could know that the Rainbow Bridge really exists? That we can all be reunited again one day? Isn't that something we should celebrate?"

Jack took a deep breath and sank to the ground. His long speech had obviously exhausted him as he lay panting.

The Keeper strode around, deep in thought.

Without warning, a piercing beam of light illuminated the field, and a voice spoke from the sky. A break in the clouds appeared, and it was as if I could see into heaven itself.

"Laura is to be thanked. Not attacked. What she has done is incredible. You must release Molly immediately."

It was Iris, sat cradling Poppy in her arms. The intense brightness of the light surrounding her was almost blinding as a host of other animals slowly emerged behind her.

The Keeper bowed his head. "So be it. But there must be consequences."

He turned to face me, and I trembled. "I will let Molly go free. But this has to be the end. No more visits. No more paintings. I will remove the mirrors that bind her. But on one condition. You must say goodbye to her today. And never return until it is your allocated time to cross the Rainbow Bridge with her. Do you understand?"

Iris' gaze fell upon me as my face crumpled, a silent scream trapped in my throat.

"My dear, you know what he's saying is right. Be brave, do this now, and then return home to tell the world about the wondrous life that awaits us in the future."

She faded from view as I sobbed, my heart fit to burst.

CHAPTER THIRTY-NINE

Molly raced over to me as soon as The Keeper released her, and I collapsed onto the ground, wrapping my arms around her so tightly I feared she wouldn't be able to breathe. My sobs reverberated around the field as I clung to her, my heart hammering in my ears.

"How can I leave you, my darling?" I wept uncontrollably, the tears streaming down my cheeks, as she twisted round to face me.

"You must. The Keeper has spoken. Don't worry, I'll be safe here now. I'll wait patiently for you. But your time is not up yet. You have to keep living. For me. So that one day, when we're together again, you'll have lots of new stories to tell me. Just promise me one thing. Every time you see a white butterfly, pause for a second and think of me."

As she licked my face, my heart broke.

"I can't do it. Not again. I've cried myself to sleep so many nights after you died. And now I must say goodbye to you once more. It's not fair."

Molly took a step back, and I stretched out my arms towards her, already feeling the space widen between us.

"Go on living. And rescue another dog like me. Give another pup a wonderful life, just like the one you gave me. Live your life to the full. I'll be here waiting for you. And then one day, you'll return and we'll cross the Rainbow Bridge together."

I clasped my arms around her and sobbed.

"I love you so much. I will always love you."

"It is time. You must leave now." The Keeper stood before me, his feet planted firmly on the ground. But as I glanced up at him through my tear-filled eyes, his face softened for a moment. "Go now, child. Molly will be safe. You have my word. But you may never return here again. Not until it is your time. You understand that, don't you?"

"Yes," I whispered.

Tom approached me, his eyes wet with tears, as Molly walked over to the other animals huddled together around the edge of the field. They enveloped her as I stood up, reaching for the rolled-up canvas bundle that would take me away from her. She glanced back once, nodding her head in submission as I took a deep, ravaging breath, held hands with Tom and touched the shimmering butterfly.

Tom landed beside me in my studio and rocked me in his arms as I sobbed and sobbed. Enid rushed into the room and cried out in alarm when she saw me.

"What on earth has been going on? And who are you?" she said, pointing an accusatory finger at Tom.

"It's okay, Enid. This is Tom. He's been an amazing friend to me. Honestly, I'll be alright in a minute."

"I think it's best if I go now. But I'll come back again in the morning, if that's okay with you?" Tom picked up his things, then wrapped me in an enormous hug. "It's going to work out fine. Trust me. You did the right thing. Call me later if you want to, and I'll see you tomorrow."

He left as Enid stared at me. "You've got some explaining to do, my girl."

I stood up and managed a weak smile. "I'll put the kettle on."

I spent hours pouring my heart out to Enid, and I felt exhausted but resigned to the situation with Molly by the time Enid retired for the evening. I was so tired, I actually got some sleep that night, and as I rolled over in bed the next morning, automatically reaching out my hand to Molly's side of the bed, her final words came back to me.

"Rescue another dog like me."

"It's too soon," I said to myself. A phrase I then repeated aloud when Tom walked into my studio later that morning. He had Cooper on a lead by his side.

"I was just hoping... You see, I've got an important conference this weekend that I must attend. Normally, I'd leave him at the shelter. But I thought, maybe..." Tom faltered. "I'm not doing this very well, am I?"

"You want me to babysit your dog for you? Is that what you're trying to say?" I glanced down at Cooper, who had settled at my feet, his head resting on his paws.

"The answer's yes. Of course I'll look after him for you." I reached down and patted Cooper's head as he sighed and rolled over.

"Great. Thank you. I'll be back in a minute." Tom hurried out of my studio and returned a few minutes later, lugging a huge sack of dry dog food and a fluffy dog bed. A second trip outside to his car resulted in him bringing in a rucksack full of tinned dog food, two bowls, and a spare dog lead. Cooper bounded over, sniffing everything with zeal.

"Are you sure this conference is only for a weekend? There's enough food here to last at least a month." I picked up a tin of dog food, and my hand froze. It was Molly's favourite: salmon and sweet potato.

I'm not sure I can do this. I miss her so much.

Molly's words haunted me. "Give another pup a wonderful life."

Tom sat down. "If I'm honest, I thought you'd have to say goodbye to Molly yesterday. That The Keeper would insist on that outcome. And I knew how hard that would be for you. It was tough for me as well, leaving Max behind. But watching you with Molly almost broke me. I wasn't sure if it was too soon for you. To have another dog in your life. But I figured I'd bring Cooper over in case you could use some company. He's house-trained, loves a tummy rub and a long walk every morning. A bit like me, actually."

I smiled, and the ache in my heart eased a little. Cooper trotted over to me, sat down, and hesitantly lifted a paw up. I stroked his head, and he lay back down at my feet.

"Why don't I leave him here for the weekend? Just to see how he gets on? No pressure. And then, well, if you decided he can stay, you already know who's in charge of the adoption papers at the shelter. I'm sure we could make it more permanent if you wanted to." Tom patted his pockets and pulled out a bag of treats for Cooper. "And are you sure you're alright? After everything that happened yesterday?"

"I think so. It's going to take me some time to process it all. But you're right. Maybe Cooper here can help me move forward. I can't bear the thought of not seeing Molly again. But at least I know she's safe. And we'll be together again in the future. That has to be enough for me. And Iris was right. I have an amazing story to tell the world. I've always wanted to write a book, so now's my chance."

"Well, I'll leave you to it then. And I'll be back on Sunday evening if that's okay to find out how Cooper is settling in. I hope I can still be part of his life if you decide to adopt him. Yours too, if you'll have me."

"Of course. And we still haven't had that picnic you kept promising me."

"Now there's something to look forward to."

After Tom had departed, I made myself a cup of coffee, settled down on the sofa beside a now sleeping Cooper, and reached for a brand-new notebook and pen. Opening the first page, I wrote the title of my book in large capital letters.

The Rainbow Bridge by Laura Adams.

I turned over the page, then neatly wrote a careful inscription:

"In loving memory of my darling Molly."

YOUR REVIEW

Thank you for buying this book. I hope you've enjoyed reading this fictional story of the Rainbow Bridge. If you have time, I'd be delighted if you could leave a review online where you purchased this book. Even a single sentence or brief comment would be lovely. As an indie author, I read and learn something from every remark that's posted and rely on reviews and recommendations to support and promote my work to a wider audience.

Thank you,
Alyson

KEEPING IN TOUCH

If you would like to be notified when I publish future books, please contact me via email and I will add you to my mailing list.

author@alysonsheldrake.com

I also write a free monthly newsletter with my husband Dave, which is full of art, photography, book reviews, news about our rescued Spanish water dog, and our life here in Portugal. You can sign up for it here:

www.alysonsheldrake.com/news/

ACKNOWLEDGEMENTS

My wonderful team of beta readers helped to shape this book, giving me wise editorial advice alongside a detailed level of proof-reading and valuable feedback. Beth Haslam, Jodie Mann, Liza Grantham, Simon Michael Prior, Julie Haigh, Chris Moore, and Petra Deen—my sincere thanks.

Thank you to the fabulous team of creative talent at Miblart who designed the cover of this book. They took my ideas and transformed them into the perfect representation of what this story is all about.

My thanks must also go to Victoria of Ant Press publishing company for her skill in formatting and presentation.

As always, thank you to Dave, my talented and supportive husband. I love you. And finally, to Zara, our rescued Spanish water dog, the girl who helped to heal our hearts after the tragic death of our beloved Kat. Thank you for all your love, woofs, and mischief.

ABOUT THE AUTHOR

Alyson Sheldrake was born in Birmingham in 1968. She has an honours degree in sport and a teaching qualification in physical education, English, and drama. She has always loved art and painting, although she found little time for such pleasures, working full time after graduation. Alyson joined the Devon and Cornwall Police in 1992 and served for thirteen years before leaving and working her way up the education ladder, rapidly reaching the dizzy heights of a Director of Education for the Church of England in Devon in 2008.

Managing over 130 schools in the Devon area was a challenging and demanding role. However, after three years, her husband Dave retired from the police, and their long-held dream of living in the sun became a reality.

Alyson handed in her notice, and with her dusty easel and set of acrylic paints packed and ready to move, they started their new adventure living in the beautiful Algarve in Portugal in 2011.

She is now an accomplished and sought-after artist and author working alongside Dave, a professional photographer. Being able to bring their much-loved hobbies and creative interests to life has been a wonderful bonus to their life in the Algarve.

Alyson is the former editor of *Portugal Letter* magazine and a feature writer for the Algarve's *Tomorrow* magazine. She is the author of the *Algarve Dream Series* of travel memoirs and the author/curator of the *Travel Stories Series* of anthologies. Her animal memoir, *Kat the Dog: The remarkable tale of a rescued Spanish Water Dog*, was released in 2022, and is a multi-award-winning bestseller.

When she is not painting or writing, you can find Alyson walking Zara, their newly rescued Spanish water dog, along the riverbank in Aljezur.

MORE BOOKS BY THE AUTHOR

Kat the Dog: The remarkable tale of a rescued Spanish Water Dog (2022)

A captivating and emotional story of survival and second chances.

Escaping from a wretched existence on a rundown farm, a young Spanish water dog goes on the quest of a lifetime, in search of a family to love her and a place to call home.

Follow Kat the Dog as she tells her heart-warming and uplifting story. The little dog with a big heart who journeyed through fear and starvation to find her forever home.

> "The most uplifting animal memoir since *A Street Cat Named Bob*. This is the kind of read that causes hearts to ache, spirits to soar, and souls to sing with joy.
>
> Against the odds, Kat battles for survival in a world that seems devoid of kindness, with only hope to cling to as she embarks on a perilous quest for a place to call home. With the open road finally behind her, Kat faces an even greater challenge—will she ever be able to shake off

her deep-seated fear and uncertainty to embrace a new life founded on trust?

Alyson Sheldrake combines empathy and imagination to deliver a unique insight into the canine psyche. The result is an enchanting narrative which leaves the reader spellbound from beginning to end.

So much more than just another animal story, *Kat the Dog* is a tale of courage, compassion and, above all, unshakeable and unconditional love."

Liza Grantham, author of the Mad Cow in Galicia memoir series.

The Algarve Dream Series

Living the Dream – in the Algarve, Portugal (2020)

and

Living the Quieter Algarve Dream (2020)

Could you leave everything behind and start a new life in the sun?

Have you ever been on holiday abroad and wondered what it would be like to live there?

Alyson and Dave Sheldrcake did. They fell in love with a little fishing village in the Algarve, Portugal, and were determined to realise their dream of living abroad. They bought a house there, ended their jobs, packed up everything they owned and moved to the Algarve to start a new life.

Travel alongside them as they battle with Portuguese bureaucracy, set up their own businesses, adopt a rescue dog and learn to adapt to a slower pace of life.

Part guidebooks, mostly memoir; the Algarve Dream series of books are a refreshingly honest and often hilarious account of life abroad.

> "It felt like I was sitting outside a local *pastelaria* with a new-found friend, drinking a *galão* and sharing a plateful of warm, freshly baked *pasteis de nata* while she told me her story."

Tom George Carroll, Playwright.

A New Life in the Algarve, Portugal – An anthology of life stories (2021)

Meet a whole range of different people who have also made the Algarve their home. Read about the families that moved to live in the Algarve in the early 1970s, before tourism was even an idea.

Follow the artists, writers, and individuals who have set up amazing charities, innovative magazines, and new companies. Discover the stories behind the owner of an award-winning wine farm, the couple who run a yurt farm, a wedding planner, estate agent, rural retreat owners, therapists, and the Vice-Consul to the British Embassy in Portugal.

Read their stories—and be inspired.

Includes a foreword written by the former British Ambassador to Portugal.

> "This is a well-crafted collection of tales to satisfy anyone's urge to delve into the lives of others and see what makes them tick."

Lisa Rose Wright, author of the Writing Home series of books about life in Galicia, Spain.

> "I congratulate Alyson for assembling these stories, all very different but each in its own way communicating a deep affection for this enchanting place at the westernmost tip of continental Europe and its equally enchanting people."

Chris Sainty, former British Ambassador to Portugal.

The Travel Stories Series

A collection of short travel stories from all over the world.

Includes work by *New York Times* bestselling and award-winning travel memoir authors.

Chasing the Dream – A new life abroad (2021)

20 different stories. One shared dream—the chance to start a new life overseas.

Young lives, families, midlife movers, rash spur-of-the-moment property purchasers, and retirement dreamers are all featured in this book. Read about their adventures and find out what it is really like to move abroad.

> "Fabulous stories, brilliantly curated by Alyson, showing the ups, downs, laughs and tribulations of living abroad. Once you open the book, you'll struggle to put it down until you've finished and started to plan your new life abroad."
>
> *Kevin J D Kelly, author of the Midlife Misadventures Comedy Travel Memoir series.*

Itchy Feet – Tales of travel and adventure (2021)

From the Indonesian jungle, to an epic journey out of Africa, and rafting the Zambezi. Find out what Egypt is like in a heatwave, and hunt down Dracula in Transylvania. Catch a rare glimpse into the lives of the last Pech Indigenous people of La Moskitia, Honduras. Be entertained by a teenager's first glance of foreign soil, and an Australian view of England. Ride a Harley through France and Spain and find out what makes someone a perpetual nomad.

> "Itchy feet—we have all had itchy feet these past months. Inspired by these talented, including some new travel writers, I am raring to go again. How wonderful to have such fine writers building on the legacy of authors who first made travel so irresistible for us."

Neal Atherton, author of the Travels in France Series.

Wish You Were Here – Holiday Memories (2021)

We all have that one holiday that stands out in our minds, that one break or vacation we will never forget. Whether it is a childhood 'bucket and spade' family holiday, the 'once-in-a-lifetime' dream destination, your first trip abroad or the city where you first fell in love, the memories are still there today.

The authors in this anthology bring out their postcards and photo albums and invite you to join them as they reminisce about their travels.

> "These stories are so full of incredible details that I felt like I was right there with the writer. There are several places I've added to my 'have to see before I die' list. There's something for everyone in this fantastic collection of memories."

Tammy Horvath, author and Amazon Reviewer.

The Travel Stories Collection (2021)

This digital box set contains all three books in the *Travel Stories Series* and also includes 17 exclusive bonus chapters.

77 chapters—almost 50 different authors—covering locations from Africa to the Zambezi. You can travel the world with this box set from the comfort of your own armchair.

> "A wonderful collection of short travel stories from all over the world.

It is amazing to read all the splendid memories, and the authors really take you on a trip full of adventures."

Kathleen Van Lierop, author of the 'mycrazylifefullwithbooks' blog.

For more information on all of Alyson's books, please visit her website:

www.alysonsheldrake.com

www.ingramcontent.com/pod-product-compliance
Lightning Source LLC
LaVergne TN
LVHW041756060526
838201LV00046B/1022